Aftermath
A Story of Survival

LEANN EDMONDSON

With Contributions by Mike Kosinski

ISBN: 1505374316
ISBN-13: 978-1505374315

DEDICATION

I wouldn't be publishing this work of fiction without the patient support of my husband and the enthusiastic encouragement of Joyce.

If not for Mike starting the storyline and the faithful fans, I would have missed out on one heck of an adventure. Words cannot express my joy and gratitude!

CONTENTS

ACKNOWLEDGMENTS

Thank you first and foremost to the fans that read and voted for over half a year to help shape this story. I thoroughly enjoyed getting to know several of you and look forward to more stories in the future! Thank you to TinHatRanch.com for hosting the weekly serial and letting me go with the story!

To those who spent days helping me edit this (especially the Laughing Bear!) your bleary eyes and lack of sleep on my behalf is appreciated more than you know.

i

Aftermath
A Story of Survival

CHAPTER ONE

A dry ham sandwich was on the lunch menu this afternoon. Jimmy hated the way the faux wheat bread made a lump in his throat but had no one to blame. He made it.

He choked down a bite as he keyed up the mic, "CQ, CQ, THR4K". He loved to spend his lunch breaks sitting in his Jeep, talking with whoever was there to receive. So far during the first few bites of his sandwich he'd worked Florida from Indiana on 10 meters. Not bad, but he had done better. Spinning the dial on his radio across the band, he picked up another HAM. He caught him mid-sentence, the signal was almost unintelligible, something about an accident and he thought he heard the term RACES (Radio Amateur Civil Emergency Service). The signal then abruptly ended. *What? RACES?* He heard footsteps quickly approaching.

Jimmy looked up and saw Bill Allen, the plant manager, frantically running over to the Jeep. "Jimmy, you'd better get back in the plant, all hell's breaking loose. The conveyors just started running double speed, the sorters are jammed, and the electro-magnetic separator caught fire just before it quit spinning!" blasted Bill, who was obviously on the edge of a full-blown panic but keeping it together.

"What?!" was about all he could get out of the surprised look on his face. He turned off the ignition, pulled the keys and slammed the door to the Jeep. He trailed Bill through the icy parking lot towards the employee entrance. As they passed the picnic tables a loud crash and the sound of tearing metal stopped them in their tracks. About 20 yards to the left, their brand new Hyster forklift was busy ripping its way through the corrugated metal wall of the plant. The funny thing was, it was driverless. It finished chewing through the wall and headed on the downward slope towards the parking lot, finally stopping after it speared the boss's Mercedes and its wheels lost purchase on the ice.

"What the?!" This time Jimmy managed two words out of the surprised look on his face. The pair continued on back towards the plant. When they got to the main door, Bill's access control card refused to unlock it. It didn't matter; the door burst open as one of the line workers came running out trying to escape the melee inside.

His office was just inside the employee entrance door on the south side of the plant. The sound of chaos filled his ears; glass crashing, machines running out of control. He rounded the corner and opened the door and lunged towards his PC. The whole plant was run off of PLC controllers; he could quickly shut this mess down with a mouse click. The surprised look on his face didn't utter a sound when he saw the screen. His display, which previously displayed a graphical representation of the plant now had a picture. A picture of a dog taking a dump, the words "IT Happens" displayed below it.

He knew it would be futile but he hit CTRL-ALT-DELETE anyway. Nothing happened. Jimmy wasn't a rocket scientist, just a retired Marine maintenance tech but it didn't take one to figure out what was going on. "We've got one hell of a virus," he muttered under his breath. Jimmy was against connecting the PLC network to the Internet in the first place. Admittedly for selfish reasons, he didn't want remote access and 2am phone calls while he was at home in bed. But he had also considered this possibility.

As he turned to reiterate his last statement to Bill who was standing aghast behind him, the lights went off along with all power. Within a few seconds, the sounds of chaos that were echoing off the walls of the plant wound down, finishing with a single spinning Snapple bottle.

It was at this point that Jimmy's sense of smell became the top priority to his senses. The acrid smell of burning electronics and garbage was quickly filling the air. His next thought was to call the fire department but a quick glance at the dead POE powered phone told him he'd better reach for the iPhone in his pocket. He reached in his pocket and as he pulled it out a little warning light went off in his brain. The phone was like twelve degrees. He instinctively pressed the top button, but when he went to swipe, there was the dog.

As if the panic caused by the current situation in the plant wasn't enough, a new rush quickly flushed from his head to feet. This wasn't limited to the plant.

"Evacuate the plant!" he shouted to Bill.

****

Two years earlier, 16 year old Adam Philpot was again left to his own devices. Previous generations might have called him a latchkey kid, but for today it was pretty much the norm. Dad was gone and Mom did just enough to keep the lights on in-between drinks. Most people might think that Adam partook in the normal activities of a 16 year old with little supervision; drinking, drugs, general mayhem, but they would be wrong. Adam was odd. Different vices tripped the pleasure centers of his brain. Adam might be what you would call a genius in a twisted sense. If he wasn't playing X-Box he was writing code. It was a few of his quirky ideas that he posted on the black hat hacker forums that got him contacted by Khalid. The strange relationship between Adam and Khalid consisted of Khalid giving him little "code puzzles" to solve. Khalid would have Adam break in to various types of code and deposit small bits of his own code, hiding it from the ones and zeroes and working around it. Adam would quickly solve them and a few hundred bucks would appear in his PayPal account.

Over the last year, Khalid would give Adam increasingly complex puzzles and Adam would solve them. Ever increasing sums would appear in his PayPal. Even though Adam recognized bits of the code from time to time, he didn't understand the end game. He had a suspicion he was up to no good but he didn't care, just like no one cared for him. He was making more money than all of his friends combined and as far as his mother could see through her fog, he wasn't getting into trouble. The coast was clear.

Had Adam been able to ask Khalid about his suspicions regarding the types of code he was breaking, he would have been right. You see, these "puzzles" were portions of operating code for all types of computers and machines; just about every major subset of modern day life operated by software. As you probably guessed, Adam was crafting a virus, straight from the evil genius portion of his brain. The dog? It was his signature. Every common software platform was affected. Each little puzzle was another device. They ranged from PLC software, to Windows, Android, iOS, cars, and even refrigerators. You name it, everything connected was compromised, even airplanes by taking out key communication and radar reading subsystems.

****

Smoke was beginning to fill the plant and flames could be seen licking the ceiling over by the electro-magnetic separator. In a vain attempt Bill shouted at the top of his lungs, "Everybody get out!" Jimmy rounded the corner to head for the door when the ground began to shake and a deep bellowing boom shook the plant. It was followed by a rumble like thunder, only in concert with the shaking ground. Jimmy knew it wasn't thunder.

The door opened to the bright sunlight and he saw several of his co-workers all staring in the same direction, mouths agape. He turned his gaze in the suggested direction. A fireball was rising into the crisp blue sky with a plume of coal black smoke. "What the hell?!" was the most he'd been able to say since this nightmare began a few minutes ago. Sally, a line worker burst through the door as Bill and Jimmy stared and quietly said, "It just came twisting out of the sky, straight into the ground. My God," she paused. "They're all dead". Tears streamed down her cheeks.

The fireball and smoke were the remains of Southwest Flight 587 from Baltimore to Chicago. It crashed when the virus took over, the flaming wreckage shattered in a crater a mile or so out of town. Jimmy still didn't comprehend everything he was seeing; his mind was still putting it all together. The last piece of the puzzle came from the corner of his eye. He caught a glimpse of the sun reflecting off of aluminum. He swung his head around, just in time to see a twin engine jetliner in a flat spin. His eyes focused as the left wing sheared off the crippled bird. It looked to be four or five miles away. The crowd became torn as more of them noticed the second plane, two horrifying events unfolding before their eyes, not to mention the smoking wreckage of their place of work behind them. Jimmy's eyes tracked the second airliner as it disappeared below the tree line, his brain still processing his senses. Seconds later an orange orb of fire reappeared.

He was used to chaos in Iraq. He was even used to seeing balls of fire and feeling the ground tremble. But this was home! It was Hebron, Indiana! The trained portion of his brain clicked on autopilot. He looked at the gathering crowd of his co-workers and a grim reality began to set in. Scanning the crowd from left to right he realized they didn't have a clue. The clock had begun. He sprinted to the Jeep, jumped in, and put the key in the ignition. He wondered if anything would happen when he turned the key. To his half-surprise the 4.0L six sputtered to life. He backed out of his spot and drove past the crowd, passed Hargrave's speared

Mercedes and as he pulled on to Route 2 he could see smoke starting to come out of the roof at the Waste Enterprises main recycling building.

The roads in a small town like Hebron are never really packed with cars so it was easy to drive around the ones that were seemingly broke down in the middle of them. Strangely enough, not every car was disabled. The Jeep was running. Even Jimmy's initial deduction that it was only new cars didn't pan out. Some of the cars still driving were new or appeared to be, anyways. His thoughts were racing. Jimmy was a prepper and knew what was about to happen. Being a faithful prepper he had a few things. First, he was only about 25 miles into a full tank of gas. In the Jeep he had an AR-15, a Sig P-226, and a get-home bag that was more like a full on bug out bag (BOB). He also had a bug out location (BOL), north across state lines, a three hour flat-out run from his house just outside Hebron. There was where plenty of supplies and self-sufficiency waited. Getting there was going to be the ultimate goal. Yet his mind reviewed the fact he had more ammo, a few months' worth of freeze dried food, and other survival gear at his house.

The traffic lights were completely out as he pulled up to the intersection of County Road 231 and Route 2. He realized he had a choice. To his right was the distant column of smoke from the burning airplane, the same in his rear view mirror. To the left was his home, 4 miles away. Straight on was where he needed to be. He took a few deep breaths to clear his head. He needed to take stock of what he had before making his next move.

CHAPTER TWO

Jimmy paused at the intersection and reflected on the three days' worth of supplies in his BOB in the back seat. His nerves were already beginning to tingle in anticipation of what might happen next. Instinctively he flicked on his left turn signal. He chuckled as he realized the futility in indicating his next move. He hesitantly executed the turn and then pressed the accelerator with a little urgency. He began to speed down Highway 231 towards his home about four miles out of town.

The story was much the same down the 2 lane highway, some cars still driving, some completely disabled in the middle and on the side of the road. He flicked on the radio, static. He hit the scan button and the tuner began to rise up the dial and found nothing. Nothing, that is, until he hit 1630. Jimmy didn't know it but 1630 was an emergency alert station out of Schererville, Indiana. The radio stopped on 1630.

"...Difficulties with the power grid. Please stay in your homes until further notice. The National Guard has..."

He shut it off. This was for real. He depressed the accelerator a bit more. Just a minute later he was coming up on County Line road where he rented a house a mile to the south.

His rented house consisted of what was basically an old converted garage on an abandoned farm. This time of year it was drafty as hell and sucked down the propane, even when supplemented by the wood stove. It was supposed to be temporary until he could get a permanent place up by his folks' BOL. After leaving the military he figured he'd spend a few years saving up some cash. He, like many preppers, ended up dumping more and more money into gear and gadgets. Every year he'd consider the possibility of moving off the grid, then he'd push it back one more year. He should have been there by now, but then again, he always had his folks place as a fall back.

When Jimmy was a kid, his parents bought a place just east of a little town called Freesoil, Michigan, right smack dab in the middle of the Manistee National Forest. His dad was a prepper before the word had a meaning. 25 acres, surrounded by hundreds of acres of Federal land. Twenty-five years of preparation and today seemed to be the day for which his dad had been preparing. All he had to do was get there.

As he pulled into the drive he figured he had just a bit of time to grab what he could. IT had started just less than 20 minutes ago. As he stepped out of the Jeep he again felt the ground rumble, but this time is was low and growing. He knew that rumble. He glanced up to see the F-16's flying low, 500 ft. off the deck, tearing towards Chicago. An instant later he could hear the sound of air ripping in half. Something didn't sit quite right as he was southeast of the city and Chicago was covered by the Wisconsin Air National Guard out of Madison, Wisconsin. *No time to worry about that*, he thought. As he ran to the house the rumble faded into the distance.

Hebron, Indiana was still technically a "suburb" of Chicago, which was 45 miles to the northeast as the crow flies. He knew that enough of the unprepared hordes would be emptying the city to clog the roads within a few hours. Hell, on a Friday afternoon the weekenders would jam I-

80/94 on the way towards their summer homes in Michigan, and that was just the direction he would be headed. On a normal Friday afternoon they might add a few hours the trip up to his parents. This particular Tuesday afternoon, who knew what it would mean? He had run through this scenario in his head over and over. He was always overly cautious; he had enough gear, food, and supplies on hand to wait it out for months. So much in fact he couldn't cram it all in the jeep. This was a scenario he felt would require him to get out, to 'bug out.' He might have to leave a great deal of it behind.

He didn't leave things to chance, he'd never let his tank run under half full but he still kept enough gas in the shed for the trip. In the old Jeep's case it'd take just over twelve gallons to traverse the 250 miles to the ranch. Three, 5-gallon gas containers awaited in the shed. Every fill-up he'd haul one to the gas station to keep them fresh, putting one in the Jeep and refilling it. With what was left in the tank and the gas cans he figured he had a 650 mile range if he needed it. He quickly grabbed two of the containers and trudged back down the driveway towards the Jeep. Just as he was opening the hatch he caught the reflection in the glass of a car turning into the drive.

It was Eugene Ott, the neighbor from across the way. Eugene could have walked the 500 feet but he didn't like to walk. He didn't ever want to do anything to help himself. He pulled his beat up old Chrysler right behind the Jeep and rolled down the window, sticking out his fat head. "Jimmy! Must be the big one," he said in a half sarcastic tone.

"I don't know, you tell me?" Jimmy's replied.

Jimmy kept Eugene at arm's length at all times, he didn't trust him. He was cordial but never offered him more information than he had to. Eugene was the type of guy always looking to game the system, or a neighbor for that matter.

"Where you headed?" asked Eugene. Jimmy was aware that Eugene knew exactly what he was doing short of an address. They'd been neighbors for quite a few years and Jimmy had made the mistake on occasion of trying to awaken Eugene to the need to be more self-reliant. Eugene lived in another world and had full faith in the Government. Getting caught loading gas cans into the Jeep didn't help.

"I'm gonna see if I can't get some more gas for the generator, just in case something is going on," Jimmy finally replied, hoping Eugene would bite.

"They looked pretty full to me" Eugene quipped.

"I'm going to use them to fill the Jeep when I get to the gas station." He replied.

The statement seemed to pass right through Eugene's ears, "Power is out and so is the phone. And what's going on with those fires?" Eugene asked. Jimmy was well aware of what was going on but neglected the fact that Eugene probably had his head ensconced in the latest episode of Maury when IT began

"Don't know Eugene, looks like the power's out." He restated the obvious, realizing there was a question on Eugene's mind that wasn't making it to his lips.

Jimmy had been so focused on trying to read Eugene's intent he neglected the fact the Chrysler's radio was set to the Emergency Broadcast station. He realized it just in time to hear "The President has declared a National Emergency" emanate from the speakers.

"You're not thinking of leaving? Are you?" There was the question. "The President has declared a National Emergency, we're supposed to stay in our homes".

"Looks like you're the one breaking the law, Eugene." He sarcastically chuckled.

Jimmy knew far too well that Eugene didn't give two craps about him, or his well being, or the law for that matter. Jimmy was a nice guy; nice to the point that he'd let Eugene take advantage of him for a while when they first met. He plowed his drive in the winter, chores in the summer, never receiving a thing in return. Not that he expected anything, but that was the problem. Whenever he'd help his neighbor out it was almost like it was expected he do more. Eugene wasn't stupid; he knew how to manipulate everything around him to his advantage. He didn't work much, but judging by his rotund frame he never missed a meal. No, at the very least he wanted Jimmy to stay put for his own comfort and security. Eugene equated a situation like this with needing Jimmy's skills and supplies. *Even though the world is full of them, it would take a moron not to realize something big was happening.*

Eugene poured himself out of the car. He was a full 6 inches taller than Jimmy and had him by well over a hundred pounds. Jimmy despised the sweat suit and the greasy black curly hair he usually wore. It dripped of laziness.

Jimmy stood between the hatch of the Jeep and the front bumper of the old Chrysler. Eugene's towering (if rotund) figure composed itself to as formidable threat as it could.

"Jimmy, I think you should stick around," ordered Eugene. He took a step forward.

Wow, thought Jimmy. He'd run scenario after scenario through his head. This one never hit the radar. He'd never imagined his first threat in SHTF would be his lazy conniving neighbor threatening him not to leave. Eugene definitely had a sensible idea of what was going on. There isn't much you can hide from neighbors over years. He knew Jimmy was prepared but he was pretty sure he didn't know to what extent.

"Look, I'll be back in twenty minutes. I'm just headed to the gas station to top off the Jeep," He said, hoping his nerves weren't starting to give away his position.

"Come on Jimmy, I'm not a moron. The power is out everywhere. You aren't going to be pumping any gas. Besides, you've got enough gas here to run the generator for a few days and I just bought a bunch of steak and lobster. I'm gonna need your generator again to keep the refrigerator running. I know you are leaving and I think you need to stay!" asserted Eugene.

That's right, Jimmy thought. Yesterday was the first of the month. Eugene always "stocked up" on the first of the month and off of Jimmy's taxpayer dime, nonetheless. It was then that Jimmy saw the glint of the pistol haphazardly stuffed into the fat bastard's waistband. For a brief instant his heart misfired and beat a few times backwards.

Jimmy's mind presented itself with two choices. It was the way he had trained it to react in situations like this. It always had two possible ways out of any scenario. He had more supplies than he could take with him, he didn't need the generator as the cabin was on alternative energy. He could probably buy his way out of the situation, but that was going to take precious time. He also had a .40 caliber handgun in his waistband holster.

CHAPTER THREE

Eugene made the decision for him when he took another step closer, crossing the border into Jimmy's personal space. Jimmy's hand, already close to the gun inside his waistband, moved accordingly. He could see the shock and surprise of what was happening on his face in the reflection of Eugene's glasses.

At nearly the same instant, Eugene's intent stare focused on Jimmy suddenly darted over his shoulder as an immense flash illuminated his face. His pupils shrunk to pin pricks. The hair on the back of Jimmy's neck stood on end and it warmed instantly as if in a hot August noonday sun. For a brief moment Jimmy experienced sensory overload. Eugene's jaw began to drop as his synapses began to fire in disbelief. His attention was no longer on Jimmy, but on the fiery orb growing over his shoulder in the distance. Jimmy's window of opportunity was opening.

He grabbed the pistol from his waistband and in one smooth motion, struck Eugene on the side of the head. The fat man fell to the ground like a pile of wet towels. When the heat on Jimmy's back continued to increase, he dropped to the snow covered driveway between the Jeep and the Chrysler. Was it two seconds or three since the window opened? He continued to count, 5, 6, 7, the intense light and heat appeared to have no end. 8, 9 and he noticed the intensity wane just a fraction. At 10 the magnificent pulse was fading, and by eleven it felt as if an equal to the overhead sun.

My God. What was happening? Thoughts raced through Jimmy's head. Even though he'd whacked him ten seconds prior, he'd forgotten about Eugene. He laid sprawled out on the ground next to the left front tire of the Chrysler, a huge knot forming on his right temple.

As the intense heat regressed into a cold winter day, Jimmy stood up and looked to the northwest. He observed the massive fireball rising into the frigid blue winter sky. He intently stared as it rose majestically above what was once Chicago. As the fireball climbed it began to cloak itself in smokey billows. Barely a stem was visible below the off-white cloud racing towards the heavens. The slight icy breeze blowing directly into his face started biting his motionless figure.

It was this chilling wind that snapped Jimmy out of his stupor. Jimmy was a prepper and a retired Marine with NBC (Nuclear, Biological, and Chemical) training. His scrambled brain began returning calculations on his observations filtered through his training. A ten second flash equaled a yield in the vicinity of hundreds of kilotons. The stemless mushroom cloud revealed an airburst. The gentle breeze directly in his face told him the fallout might arrive in six or seven hours. Jimmy's desire to bug out suddenly took on a dire urgency. The masses formerly confused by the computer virus would suddenly begin to panic on the latest development. The roads would now be shortly clogged with the irrational, trying to escape to an undetermined destination. Time was of the essence.

Jimmy sprang to his feet. He pulled his Leatherman out of his pocket and cut the wiring for the trailer hitch out of the back of his Jeep. Pulling Eugene's fat-laden arms behind his back he tied them together. He attempted to pick him up but the 300 pound mass was just a bit much. He pulled Eugene's pistol out of his pants and opened the passenger door, gently placing the weapon deep under the driver's seat of the man's car.

He sprinted back to the house, the urgency to get *going* increasing as the seconds ticked by. His first grab from his prepping room was four 5 gallon jugs of water. He ran back to the Jeep and threw them in the back. Next was the tote full of the large cans of freeze dried food (with a high ratio of Beef Stroganoff) and a tote of varied pouches. Given the nature of what was happening, a few gas masks, some rolls of plastic, duct tape, and a couple of surplus German rain ponchos found themselves added to the pile. He selected a few choice weapons; an AR, a shotgun, two dozen or so magazines, and few thousand rounds of ammunition in ammo boxes. Some spare clothes, tools, documents and copies on a thumb drive rounded off the list. With the extra supplies and what he had in his bug out bag (BOB) he could make a pretty good effort at getting to the cabin. Just a few minutes had gone by and the Jeep's cargo area was pretty well packed. There was still plenty left for Eugene to rob when he came to.

As Jimmy opened the driver's door he glanced at his watch, three minutes and thirty seconds, not bad. It was then that the air crackled like lightning and the low rumbling thunderous roar began. It was the sound of hundreds of thousands of people and the City of Chicago succumbing to a nuclear weapon. Jimmy paused to look at the mushroom cloud that was now clawing its way through the Stratosphere. All that was left of the bomb's blast energy puffed his face like a quick stiff breeze.

"Oh, crap," he muttered under his breath. He'd forgotten about the EMP! He had read studies that showed even modern cars may not be as affected by an electromagnetic pulse as previously though. Plus, he was about 45 miles from the detonation point. Nevertheless, the turning of the key was a tense moment. He might be screwed if it didn't start and there was significant fallout. A sense of relief washed over him as the starter clicked and the engine came to life.

Not even bothering to with the driveway, Jimmy swung the Jeep around and punched it up over a snow bank. Slowing briefly at the end of the driveway he made a quick left and was on his way.

A quarter mile down the road he saw the planes again, this time moving with even more fervor. They were about 500 feet off the deck, probably just beyond the sound barrier. He tried to pay more attention than he did the first time, but they were moving way too fast. If they had tail numbers or identification, Jimmy couldn't tell. They were screaming off to the southeast. *Did they do this?* Jimmy wondered.

He quickly reviewed the last hour of his life. It started with a ham sandwich, there was the virus that brought down nearly every microprocessor he was aware of, a confrontation with his conniving neighbor, and a nuclear bomb.

What could be next? He figured he was way ahead of most people's reaction time. He could try the interstate; maybe he had that much of a lead on the masses. Alternatively, he could head further east and then cut north using the back roads. Either way he'd be dodging the virus-disabled cars. The 250 mile trip to the cabin normally took a little less than 4 hours on an open freeway. Taking his backup route would take 5 or more. It was close to 1 o'clock and the sun would be setting in 4 hours. On top of that, fallout was headed in his direction.

\

CHAPTER FOUR

Jimmy considered his options, taking one disaster event at a time. The virus that shut down electronics followed by a nuclear bomb being detonated in the air over Chicago would send people into a state of panicked chaos. The interstate might be faster since he had a jump on most people's ability to react. Being a retired Marine with nuclear, biological, and chemical training along with a long time prepper gave him many advantages. He understood what was going on better than most and knew the time was counting down when the fallout would reach him. He took a deep breath. The back roads would make the trip take longer but would have less of a chance of being clogged with panicked people. *Well'* Jimmy thought to himself, *Either way I go, it will be dark by the time I make it.* His top priority was to make it to the land his father bought years ago that he turned into his bug out location (BOL), some 250 miles north of his current location. That decided, he turned east and laid on the gas.

Here and there, cars were stopped in the middle of the road or had been pushed off to the side. His training was on autopilot in the back of his mind, constantly taking in his surroundings and considering other route options if they were needed. He felt a little uncomfortable resorting to his back up route from the start but after making 40 or so miles with little issue, he felt he had made the right choice. He was on a particularly long straight stretch with no other cars on the road. Jimmy punched it and drove in the middle without thinking, his training taking over. As he made his way, he wondered if Eugene had woken up yet and then remembered the emergency radio station. Scanning the area again for any threats, he flipped the switch on.

"...Has declared a state of emergency. Martial law is now in effect nationwide. You are ordered to immediately return to your homes and comply with authorities. National Guard will be enforcing a 6pm curfew. You may detained for non-"

He turned the station off, the sense of urgency increasing. With the Guard being deployed and martial law in effect, he wondered if there would be problems crossing state lines. He hoped he was far enough ahead of the waves of people to make it across. Slowing down to make the turn north, Jimmy glanced at his watch. Just less than 2 hours had gone by since IT happened. He knew he would be out after the curfew and in the dark, which would make him easily spotted. "Deal with one thing at a time," he muttered. He saw some people on the sides of the road here and there. A few reached out a hand imploringly for him to stop while others looked to be in shock and unresponsive to anything around them.

As he neared Plymouth, he noticed more cars on the road and had to slow down to maneuver around them, sometimes going onto sidewalks. The smell of smoke was in the air and Jimmy could see clouds rising from the west. He saw people walking around with dazed looks in their eyes, wounded from car accidents. Others were simply sitting and crying. Jimmy knew he couldn't stop though it pained him to keep going. Taking a few side streets, he was able to get through and continue north on Hwy 31. His adrenaline pumping, he reached into his bag for a bottle of water and a granola bar, considering the best way to go. If Plymouth was affected like this, South Bend would be even worse. With a population of over 100,000 and the suburbs besides, it might be best to go around and cross into Michigan at Granger. Checking his fuel and going through the mental lists again, Jimmy focused on driving. As he progressed, he noticed more vehicles clogging the road. People began approaching the jeep with hands stretched out imploringly. He pressed on, going over road maps in his head and realized a mistake in his line of thinking.

Granger would not be an option since there was access to Interstate 80/90 and a truck stop with fast food places and strip malls being built. As he neared the turn off for state road 933, he made a decision and turned right. He would instead take a series of back roads and cross into Michigan on state highway 5. It was 'in the boonies' and was not a major access hub to the interstate. He set the plan into motion. He was never more thankful for his Jeep as he was during that drive and its ability to handle curbs, raised medians and even evading a cow that had gotten loose.

The going was considerably slower and by the time he was approaching the state line, there was only about an hour of daylight left. He was able to see down the straight road, a line of cars for at least a mile. He opened a bag on the passenger seat and grabbed a travel set of binoculars. Focusing in, he could see the iconic vehicles and stance of soldiers walking between cars, weapons slung over shoulders. They were making their way down the line. Jimmy knew this might be a problem. Flashing the I.D. of a retired Marine, the guys may just let him through. Then again, his driver's license had an Indiana address and they might turn him away. If he turned around, he may be followed and possibly detained; especially if they saw all of his gear stowed and the ammo cans. After all, martial law was in effect. He took a deep breath and sat for a second to ponder his situation.

He found it odd that the National Guard was already on border crossings; even at small ones like this. It made him wonder how long the government had had plans in place for a disaster of this magnitude. He knew he needed to keep moving though. He could cross the line on some railroad tracks, but he had put himself too close to population. He could attempt to drive the Jeep on a frozen river. The winter had been cold enough. He'd considered rails, rivers, and hiking trails as alternatives for bugging out but he had always considered them on foot.

The walls started closing in on Jimmy. It was a quarter after three and the sun would set around five-thirty. It was February 15th and cold out there. He would never make it to Freesoil by dark at this point, even if he could get over the state line. He was 180 miles away still. The few options available to him would add even more time and distance to his flight. Jimmy wondered if all of the people around him were aware of fallout that would be raining down in a few hours. One thing was for sure, he knew, and he had to get away.

He lay back in his seat, his head against the headrest as he closed his eyes. What should he do? Land travel was a problem and would be worse tomorrow.

His eyes snapped open and focused on the side mirror, as if a light went on in his head. A faint sound had woken him and an idea began to form. A small grin turned up the corners of his lips. *Naw*, was his first thought, followed by, *What the hell, the world is ending anyways.*

Jimmy quickly spun the wheel to the left, reached down and put the Jeep back into drive. The pedal went nearly to the floor as if to coax the Jeep into a 180-degree turn in one motion. If land travel was not the best option, perhaps it was time to take to the air. Right smack dab in the center of the windshield was a Cessna 172 taking off from the Elkhart Municipal Airport two miles away. Jimmy was about to become a felon.

For the first time in his life he could write off all of the people that told him he had wasted his money on those flying lessons. He never did get his license, he had to "put it off" when money got tight. Nevertheless, he had soloed a few times. He had always wanted to add "pilot" to his list of bug out attributes. The thought just hadn't crossed his mind up to this point because the "box" hadn't been checked on his list of accomplishments.

When he was a student, the first thing he learned about small airplanes in the context of bugging out was they never locked them. If someone wanted to steal something out of the airplane they would cause more damage breaking in then the value of what they might steal. The second thing was, if they didn't leave the keys in the plane, the ignition was easy to hotwire. Jimmy reached over and opened the glove compartment of the Jeep, just to make sure his tool set was still there. *Bingo.* Jimmy was still gambling, even with the latest decision. He needed two more stars to align. First, he hoped a Piper Warrior was on the tarmac and second, that it had enough fuel in the wing tanks to get him where he was going. Now was not the time to "borrow" an unfamiliar airplane, especially for a pilot with about 40 hours of total experience. The Piper Warrior was the plane in which he took his lessons and were common.

Jimmy made a left onto Route 6, which spanned the north side of the airport. He carefully scanned the parked planes until he found his prey, a white Warrior with a green and gold stripe. As luck would have it, the gate was still opened to the airport entrance. He quickly pulled in and put the Jeep in park next to a hanger. Jimmy figured the cops in town were pretty busy at this point but he would still have to make this quick.

Jimmy had packed his crate of survival binders right behind the passenger seat. He rifled through them until he found the one labeled "Miscellaneous". He really should have committed this information to memory but he didn't. He had some more decisions to make that were critical to the next part of his journey. He found the specs on the

Warrior. The sheet confirmed he had 940 pounds with which to work. Jimmy weighed in at 180, so that left 760 pounds for fuel and gear. Even worse, the cramped cockpit would severely limit what Jimmy could pack in the plane. He had to make some quick mental calculations. He'd have to carry whatever he brought so that narrowed his choices.

Jimmy pulled the Jeep up to right behind the plane and got out. He took a quick look around and didn't see anyone. With a quick prayer he put his hand on the door handle and turned it, sighing relief when it opened. He grabbed the fuel dipstick next to the pilots seat and went over to the left wing tank filler cap. If there wasn't enough fuel it was game over. A feeling of relief again washed over Jimmy. There was enough to get him where he was going. Roughly 40 gallons of fuel removes another 240 pounds from the planes capacity, leaving Jimmy with 520 pounds to work with. Thankfully, he'd probably run out of space in the small plane before he overloaded it.

He quickly ran through pre-flight of the exterior of the airplane from his survival binder checklist, at least all of the stuff that mattered to this one time use; Flaps, elevators, Pitot tube, ailerons, etc. He removed the tie downs, hopped in, and set the parking brake. He was just about to break out the tool set when he noticed the keys. *Wow, it's my lucky day, sort of,* he thought to himself. He turned the master switch and fuel pump on. He yelled "clear" to nobody and after another brief prayer, turned the key. The Piper's engine sputtered to life and it was a beautiful sound to Jimmy's ears. He glanced at all the gauges to make sure they sprang to life and set the altimeter.

He had to get moving. It was like some unseen hand was pushing him to go faster, to get out. He ran back to the Jeep and grabbed his BOB. Jimmy would be walking from the airport to the ranch.

His newly formed plan was to get to Baldwin Municipal Airport but that was still a good 15 mile hike. He quickly shoveled in some of the extra food, clothing, and his snowshoes. Right now there was snow waist deep at the ranch. He could walk on the roads but figured he would need the snowshoes to disappear into the woods if need be. Considering the snow he only grabbed a 5 gallon jug of water. There would be plenty of available water through melting ice and snow.

The space in the small airplane was quickly filled. The tight back seat contained his bag, the clothing, snowshoes, and the extra food and water. All that was left was the tiny baggage area. This space was filled by his survival binders, a little more food and a couple of ammo cans. Jimmy figured the engine was somewhat warm at this point. He took a sorrowful last look at his trusty Jeep; he figured it might be somewhat of an even trade to the owner of the airplane he was borrowing. It had a few months of food; some fresh water, gasoline, and the keys were in the ignition. If the fallout wasn't too bad it might be put to good use.

Jimmy pulled the mixture a little leaner and unlocked the parking brake. Giving it a little throttle, the plane started to roll forward. The rudder pedals were always the toughest to Jimmy, he could never quite get the hang of steering with his feet. He taxied the plane to the end of the runway, pointing the nose of the machine into the wind. After checking the magnetos he took a deep breath, set the flaps, gave the plane full throttle, and released the brakes.

The Warrior began to barrel down the runway. Jimmy was rusty, but managed to keep the plane straight. At 55 knots he pulled back a little on the stick and at 75 he was off the ground. Jimmy would be flying by the seat of his pants, staying under 500 feet to avoid radar contact, if there were any radars left watching. As the plane rose off the ground he could see the smoky mess that was formerly Chicago. The black fallout was fast approaching and he needed to get away, and quickly. He turned the plane due north and began looking for route twelve. He would follow twelve slightly east until 131, which would take him north towards the Baldwin Airport. The air was pretty tranquil, even at 500 feet on this frigid day. Jimmy could hardly believe stealing an airplane would be the easiest part of this day. It was almost relaxing.

It was about 25 miles out of Grand Rapids that Jimmy's streak of good luck gave out. Although the weather had been perfectly clear to this point, the west winds had stirred up some lake effect snow. Jimmy could see it to the north-northwest, creeping across the ground like a thick fog. He was about 30 miles or so out of Baldwin and it was closing in on a quarter to five. He could head straight west and land at one of three airports closely clustered together or he could take a chance and hope he could beat the snow and land in Baldwin. Landing to the west would add another 30 miles or so to his journey on foot.

CHAPTER FIVE

Jimmy sighed and resigned himself to spending at least one night out in the frigid cold. He couldn't stomach the thought of adding another couple of nights by adding 30 or so miles to a journey on foot through the deep snow, though. He pushed the throttle just a bit and turned the nose of the Warrior slightly, so as to align with the Baldwin airport. The snow wasn't there, yet. The engine began to buzz at a slightly higher rate and the plane added a few knots of airspeed as he pushed on to his destination.

He continued to fly for the next fifteen minutes up M-37. As he approached the airport, Jimmy's stomach sank all the way below the seat to the floor of the airplane. The flakes began to dance around the cockpit. He saw a single Cessna at the west end of the airport, completely covered in snow, but no runway.

What Jimmy didn't realize was the Baldwin airport was closed from November to April, due to lack of snow removal. This winter had already been a doozy; there was over 70 inches of compact snow between the wheels of the Piper and the runway.

Jimmy panicked as the snow was beginning to swirl around the plane. He passed over the airport and began to look around. He would be in the lake effect snow squall in a matter of minutes and it was getting dark. He could belly flop the airplane where the runway should be, but he wasn't quite sure what would happen. His only other option was to put it down on M-37 that ran next to the airport.

Jimmy pulled the throttle out and banked the plane into a hard left turn, his airspeed began to bleed, 105..100..95..90. The turn put the town of Baldwin behind him. He wouldn't find anything open enough for a crash landing in that direction. Jimmy quickly glanced at the instruments. He was 200 feet above the ground that was beginning to be obscured by the snow. He reached down between the seats and pulled the flaps up all the way. The road was beginning to disappear just below him as he pushed the throttle to maintain airspeed. The snow burst forth from the sky just as Jimmy needed to find a safe place to put the plane down. That's the way it was in Michigan; one second you see the clear blue sky, the next second it is snowing like a blizzard. *But just on your side of the street,* Jimmy chuckled wryly as his mind darted around for an option that didn't end up killing himself or anyone else in the process.

Time slowed as Jimmy's options began to run out. The whiteout lowered visibility even more and his heart dropped through the bottom of the plane as he was blinded. Jimmy could faintly see the blue sky just above him. There was the slightest let up in the snow, and just south of the airport there was an area devoid of trees on either side of M-37 for about an eighth of a mile. Jimmy aimed the plane for a touchdown, on the road, in the clearing. Two seconds after spotting the clearing, the whiteout ensued again.

He killed the throttle on the airplane and kept the nose of the plane level. As he sunk through the air, the tops of the trees could be seen through the falling snow on the sides. The road was straight with the nose of the plane, and Jimmy added a little rudder to counter the slight crosswind to keep it that way. The speed was bleeding off, requiring him to pull back further and further on the yoke. About 20 feet off the ground, the trees disappeared but so did his ability to pull back any further on the stick. He was concentrating so hard on trying to get down in the clearing he completely missed the stall warning screaming in his ears.

The Warrior fell the last 20 feet as if it had brought a parachute that was a bit too small. It hit the ground with a loud thud and bounced a few feet back into the air. On the second touch down, the wheels stayed on the ground but Jimmy was not in control of the direction it was travelling. The plane began to slide ever so slightly to the left side of the road. Through the snow on the pavement, the tires offered suggestions of which way the plane should be going, but nothing more. Jimmy had been knocked around by the bounce and was calculating in his noggin' what to do with his feet (which you may or may not remember steer the plane on the ground). Like a skid in a car, you should steer into it. He mashed his right foot down on the pedal...nothing. The plane was still traveling down M-37 at about 40 miles an hour and headed for the six foot plow embankment on the left.

Anyone who has ever driven in Michigan in winter, and had the misfortune of meeting a snow bank, can attest to what happens to Jimmy's borrowed airplane next. As the left wheel dropped off the pavement onto the shoulder the slightly deeper snow instantly snapped the nose of the plane straight towards the embankment. The prop would have hit it first, if the left wing wasn't so overreaching. It clipped the bank and rendered the airplane no longer airworthy.

As the prop hit the bank, it dug in and gave a spectacular display of bending metal and snow spray. For a finale, killing the last few miles an hour, the right wheel dug in just a bit, causing the left one to rise about a foot off the ground, where it teetered for moment, before it settled down as the plane came to a full stop.

Jimmy was unsure of whether or not surviving a plane crash could be checked off his list. He sat there for a moment trying to compose himself, the flakes beginning to stick to the slightly cracked plexi-glass windshield of the Piper. The whirring of the instruments caught his attention and he flicked off the master switch, just in case there was fuel leaking somewhere. He took a deep breath and tried to relax a little. He was thankful to have made it this far in such a short amount of time - and overcoming so many obstacles. The light of day was fading through the snow squall and as tired as he was, he was going to have to make another decision. The plane was off the road, more or less, with the nose buried in the snow bank. He was thirty miles from a familiar warm bed. It was only twenty miles as the crow flies, but the crow was broken. The previous night had seen a full moon, he could continue on and set up camp off of M37 in the trees, or he could just rest his nerves somewhat and spend the night in the plane. Either way, Baldwin lay three miles to the north, between him and nothing. He shook his head to clear it some and went through it all over again, focusing in on the details and getting things in perspective.

CHAPTER SIX

Jimmy sat in the fuselage of the 'borrowed' plane and took stock of the situation. Today he had already survived a recycling plant tearing itself to bits after a virus took down all modern electronics. He survived his pudgy neighbor Eugene who laughingly tried to strong-arm him into staying, a nuclear bomb, and a plane crash (of sorts). He was 30ish miles away from a safe place with a warm bed. It was getting dark and the snow was not showing any signs of slowing down. He was more or less on state highway M37 and knew he was close to Idlewild which was cause for concern.

Idlewild was the kind of place not many would expect to find in the countryside. Located in the middle of a national forest, the town was made up of burned down buildings and gangs that were known for violence and reveling in chaos. Most people stayed far away from the area due to the reputation. He could go around, but that would add to his already 30 mile hike through deep snow to get to his BOL. Still, he figured he was far ahead of most people's reaction times and though he had lost a lot in supplies to get to where he currently was, he was not without resources. Stretching a bit and making another mental check for injuries, Jimmy unbuckled himself from the seat and looked to the gear that had been tossed around in the crash. His BOB and snowshoes looked fine but the 5 gallons of water had gotten a hole in the side and water had dribbled out until it was below the line. When Jimmy picked it up, he estimated there were about 2 gallons left. Carrying a 5-gallon water container for 30 plus miles in deep snow was not something he really wanted to do. Opening his BOB, he pulled out his CamelBak water container and filled it, along with some empty plastic bottles that were in the plane. Double checking everything one last time, he glanced out the window as he was struggling to put his pack on and noticed the snowfall had increased: visibility was going to be a problem.

Jimmy used his shoulder to get the jammed door open and ended up spilling out of it into the deep snow. Standing up and brushing himself off, he looked around as best as he could and listened for any noises. He wanted to get out of there before anyone came to investigate the plane crash area. Heading in the direction of Baldwin, Jimmy kept to the road for a bit while he planned his next move.

After about half a mile, he thought he saw lights, unmoving in the snow and was torn on what to do. Should he try and help or continue on? *I am no help to anyone until I get to my bug out location, that must be my main focus right now.* He trudged away from the lights. It was dark by this point and he knew he needed to get some rest if he wanted to make it to his cabin tomorrow. Strapping his snowshoes on, he headed off the road and into the woods to find a spot for camp. He wasn't too worried about anyone following his tracks with the wind whirling the snow around. After another 3/4 of a mile off the road, he found a spot with some trees that sheltered one side of a little hill. He knew he would need shelter from the wind and snow but he also needed a way to make a fire that would not be easily seen or go out in the weather.

Jimmy was ever alert, listening for sounds of humans or animals but all he heard was the wind and snow in the trees. Getting into his BOB, he pulled out his hatchet and paracord. Making a small lean-to shelter out of evergreen branches and binding them together, the shelter was completed in short order despite the poor visibility. Jimmy lined the inside with more evergreen boughs and laid a Mylar blanket down as a barrier to reflect his heat back at him instead of being sucked into the ground. He didn't want to wake up as a popsicle. As soon as the shelter was in place, the next step was a fire that he could heat food or water without being seen. Again using his hatchet, he hacked at the frozen earth until he dug a shallow hole to build a fire in. Using supplies from the bag, he was able to make a small fire that reflected heat back to him and give off very little smoke. After an hour, Jimmy was warmer than he had been almost all day. With shelter and some Mountain House Beef Stroganoff cooking inside its bag, he started to feel better. After eating and drinking some warm water, he put the fire out to avoid being seen and climbed into his shelter to get some sleep. He didn't think he would be able to sleep much but as soon as he found a comfortable spot he slept deeply.

Some hours later, he woke with a sudden jerk and was confused with his surroundings. Memories of the previous day came back to him in a rush and he relaxed a bit, and went through the goals for the day. A glance out from under the lean-to let him know several things: it was about an hour before dawn, the snow had built up against the side of his shelter that provided great camouflage, and it had stopped snowing. As he began preparations to make another small fire, he heard voices in the woods. *I wonder if that is what woke me up*, he mused to himself. All his senses were on high alert as he began to quietly get his gear in order in case he had to make a quick exit. He heard a shout and a replying answer but could not make out the words. Blood pumping in his ears, he worried that these may be some thugs from Idlewild and then laughed at his moment of panic. He was miles away from there and with no cars running, it was unlikely anyone from there would be near him. Still, he mentally prepared for a confrontation. Risking another look, he was met with nothing but shadows in the trees and the sounds of footsteps coming closer to his location. He needed to get going and make it to the BOL today; the idea of spending another frozen night outside was plenty of motivation in itself but so was the security and comfort of the cabin.

Assessing the situation more closely, he knew there were two people out there at the least and they were getting closer. There were no tracks leading to his location thanks to the wind and falling snow but his senses told him it would be best to avoid these people. It was an hour before dawn the day after everything went to hell. They could be people just trying to get home but he had gear they didn't including food and that could be just enough to cause a real problem. Gathering his gear, Jimmy waited to hear the shout and reply again and made his move out of the shelter and away from the voices. There was little he could do about his tracks at this point so he just kept marching with a determination borne of military training.

No one followed him and after a couple miles, he knew he needed food and some warmth. Finding another sheltered spot was easier and it took less time to get something warm to eat. While he was enjoying his food, he considered his path. Pulling out a smaller map of the BOL and surrounding area, Jimmy decided that he would not go too far around Idlewild. He was banking on his military training and experience to see him through any confrontations. It was either that or add five miles to his travel time. He packed up his gear and headed out once again. The day was cold and clear and…quiet. Really quiet. No machinery of any kind could be heard. No airplanes overhead or cars, tractors – nothing was making a sound and he had to shake off a feeling of unease. It was a little surreal. The next eight miles were fairly uneventful as he crossed forested areas and country roads. He could see people in the distance here and there but overall there was not much movement. *I bet people are really starting to freak out now. I wonder if there are any news reports being broadcasted. With the EMP, it could be sketchy*, he mused to himself as he went along. Even though he was still some 20 miles away from his BOL, Jimmy felt pretty good considering how things had progressed. At any point along the path, he could have been injured or died from various threats and yet, he was still here. He pushed on, eating a protein bar to keep his strength up. *Well, the upside of all of this is I will lose the extra 15 pounds I have.* As he neared what he considered the borders of Idlewild, he stopped and took stock. Getting his binoculars out of his bag, Jimmy set down to do some recon to see what kinds of threats were visible. What he saw was like something out of a Mad Max movie. People were pushing vehicles along the road into the town and men with AK 47 and AR 15 assault rifles were patrolling the area. *Well, that didn't take long,* Jimmy thought. *They are really getting into this.* He knew some people would actually look forward to a world without the rule of law (WROL). From the looks of it, these people fit into that group. He saw them hanging a sign that read "Looters welcome, we need the target practice" on a tree next to the road where they had blocked it with cars. *I need to get out of here before they see me. If I backtrack and go around, I will spend another night out in the cold but if I go around closer to their borders, I risk being seen. I need to get to the cabin ASAP! Here we go!*

CHAPTER SEVEN

Sighing heavily, Jimmy put his binoculars away and cinched up his pack. *I wish I knew what was going on out there. Did they figure out who did what? Or what happened to trigger it all?* He began his backtracking and then turned, taking a wider path around Idlewild. There wasn't much he could do about the tracks he was making but it looked like there might be more snow today. Pulling his water bottle from the side pocket of his pack, he took a drink and kept moving forward while keeping aware of his surroundings. After about a mile of slow going, he found what was likely a country back road though it was hard to tell. It was a cleared path wide enough for vehicles. He guessed it was either that or this was a 4 wheeler track for recreation, given the tracks that were mostly filled in with snow. Either way, it was easier traveling and took Jimmy in the general direction he wanted to go. It was just after noon and he had only made it about 5 miles since he woke up, three of which were added to the original tally by going around Idlewild.

As he trudged along, he thought he heard a faint noise. *A machine?* He wondered. *Maybe it is a 4 wheeler or something. Time to disappear!* He looked down at the tracks his snowshoes were making and felt foolish. Anyone who may be coming down this path would notice tracks that suddenly turned off into the woods. The sound grew louder and Jimmy made up his mind right then that he was not going to run anywhere. Turning fully toward the sound of what he knew to be a snow machine, he changed his stance to one of a tired traveler; non-threatening and just looking to get to his cabin to check on things. He had no idea what mental state the person or people might be in and if they were from Idlewild, it could get ugly real quick. Best to make whoever it is think that he was resigned to whatever lay ahead. About a quarter mile away, he saw the snow machine with a single rider on it making way down the same trail he was on. Deciding that standing there made him look like a dumb oaf, and knowing the rider had seen him, he brushed the snow off a stump and sat down to wait.

As the mystery person got closer, Jimmy started feeling like a sitting duck and was just about to get up and move off when the machine made a funny noise and stopped just behind a clump of trees around a bend in the trail. *Oh great, either they are hurt or are setting up an ambush. Or they are* pretending *they are hurt to lure me in.* Sighing heavily again, he cinched his pack up and went in the direction of the noise. It was not easy to poise on the balls of your feet in show shoes but he was tense all the same as he came around the bend in the trail. He was just about to call out when he saw movement on the backside of the overturned machine as the rider came popping up from the snow. Standing there, Jimmy wasn't sure they knew he was close and didn't want to startle them. As he was about to call out again, the rider flipped up the visor on the helmet and kicked the machine. Later on, he would wonder what shocked him more: the fact that it was a woman, or the string of cussing that came out of her mouth. "I swear to all that is holy!" she muttered. "They claim to worry about my safety and then give me the crappiest machine they own!" She kicked the machine again and muttered something that Jimmy didn't catch, and then shocked him as she looked up right at him.

"Well, are you just going to stand there or help me out?" Hands on her hips, she gave off a no nonsense air that made Jimmy chuckle as he walked toward her. As he got closer, he couldn't believe how…small she was. *I can't believe something so small can handle that machine.* Still saying nothing, he moved to the other side of the sled and helped her flip it right side up. *Stronger than she looks too,* he observed. Something about her looked familiar but it was hard to place it. "Thanks for the hand on that. Can I give you a lift down the trail a bit? I am only going another couple miles or so but it will get you there faster. I don't have another helmet but sunglasses and a kerchief will give enough protection for the distance I am going. Hi, I'm Amie." She took off her glove and offered her hand.

He smiled and shook her hand replying, "I'm Jimmy. I will take you up on that offer and thank you for it. I am trying to get to my cabin and check on things but it has been slow going."

Amie eyed him as if to say she knew better but said nothing and readied herself back on the sled, moving forward to make room for him. *Not much gets past this one,* Jimmy thought to himself as he settled in, strapping his pack closer to his body. "Ready?" Amie asked a split second before revving the machine and taking off down the trail. Lurching forward, Jimmy held on and was almost giddy with how quickly the terrain was going by. He saw animal tracks along the sides of the trail here and there and hints of other snow machines. Amie slowed the machine down and came to a stop just before a turn down another trail.

"Okay, here is your stop," she said as he climbed off the back. "How much further is your cabin?"

"Well, I am not really sure unless you can tell me where we are exactly?" He didn't trust anyone or anything right now and didn't want to give much away.

Amie grinned from inside the helmet and said, "Ok Jimmy or Jack or whoever you are, level with me here. I can tell by looking in your eyes you are not stupid and I am pretty sure you know I am not either. The whole world has gone to hell except no one knows how badly because communication is just about out except for the odd HAM. I expect there will be a lot more people "checking on their cabin" in the next couple days around here. You are just the first one I stumbled on. So, since it will be dark and cold soon how about you consider coming up to my place for the night. I have warm food, and maps you can look at. I am not offering it for free, mind you. Always something needing done around the place." Amie glanced at the sky, "If those clouds make it over here, firewood will be first on the list. What do you say?"

He weighed his options and took a close look at Amie, sizing her up. She spoke a lot of sense and sleeping inside sure sounded better than another night in the cold. The flip side was that Jimmy would be in unfamiliar turf and vulnerable. On top of that, the nagging voice in his head kept whispering urgency to get to the cabin. Jimmy met Amie's eyes and focused, dropping his weary traveler front trying to decide what to do. Amie held his eyes and smiled a wry grin.

"I knew you were not what you pretended to be. My guess is military and you know it is bad out there."

Jimmy could not keep the shock from his expression and replied, "Marines, retired. How did you know?" Amie grinned again.

"You'll get along just fine with Dad. Let's get going, I've a mind for something hot to drink." She climbed back onto the snow machine and he knew his choice had been made. He just wasn't sure if he was the one that made it.

The snow machine lurched into motion and they headed off down the trail. He on high alert and taking in his surroundings in case he needed to get out quickly. Though he may have been machine maintenance in the Marines, they still drilled situational awareness into every soldier's head to the point of becoming second nature. Thanks to that training, he noted there were lookout points in the snow that

37

gave excellent view of the trail, game cameras mounted in a few locations, a fur trap set here and there. The going was faster on this path; it was used more often from the looks of it. After a couple miles, he could make out smoke against the twilight sky and guessed it was less than a mile away. Mentally preparing himself for anything as best as he could, the thoughts of warm food and a warm place to sleep kept creeping into his head. He was shaken from his musings when Amie pulled out a bullhorn and let two short blasts out.

I wonder if that means two people are coming and be ready to take one out. Deep down though, he didn't think that this woman or her family would harm him. He learned long ago to listen to his gut on things like this but even so, he still didn't let his guard down. As they came around another corner, the site of the a cabin came into view. A nicely built two-story number, tucked amidst red oak and white cedar trees. It was easy to tell this was not a vacation cabin; it was lived in year round and well kept. Amie pulled the sled up to the side of an outbuilding and waited for Jimmy to move. He was adjusting his pack and opened his mouth to ask about the horn when he heard a booming voice holler, "What, you find a stray already Amie-girl?"

Jimmy turned to see a bearded giant of a man who looked like he was cut from the very forest they stood in. At least six feet tall (likely closer to six and a half), he walked over to where they stood and openly sized Jimmy up. When the man suddenly stuck out his hand to shake, he jumped a bit and stepped back. The man roared with laughter and, to Jimmy's dismay, so did Amie. "Twitchy eh? Or maybe just on alert, hmm? Name's Mike but everyone calls me Captain. Dunno why though, never made the rank." His smile was sincere and Jimmy felt the fool as he grasped Captain's hand and shook it firmly. "Jimmy, Jimmy Walker. Nice to meet you, Sir."

"Well, I know a fellow military man when I see 'em. How about we get inside and get some warmth on you before the night's chores." Captain turned and headed to the cabin with Amie just behind. Jimmy followed along and noted that things seemed well in hand here. The biggest thing of interest he saw was the antenna and satellite dish mounted. *May be a good place to get some information. Amie mentioned that HAM operators were active. Maybe I can get some real information.* Stepping into the entry, they shed their jackets, boots, and gloves. Jimmy felt 50 pounds lighter just getting the boots off. Keeping his pack with him, he followed Amie into the main living area and was immediately drawn to the wood stove. The heat it was giving off was like a siren's song and made him realize he may be slightly hypothermic. After a few minutes, Amie came out from what must be the kitchen area with a tray of coffee and some kind of fruit pastry. Captain asked Amie about the conditions out there and how it looked while he gratefully sat drinking coffee. He could feel the warmth of the fire seeping into his bones and the coffee was helping the rest. "Well, looks like the snow arrived early," said Amie, looking out the window. "Guess we better get to that firewood before we get to those maps." Jimmy nodded and stood up, following her out to put boots and gear back on. When he looked at his pack and then her before heading out to the woodshed, Amie smiled and said, "Honestly Jimmy, what could you possibly have in there that we do not already have here. Cut through the paranoia and come help me." She turned and headed outside, leaving Jimmy to follow or look the fool. He followed.

They fell into a nice working rhythm; he split rounds and she stacked the cuts. They spoke about what had happened, what they knew and didn't know. Jimmy decided he could trust these people so told her about how he ended up chopping wood for her and the Captain. "I knew you were military and not some yahoo lost on the sled trails! There is a certain way they carry themselves, you know?" She smiled and Jimmy found himself returning it before turning to grab another round only to find there were no more. He looked up and saw the wood shed was filled and it was full dark outside. His stomach growled and Amie laughed. "I would say you earned that meal. Let's go inside and see what Dad has cooking." When they opened the door, smells of roasted meat and garlic potatoes, gravy and steamed vegetables made Jimmy's mouth water. They sat down at the table and tucked in. There was not much conversation while they were eating but as Jimmy was clearing his plate, he heard static coming from another room. "Excuse me," said Captain and he went off toward the noise. Glancing at Amie she answered his unasked question.

"Remember the odd HAM operator I talked about? Dad would be the one. Well, one of them anyway. I don't know much about it but I suppose I will have to learn."

He smiled amiably and replied, "It is easier than most people think. I have been playing with radios since I was a kid." He badly wanted to get in there and get some information but knew that would be overstepping himself. He helped Amie clear the table and set the dishes in water. Before he asked if he could help wash them, Captain came out with a roll of maps in his hands and handed them to Jimmy. "Amie says your cabin is close but you aren't sure where you are." He plucked one of the maps and spread it on the table, pointing to an area. "This is where we are, and this is where Amie found you."

He studied the map and pointed. "Idlewild?" Captain nodded.

"They will be trouble sooner rather than later. Naught a good thing ever came out of that hovel." He told him about what he saw which seemed to confirm the older man's assessment. "Well, what about you now? Where is the cabin?"

He stood up and locked eyes with Captain who looked back with an unconcerned and open air around him. After a moment, Captain chuckled and said, "Look, we are men cut from the same cloth. We have taken stock of each other and likely consider ourselves to be a fair judge of people. Trying times are ahead and there will be few you can trust and even fewer you can turn to. Idlewild will explode onto the countryside before long and if there is no resistance they will either enslave or kill everyone in the area. I saw your interest in the HAM and I am sure you are beside yourself wondering what is going on. I assume your cabin has communications, too?" Jimmy nodded but said nothing. "Good. I have always thought there is a reason things happen the way they do. I am thinkin' that you stumbling on Amie's trail wasn't just a lucky chance. Depending on how far away you are, might be we could team up and exchange information. Maybe patrol and keep tabs on the area. You know it will get worse before it gets better. How about you sleep on it and let me know in the morning. It is late and I am wiped out." Captain nodded to Jimmy and turned to go to bed.

Amie came down the stairs with her arms full of bedding. "Couch is a hideaway, here are the sheets and whatnot. If you want a shower beforehand, it's through there," she pointed. "Dad is usually up around 5am. Old habits die hard, I guess. Good night." Jimmy thanked her and she turned, going back up the stairs. He went to his pack to get items for the shower. *I bet I reek*! Two days trekking through the snow and sweating was enough to make anyone ripe.

After the shower and making up the bed, he checked the fire and put another log in to hold until morning. As he climbed under the blankets, he considered all that had happened that day and the Captain's offer. He never said where his cabin was and didn't reveal anything about supplies. The only real slip he made was about communications but didn't tell Captain about the full HAM set up he had. *Things happen for a reason, hmm? Well, perhaps he is right about at least communicating.* Jimmy had seen from the map that he was roughly twelve miles from his own cabin. He was a little off the course he wanted to take but this may prove to be an important opportunity. He hadn't thought much about what he would do when he actually got to the cabin other than survive, of course. Communication and a support team was vital in any combat situation and he knew it wouldn't be long before he would be faced with armed, hungry people at his doorstep. *If they haven't looted it already*, he thought. I will decide in the morning. The blankets were warm and faint sounds of popping wood in the fireplace lulled him to sleep.

CHAPTER EIGHT

He woke up to the smell of coffee and sleepily wondered if he had set the timer the night before. He heard someone whistling in another room and his eyes snapped open, momentarily confused. *Oh yes, Amie and Captain's place*, he thought to himself. Relaxing back into the hideaway bed, Jimmy took stock of his situation. Jimmy ran through all the steps he'd taken that got him here. He was about twelve or so miles away from his own cabin and an opportunity for an alliance of sorts had been presented. Amie and the Captain seemed to be good and honest people. He hadn't thought much about what he was going to do after he made it to the cabin other than survive and help rebuild after the chaos settled. Sgt. Harrand's voice kept coming back to him, "One man is not an army, private! You aren't superman, no matter what your girlfriend tells you! You have a team for a reason!!" He smiled at the memory. He had always preferred his own company to large groups and gatherings. Sometimes, like now, Harrand's voice would get into his head and start ranting and he knew it was the right thing to do. He knew communication would be vital during these times and that steps should be made now to establish a code with Captain, show him where the cabin was located and discuss a schedule for checking in.

Guess my mind is made up. Getting up out of the bed he realized he felt good. Really good. He was well rested, clean and had a plan forming with some likeminded people. Until he ran into Amie, his primary focus was to bug out to the cabin and figure it out from there. Things had changed, there was no denying that. He was going to have to change with it. He was stripping the bed down when Amie came in with a mug of steaming coffee in hand.

"You strike me as the kind who prefers their coffee strong and unsweetened," said Amie, leaning against the doorframe.

"Yes'm, you would be correct on that," replied Jimmy as he folded the bedding and stacked it neatly on the coffee table. Offering the cup of coffee with a smile, Amie let him know that Captain was outside patrolling around the area and breakfast would be ready in about half an hour. After deeming the coffee 'the best he ever had,' Jimmy went outside in search of Captain and found him coming back to the house.

"Ho, there Jimmy! Sleep ok?" Captain asked with a smile. Jimmy guessed he was somewhere in his early to mid 60's. "Slept like a baby Captain. Thank you for it." Jimmy cleared his throat and waited for Captain to come closer to the house before saying, "I've thought about your offer and I agree it is a good idea. Establishing communications now will give a great advantage." He told Captain about his full HAM radio setup, let him know the cabin was only about twelve miles away, and that he was provisioned enough to get through the rest of the winter. "I think it would be best to make a code for communication security and have a check in schedule," he told the older man. Captain was about to respond when Amie called from inside to get ready to eat.

"Best not let it get cold, she gets grumpy - bad as her momma ever did. Let's get settled and iron out some details," Captain said as he made his way into the house.

Over breakfast, the three of them talked about

communications, schedules, and code words to keep security levels high. They didn't want to be pinpointed and targeted by angry mobs from urban areas nor did they wish to deal with martial law and soldiers coming and taking everything. "You know it will come to that, right?" said Captain, "Most likely it has already been declared and is being enforced now." Jimmy told them about what he had heard over the radio while he still had his Jeep and the National Guard being in place on the state borders. Captain gave a low whistle, "Makes you wonder if they were expecting it, eh?"

Jimmy shrugged while handing empty dishes over to Amie. He got up and plucked the map they were looking at the night before from the chair and unrolled it. "Here is where my cabin is," said Jimmy, pointing to a spot. "It's a fair distance to cover between here and there. I hope to make it there by tonight but it may be tomorrow morning."

Amie came over to look where he was pointing and said, "I can run you up there on the sled, be there in no time and get a lay of the land at the same time." Jimmy mentally cringed. For so long he kept his cabin and activities to himself. *These people have given me no reason to distrust them.*

He looked at both Amie and her Dad and said, "That would speed things up. I want to make it clear that I am coming to this with an open mind, considering all that has happened to get me here it wasn't easy." He looked at Captain. "You're right. I do consider myself a good judge of character and I do think some things happen for a reason. Now more than anything, we need people we can trust and rely on. It's going to be rough out there. I can be ready in 10 minutes." Amie and Captain smiled.

"We are the people you think we are, Jimmy," said Captain. "I think we will need each other before the end. Amie will meet you outside in ten. I need to get on the HAM and see what I can find." Everyone went into motion.

Fifteen minutes later, Amie and Jimmy were riding down the trail. Captain had told them there was some rumors of nuclear bombs being fired on the west coast but there was nothing solid on it yet. He had given Jimmy a shotgun and some shells to take with and send back with Amie. They had to stop a couple times to get their bearings but were making good time. Jimmy kept his eyes open for signs of cabins, smoke, tracks; anything that would indicate trouble up ahead. The snow deepened the closer they got to his cabin. About a mile away, Jimmy tapped Amie on the shoulder and she slowed to a stop. Jimmy climbed off the snow machine and asked her to wait so he could get closer. "No more than half an hour," he said as he was strapping his snowshoes on. "I want to be sure no 2 or 4 legged animals are lurking. Might want to kill the engine so you can listen, too. I'm going to get within sight, assess, and return. Amie eyed him a moment before nodding.

"Takes trust to build trust," she said and turned off the machine. He flashed a smile and got to hiking. He was on high alert as he made his way toward the cabin. After a quarter mile, he bent behind a large tree and checked a snag line placed there. He exhaled a sigh of relief to find it untouched and continued to the next one. When he had made it three quarters of the way he turned and trekked back, satisfied that no one had been there. Smiling when he saw Amie, he gave a thumbs up and she drove him up the rest of the way.

His cabin was set against the hillside and looked to be roughly 20 feet x 30 feet with a semi wrap around deck. It was hard for Amie to tell with all the snow built up. Eyeing the roof, Amie said, "I would be looking to clear that roof, first. That is a lot of weight."

He nodded his agreement. "I can handle it from here." He slung the shotgun off his back and handed it and the shells over to Amie. "Tell Captain thanks for me and thank *you* for the ride. I would have had to walk all day and more." He tossed his pack on the snow-covered stairs. "I will make contact to let Captain know you are on the way back"

Amie smiled and nodded. "You're welcome. I am sure we will see each other again. Be careful, Jimmy. It's hard being alone at any time up here, but now more than ever."

Jimmy saluted and grinned, "Will do, Ma'am."

Amie shook her head with a smile and turned around. Soon the sound of her machine was lost. He had made it to the cabin. He took a deep breath and looked around. *Time to get to work*, he thought. He cleared the roof as best as he could, got a fire started, found his handheld HAM radio and messaged like he promised.

"Sounds good, I'll be watching for her," crackled Captain's voice over the speaker. "Until next time, Cap out." He was relieved to find everything as he had left it and thanked his lucky stars that he moved when he did.

He focused the next few days on getting things in order before he could patrol the area, but was able to spend an hour or so each day listening on the HAM. What he heard was not comforting. Blame and accusations for the virus and nuclear attacks were being flung against every country against every other country. Chaos, panic, FEMA, National Guard deployed, talks of WWIII starting; it was hard to tell the truth from rumors. The only time he transmitted was during his scheduled check-ins with Captain and Amie. He was just finishing up a can of chili for dinner when he heard someone call out, "Hello!! Anyone in there?! HELLLOOOOO!!" Jimmy froze, trying to decide which approach to take. He knew they saw smoke but wondered how they got passed the trip lines. *I could come out guns blazing or play the regular citizen again. Worked before but it's now almost a week after IT happened.* He glanced at his rifle next to the door.

CHAPTER NINE

"HELLLOOOOO!?!," came the call again. He reflexively checked for the sidearm on his hip and reached for the loaded shotgun, ready to go out guns blazing. *Wait,* thought Jimmy, *I need more information before going out there like this.* Setting the shotgun down, He grabbed his infrared binoculars, thanking himself for splurging a couple years ago on them. They weren't cheap but were paying off in spades now. He moved to the door and hollered out, "Hold your position. Any threatening motions will be replied to in kind!" Moving to the darker side of the cabin for a better view, he kneeled down. Flipping the infrared switch on, Jimmy spotted one person with arms up in the open and 2 more back in the trees. One looked like it may be a child. *Shit, I knew this day would come. Just not this soon!*

A man hollered back. "We aren't looking for trouble, just a place to hole up for the night. We have our own food and water so won't be a drain. Just a warm place to sleep and we will be on our way come first light."

Jimmy relaxed a little and let his breath out, not realizing he had been holding it in. He got up and checked the back side of the cabin through another smaller window to check for anyone sneaking up the back or sides before heading back to the front door. Before opening it, he called out, "I see the three of you. Have your wife and child come out to join you. I am armed and will shoot if needed." Jimmy waited a few moments, listening intently and heard a woman sneeze.

"Okay, we are here together! We are taking a risk here, too, you know!" the man called out. Jimmy checked through the binoculars again and confirmed the three heat signatures standing about 700 feet from his front porch. *Well, if it's a trap, they are playing the beginning part very well*, thought Jimmy before opening the door slowly and coming out with shotgun aimed mostly at the ground but high enough that it would take a split second to aim. He could see them clearly enough and guessed the boy to be about eight to ten years old. The couple was likely in their late 30's and the man had a Hispanic look to him. The man had a shotgun slung across his back and they looked to be carrying well-provisioned packs, not to mention walking on snowshoes. Hmmm, fellow preppers?, Jimmy wondered. A spark of hope ignited. He cleared his throat.

"Hello. My name is Jimmy Walker and you are on my property. From the looks of things, you aren't just traveling to some random location, hmm? It takes trust to earn trust. Tell me where you come from and where you are going. I have been here about a week now and you are the first people I have seen or heard since." Jimmy hoped he wasn't making a huge mistake.

"Jimmy, I am Alvarado and this is my wife Sarah and our son, Austin. We come from Detroit and are heading to our cabin that is about 10 miles north and east of here. We are bugging out much like it seems you have done. I smelled the smoke and saw the antenna and decided to take our chances. Sarah is about 3 months pregnant and I would prefer not to sleep in the tent again. I know you have no reason to trust us. We have no reason to trust you either but here we are in the middle of a forest and it is cold and I would dearly love to drink something warm, even if it is just water." He took a deep breath and Jimmy mentally admired the straightforward way Alvarado spoke. Plus, the man made sense. Jimmy nodded. Just a few days ago, some people took in Jimmy and now it was time to return the favor.

"Well, hard to argue with that kind of logic and I can do better than warm water. I'd appreciate you unloading your shotgun, though." Alvarado nodded and made quick work of flipping the shells out. "Come on in and get warmed up, I'll get the water going." Jimmy could see the relief on the boy's face as he walked up first, fearless as you please. He walked right up the steps and stuck out his hand to Jimmy. With a wry smile on his face, Jimmy shook his hand and the boy said, "Pleased to meet you Mister Walker. Thank you for the place to sleep." The child had dark hair like his father but deep blue eyes that were striking to look at. He was impressed with his manners and nodded.

"You're welcome, now go on in and get warm." He watched the child stroll inside without a care in the world.

If they kill me in my sleep, there are worse ways to go than that. He went in after the others and got water heating up on the stove while the family peeled off layers of clothing. He learned a long time ago in the military how to keep his head down but still know what was going on around him. Situational awareness kept people alive. From all he had been able to piece together over the last few days on the HAM radio, it was pure chaos out there. Just this morning he learned Martial Law had been put into effect in both the United States and Canada. The virus that affected all of his electronics had spread across the globe but there were some conflicting reports on that. He did not do much more than listen, except for his check ins with Captain and Amie. They were faring well and hadn't had any issues. Some family had made it to their cabin, but they were expected and planned for.

The lady coughed and brought Jimmy's attention back to the present. "You'll be wanting something for that cough. I have tea and some instant coffee." Sarah smiled and replied, "Some tea would be wonderful." Jimmy nodded and moved to get some cups and tea bags from the reclaimed cupboard he installed last year. "So, what news Alvarado?" asked Jimmy.

"Please, call me Al. Well, I am sure you know about the virus." He nodded and poured hot water over the tea bags. "That was the first clue, of course. There was no happy romantic phase. With all the media covering 'preppers,' people knew it meant chaos. Especially when the lights went out. There were nukes exploded in the air all over the place and no one really knows who did what or why for sure. That is the last I heard about the situation overall but the cities are hell holes, plain and simple."

Jimmy brought tea cups to everyone and put some sugar packets on the roughly made table. "That is pretty much what I am hearing as well. You said your cabin is 10 miles north and west?" asked Jimmy, looking Al in the eyes.

Al shook his head and smiled, "No. north and east. We have enough for about 6 months and the wife here has seeds in her pack to plant, if we even dare to. I worked in construction and went to some third world countries on volunteer jobs..." Al chuckled with a look of disbelief and shook his head. "I guess everywhere is a third world country, now. Won't be long before people start making for the hills, even if they don't have a place to go. And they will be hungry." Jimmy nodded and sipped some tea, considering.

Ten miles up the way and Amie and Captain about twelve miles down. That would be able to cover a nice area. Jimmy felt like a piece of a puzzle clicked into place. He wasn't one to make quick decisions unless needed and he could sleep on it tonight. He would need to find out some more information first and talk to Captain. Construction skills were important but this family could also be a loose cannon or worse, tell the wrong people the wrong information.

"What kind of communications do you have?" asked Jimmy. Al looked at him and he realized that the man was sizing him up just the same as he had to Captain. His respect level went up a notch.

"We have a short wave radio system and a set of walkie talkies that get up to fifteen miles on a clear day. We keep 'em in a faraday cage." He nodded, meeting Al's eyes square on and said, "Maybe we could keep in touch then."

Al nodded and drank some more tea. "We could use about 4 cups of hot water there for a dinner before we bed down. Want to be going at first light." Austin yawned and Sarah was sitting quietly, listening. She gave an air of quiet strength, a woman who was taking things as they come and adapting as best as she could. He stood up. "Should be enough in the pot there," he pointed to the iconic blue and white speckled camp pot on the stove. "I'll get you some padding to sleep on." Al nodded his thanks.

He went outside to get some more wood for the night and looked up at the stars twinkling in the clear sky. *Amazing how many there are without any electricity from the cities*, he thought to himself. *I'm not really sure which way to move with this opportunity. Having communications further north would broaden the area that can be covered but the more people who are part of this, the greater the threat of some other group trying to come in and take what we have.* He decided to sleep on it.

CHAPTER TEN

Jimmy woke with a start, unsure of where he was or what woke him up as he slid his hand under the pillow to get his 9 millimeter. It was still dark out though it looked like dawn was only about an hour away. Suddenly a THUMP came from the front porch and he heard scuffling sounds. As he moved quietly from the bed, he heard other noises from the front room. What the heck is going on out there? He moved cautiously to the door and eased it open. He heard the sound of a shotgun being cocked and froze. "Al?" he called quietly. "Something on the porch," Al replied just as quietly. His shoulders eased a bit, relieved that Al was not trying to shoot him and stepped into the front room. They both stood and listened to the noises coming from the other side of the door. "Sounds like an animal," he whispered. Al nodded. "Big, too," said Al. Sarah had Austin up and moved out of the men's way. Jimmy moved to the window and peeked out of a slit on the side of the shade.

"HOLY CRAP!" he yelled and jumped back so fast he knocked over an end table with loud BANG! and fell solidly on his backside. Even as he was falling, Al moved to the side of the door with the shotgun aimed between the door and window. "What the hell is it? What IS IT?" Al asked.

Red-faced, Jimmy got up and replied, "That… is a black bear, maybe 2 years old." He coughed a little and continued. "When I looked out the window, his face was about 6 inches from mine and we were eye level."

Al nodded and turned to look out the window, his lip twitching. "Well, looks like you scared each other. His tracks are still steaming on the stairs," said Al. His face twitched again with a hint of a grin. Al looked at Jimmy, whose face got even redder with embarrassment. Jimmy looked over to Sarah and Austin who were sitting on the floor. Austin was biting his lip and when their eyes met, the boy lost it and started laughing. Jimmy grinned, Sarah giggled behind her hand, and Al chuckled.

"Wasn't sure I could still move that fast," said Jimmy after recovering. "How about we go take a look around, just to be sure." Al agreed and they went out to check the area. Though it was still dark, they could clearly see where the bear had wandered in, coming up to the porch, and then making his hasty exit.

When they went back in with some more firewood, Sarah already had the water on to heat and had packed up her family's things. "Might as well get an early start. We are very grateful for you letting us sleep here, Mr. Walker," she said.

"Happy to help but please call me Jimmy." He turned to Austin who was watching the adults intently. "You handled yourself pretty good back there, Austin. A cool head will get you far."

Austin beamed a smile at him and replied, "My Dad said a man who reacts without thinking things out usually ends up in a bad way and I am almost a man now." Jimmy smiled and shook the boy's hand before turning to Al.

"While you get ready, I am going to see if there is anything to be learned on the waves. Won't be too long, need to conserve power." Jimmy moved to his room toward the back of the cabin. Checking the power reserves, he flipped the switches, put on his headphones, and adjusted the volume. Switching from the channel he communicated with Captain and Amie on, Jimmy slowly flipped through a few until he heard what sounded like a recording.

"…a message from the United Nations Disaster Communications Department, North American Division. Be advised that radiation levels have been reported as lethal around most major cities. Martial Law is in effect until further notice. You are required to cooperate with your local government and United Nations authorities. Trauma and relief centers are being set up as supplies become available. You will be directed to evacuate to the locations disclosed to you by authorities. Bring any identifying information such as birth certificates, passports, identification cards, and driver's licenses. Both active and former military personnel are required to report to the closest processing station, regardless of status of discharge. This message will repeat on this frequency every 2 hours and be updated as information becomes available. This is a message from the United Nations Disaster Communica-."

He flipped the switch off and sat back in shock. *It must be worldwide if the U.N. is involved. This is the absolute real deal here. Human existence - hell, even life on the whole world could be wiped out.* His heart lurched at the thought and his breath came short and quick, heartbeat quickening. They will be combing the hills for people hiding out, they will take everything I have and send me to some camp! He lifted a shaky hand and took the headphones off slowly. He heard a scuffle behind him and turned around, wild-eyed.

"Whoa there Jimmy, calm down," said Al who was standing in the doorway. He put his hands up and took a step back. "You're pale as the snow outside, are you okay? Bad news?" Jimmy realized he was tensed, hand reaching for his boot knife as Al's face came into focus. He moved his hand away from his boot slowly and let out a ragged breath.

"I am sorry, Al. Yeah, I am okay now." He ran his fingers through his hair, taking another deep breath and said, "I just heard a recorded announcement, from the United Nations of all things. The North American division." Jimmy relayed the message and Al's face went pale as well. They both heard Sarah gasp.

"What are we going to do Al? I don't want to go to some camp!" He reeled at hearing his thoughts voiced. Sarah stepped up and turned to her husband. "I will *not* go to some government camp!" Al looked at him and back to Sarah.

"Calm down honey, we will get to our cabin and figure out the next step from there." Al turned to Jimmy. "I sure would feel better if we kept in touch once we reach the cabin. We should be able to make it there tonight, unless it storms. God, we are so helpless without our gadgets to tell us what is going on, even for the weather." Al sighed heavily then turned to his son. "Austin, pack up, we need to get moving. Today will be hard but we will be better once we reach the cabin." Austin looked at everyone a moment as if studying them. He nodded and moved to get his things. *He has an old soul, that one.*

"I am thinking there will be a lot of people who will not be interested in going to a government camp. Perhaps we should try to find more good, likeminded people. You know what I mean. Form an alliance of sorts. I am not saying to just resist purely on principle, but I have a bad feeling about being rounded up like cattle." Al smiled ruefully as he slung his pack on and nodded in agreement.

"Exactly the same thing I was thinking. We will contact you tomorrow morning, say 6am? Try every 3 hours until 6pm? If you don't hear from us well…" He nodded and they moved to the door. Sarah was filling a small thermos with hot water. "I almost forgot," said Jimmy as he moved back into his room. He came out with a rolled up paper and a baggie filled with tea packets. He handed them over with a smile and said, "I had an extra map, though it is on a larger scale, that you can have and the tea is to help with the cough." Sarah smiled and thanked him. They said their goodbyes and as suddenly as they had come, they were gone. Jimmy was alone again and his mind was racing.

He needed to talk to Captain about this. He wondered if Captain had heard the broadcast yet. Being ex military, Jimmy was being called up again to serve but felt completely torn about it. He knew what sort of 'duty' he would be asked to do. Cleaning up the dead, taking people's provisions to be 're-appropriated for the greater good,' and basically being the United Nations' armed thug while they gather the population and try to control it. He didn't make an oath to the United Nations, he made it to America, the *United States* of America. He swore to uphold the Constitution, not to be some lackey pit bull ordered to fight against the common people.

"Well, that decides that," he said aloud and checked his watch; 7:00am. He glanced outside and saw some clouds showing hints of dawn. It was Wednesday and he had a check in with Captain tomorrow. Emergency check in time was noon every day, at least until the season changed. It seemed forever from now. Jimmy was antsy and needed something to do. *Chopping wood is always good*, he thought. Grabbing his ax and splitting maul, he headed outside to the rounds he had set in back and got started. Before long, he found himself lost in the work.

They won't be able to do much searching until full spring, especially up here. We could make a larger alliance but it's hard to trust people, especially now. They can and will turn on you if they think it will improve their own situation. With a rhythmic swing, he split another round in half and bent to set it upright. *Not everyone will be bad, of course and those are the ones we need to find. They will need someone they can trust, someone who is strong but non-threatening to lead them into working together.* CRACK! Another round was chopped and tossed into a growing pile down the side of the cabin. *I got it! Captain would be perfect. Plus, I myself would follow him. Trouble is, once people get comfortable they start to complain. On top of that, if we organize we will become a target. Then again, other people will be organizing, too.* CRACK! Another round was chewed up by the swinging axe and tossed onto the pile. He thought of what he had seen at Idlewild and knew that they were already more organized than he was. His thoughts chased each other around in his head as he kept himself busy. After another half an hour, he stopped and went in to get some water and something to eat.

Standing alone in his cabin, he was still reeling from the recorded message he heard only a couple hours ago. He took a drink of water and hoped Al, Sarah, and their son Austin made it safely and also hoped they would make radio contact tomorrow morning. He took a bite of a granola bar and grimaced. He had no appetite and felt antsy and full of nervous energy. He went back outside and stacked the wood in the woodshed against the cabin. When that was done, he did some busy work around the property. He walked around the outside of the cabin, checking more closely for damage or deterioration. It didn't take long and he went inside to shift some things around. Running out of things to do, he went back outside to clean off the rest of the deck.

He checked his watch and groaned, *It's only 10:15am! A little less than 2 hours still. Ugh, this is driving me crazy!* He trudged back into the house, tossing his jacket aside and grabbing his roll of maps and a pad of paper. Sitting down at his small, repurposed table, he unrolled the map of the Manistee National Forest. Putting a finger on his location, he marked the general location of Captain's place and then Al's place. He was between the two of them, almost equal distance. There were streams between them and some rolling hills, a few small bluffs and trees. Lots and lots of trees. He needed a plan to present to Captain. Looking at the map again, he marked a few places that would be good to have communication and connections with. He took his writing pad and brainstormed a few ideas;

• Most important is to establish WHY we need to gather and protect ourselves (way of life, survival, freedom, etc.)

• Plans must be in place before full spring thaw

• Use the landscape to expand 'our' territory of patrol and security. Use cliffs and impassable areas as the borders

• Signaling system needed between locations

• Central gathering area for emergencies

• Need a place to trade. Wide open, cleared of trees or anything people can hide behind to ambush.

• Training for those who will fight, patrol, etc.

• Must make some ironclad laws. Death for theft, murder, rape, etc.

• Form a council?

It's like we are a bunch of common folk dividing the land up after the Lord or King has fallen. Jimmy snorted, *I am certainly no knight, or lord, or king. I'm just a guy who wants to live.* His military training taught him that he would be called upon to be a leader of sorts and while it didn't entirely bother him, he knew most leaders ended up with a huge target on their backs when people get comfortable and start to think they can run things better. Sighing and getting up to stretch, he checked his watch again, 11:20am. His stomach rumbled and Jimmy put some water on the stove to heat, tossed a log in to keep the fire going and went back to his notes, musing over the various details racing through his mind. His thoughts kept going back to the recorded message he heard early this morning;

"...This is a message from the United Nations Disaster Communications Department, North American Division. Be advised that radiation levels...reported as lethal around most major cities. Martial Law is in effect until further notice. You are required to cooperate...will be directed to evacuate to the locations disclosed to you by authorities. Bring any identifying information...both active and former military personnel are required to report to the closest processing station, regardless of status of discharge...."

He spaced off, letting his emotions and mind run free, allowing himself to feel the fear and consider the absolute worst case scenario. He worked through the fear, eased his thumping heart rate back down and took control of himself again, feeling better. *Best to face the fear and deal with it if you can instead of being a deer in the headlights.* Part of his military training was being able to stay calm and in control. He glanced out the window and was happy to see the sun shining through the clouds, if weakly. He checked the power levels stored in his battery bank and was surprised to see he had more than he thought. Glancing at his watch again, he decided since he had the juice (and the sun was shining a bit) that he could listen in to see if there has been any change and get an idea of what the general reaction was out there.

Sitting down in front of the radio, Jimmy flipped the switches and put his headphones on. The same recorded message was being played. He switched channels. It exploded with voices.

"They are coming to herd us up, people! I warned you this kind of thing was coming but no one would listen and now-" Jimmy switched again, "All military personnel are supposed to report but I didn't swear an oath the U.N!" He stopped and grinned. Seems his brothers in arms were feeling the same way he was. He felt a little encouraged. He listened to the chatter for a few minutes more before switching to see if Captain was on early.

"CQ CQ, this is THR4K. Tango Hotel Romeo Four Kilo. Seeking the Captain."

The channel crackled with static and then, "THR4K this is CAQ7G, Charlie Alpha Quebec Seven Gamma." They covered information such as signal strength and whatnot before getting to what HAMs call the "Rag Chew." They discussed the emergency broadcast that was going out and agreed that they needed to meet. "Cap, I think we need a plan before spring thaw."

There was a sudden crackle on the line and a voice said, "N1RL, November One Romeo Lima."

Jimmy sighed and said "Go ahead N1RL, you have the line."

"...*static* need assistance near Idlewild. Looters and..*static* ...they are even taking the....*static*....for assistance please meet near the-" the line went silent. Jimmy felt a chill and thought, *I knew that place was going to be trouble, just not this soon.*

"Cap, I think you should send the skis up the hill." Captain agreed. Tomorrow, Captain or Amie would come up to get him though it would be using up precious fuel. He felt confident that Captain understood the conversation they needed to have should not be done over the air. He signed off and started to get ready for being gone a couple days. *We don't have time to deal with Idlewild just yet but if we don't help, they could grow so large that we cannot hold them back at all.*

CHAPTER ELEVEN

Later that evening, Jimmy was tightening the straps on his pack for tomorrow's trip down to Captain and Amie's cabin and he mused over how much had changed. Just two weeks ago, he was working in a recycling plant and pretty much muddling through life. He loved to hunt, hike, camp, and fish. The cabin he was now living in used to be his getaway spot and though he always thought of it as his BOL in the back of his head, even going so far as to stock it well, He never *really* thought he would actually need it. His mind drifted to his house and all that he had left behind, his overweight neighbor Eugene who he had had to knock out so he could get going…his musings were interrupted by a sound of static coming from the radio in the back room.

"CQ CQ, this is CFV5L, Charlie Frank Victor Five Lima. Inquiry, „,*static*. Tango Hotel Romeo *static* Kilo." Jimmy moved to the desk quickly, heart in his throat. He picked up the mic.

"CFV5L, this is THR4K Tango Hotel Romeo Four Kilo. That you Al?" The line was quiet for what seemed like forever and he held his breath, hoping Al, Sarah, and Austin had made it safely. *Must have made some good time, I wasn't expecting to hear from them until tomorrow morning.*

The frequency squeaked with more static and then, "…*static* and we made it to the cabin. Found a nice *static* and started walking the path. Cabin is in good shape."

Jimmy sighed relief and quickly relayed some of the information he felt safe enough to talk about over the airwaves. "I won't be on air for a few days. Sit tight and wait to hear from me. If it has been a week with no word, well…it was good to meet you all." The line was quiet again and he sat back, mind reeling. He was tired. Tired of being on edge and not knowing what was really going on out there. He felt like a rat in a trap and had no idea when the cat would show up.

Al replied, "Roger. We will be busy setting up here in any case. Be safe out there. We will be listening for you. CFV5L out."

He signed off and cut the power to the radio. Going through the house, he made sure everything was in order and got ready for bed. As he lay there, he wondered when Amie or Captain would be by tomorrow to pick him up. He fell asleep feeling troubled.

****

The next morning, Jimmy was making some instant coffee and stopped, ears straining. He thought he heard an engine and glanced at his watch. *Barely 7am. Are they here already?* He moved to the window, taking his first sip and listened more closely. As the noises were getting louder, he shrugged into his jacket and went out on the porch. Sure enough, the sounds of a snow machine engine were echoing around the forest. Jimmy unconsciously reached to his hip for his sidearm to make sure it was there and then turned to grab the shotgun, just in case. He could see a light bouncing around the bare tree limbs that were sticking up like bony fingers to the dawn spreading across the sky. The engine came closer and then stopped and turned off. He waited a few moments before going down the stairs, shotgun over his shoulder. He walked toward the area he last heard the engine and called out, "Announce yourself!"

A few seconds later he heard a reply. "The skis are clear and waiting!" Amie had been sent up. He found himself smiling and looking forward to seeing her again. She came trudging up the trail with her own shotgun slung over her back and he waved to her.

"Pretty morning but I sure could use some of what I'm smelling in that cup," said Amie as she walked up to meet him. She smiled back to Jimmy who realized he probably looked like some grinning buffoon and cleared his throat.

"Well, come on in then. I just have to grab a few more things and will be ready to go." They went into the cabin. He poured some water into a mug and gave it to Amie before moving to do a final check on his gear.

"So, how many are at the cabin? Everyone ok?" He stuffed an extra pair of wool socks into his pack.

Amie took a sip of the coffee to test it and replied, "We have 14 total. A few more than expected but they did not come empty handed, thankfully. We should make it just fine until the first greens can be harvested and foraged for. Had a couple of wanderers try to stay but they moved on easily enough. I will let Captain give the details though. I have mostly been running scouting routes and checking areas for good lookout locations."

He listened while tightening the straps down. He nodded and said, "It is all happening so much faster than I expected. We won't be sheltered for as long as we had hoped. People in the city always think people in the country have tons of food." He turned and picked up a hammer saying, "Would you spread the coals in the stove while I close up the windows?" Amie nodded and he went outside to put the boards over the windows. Before long, they were on the trail, spitting snow behind them. It was a nice morning, clear and brisk. Jimmy found himself relaxing, happy to be doing something. He watched the terrain go by behind his goggles and let himself revel in the moment. He felt like he had a purpose again, and that was a precious thing after the last two weeks.

He lost himself in the scenery until he started smelling wood smoke and seeing signs of habitation more often. From the last trip, he was able to correctly guess they were only a couple miles away. Amie expertly wove the machine around a stump and before long was pulling up to the fence that had been built. Jimmy saw 2 armed men at the entry point and spotted another one on a platform in a large pine tree. "I see you have been busy," he commented.

Amie nodded and smiled, turning to the men, "Sam, Tanner; how goes the watch?" The men assured her everything was good and she led him through the gate, leaving the snow machine behind for the guys. "We built a three layered perimeter system with each circle being further out. We just passed the second one. The first one was back by that stump. Did you see the guy by the stump I drove around? We moved a rock in the way to force people to go around it." She grinned at him and it showed her dimples. *I don't remember the dimples*, he thought to himself as he followed her to the main cabin. Looking around he saw all sorts of changes. The makeshift fencing went around the property in a wide arc. Areas had been taped off, presumably for farming in the spring. He saw a couple teenage boys pulling on a chain, trying to get a stump free out of the frozen ground and called out to them.

"Try building a small but hot fire on either side to thaw the ground. It should come out easier." They stopped and looked at each other, then back at Jimmy.

"See? I *told* you it was a good idea!," said the taller one who popped the shorter one on the shoulder. The young man waved to him in thanks and smiled. They went into the entryway and shed their outer gear.

"JIMMY!" hollered a booming voice as he stepped into the main cabin. Captain looked to be in fine form. He was sitting at the table, maps spread out in front of him. His long beard scratched the paper lightly as Captain moved some rolled maps off of a chair and offered it to Jimmy. A lady Jimmy hadn't met came to the table and asked him if he was hungry.

"We have some oatmeal in the pot still. Interested?" She was a tall, slender woman who looked to be in her late 30's at first glance. The salt and pepper weaving its way through her hair and smile lines put her closer to 45.

"I would love some, Miss…" Jimmy smiled and glanced at Captain with a question in his eye.

"Oh! Where are my manners? This is my baby sister Denise. She came with her two boys you saw outside. Her husband is down by the gate."

He thanked her for the hot food and looked across the table. "Cap, we have a lot to talk about, and a lot more to do afterward. You heard the recording, and the guy asking for help near Idlewild. You ever talk to N1RL before?" Captain shook his head. "Never heard of them until yesterday, you?"

"I did have some people wander up to my cabin though," he replied. "A small family on their way to their own cabin about 10 miles further up than mine." He went on to tell Captain about Al and his family and his thoughts about bringing them into the group. He left out the part about the bear, though. He grabbed a map off the table and pointed. "Here is where I am and about here is where they are. They made it, I had radio contact with them last night. They are doing ok. Sarah has seeds and other things to plant a garden. They intend on making that their new home. She is terrified of being sent to some United Nations camp. From what I hear, most people are not too keen on the idea."

Captain took it all in, nodding. "Well, way I see it is we do not have the luxury of time. We need a plan set in place before the thaw and that isn't too far off. We need to get more folks into the group but that has the risk of being a target. I'll need you to stay a couple days while we iron this out." Captain chuckled, "Looks like you just promoted me to the leader position. Well, you'll pay for it by being my 1st officer."

He gave a small salute, "Yes, Sir."

Captain laughed and they got down to business. Captain agreed with most of what he had listed but disagreed that they should send scouts to N1RL's location. "Whatever was happening is already done and there is nothing we can do to help. We are too weak right now to be on Idlewild's radar. Maybe in a few weeks, we can send some scouts for a sitrep (situation report)."

He shook his head. "Captain, I disagree. Yes, we are weak right now but one or two people to see what is going on is worth the risk. We need information so we can do more to be ready than just having the basics. If we have some solid intel, we can have a few surprises of our own for when they come."

Captain grinned at him. "Freshly promoted and already questioning authority." He slapped Jimmy amiably on the back, "I prefer a man who speaks his mind. You have good points but we need more people first. Many hands make for less work. If we send two people off to scout Idlewild, we won't have anyone to reach out to the others who are hiding out and that mission will be dangerous enough. People are scared to talk to strangers and rightly so. We need a plan on how to approach them and we will need ways to communicate with them that will not give us away. Plans take time. Establishing a group is more important."

He sighed and nodded. "You are right but some of the people from N1RL could be part of that, too. We could try a bit of both? Find people on the way down to scout for N1RL?" They talked throughout the morning and into late afternoon. By the time Jimmy went to sleep that night, he felt like there was a good foundation put in place.

CHAPTER TWELVE

Jimmy grunted as he heaved a beam into place on the last of the lookout points. It was about a mile away from Captain's place and gave a full view of the area. He nodded to Tanner and held on as the other man swung a sledgehammer to set the beam. Once it was done, they stopped a moment to wipe their brow and get a drink of water. It was late February and he had been here 4 full days helping to get basic things into place. It was agreed that this would be the rally point for the group in the valley in case they were overwhelmed by whatever may come out there. *Out there*, Jimmy thought to himself. *Not a month ago people's definition of 'out there' was the next state or another country.* He bent down to pick up some scrap wood to use as a windbreak and held it in place while Tanner nailed it in. After 10 minutes, the job was done and they were hiking down to the main camp.

"Sure appreciate the help Jimmy. It would have taken us over a week to get them all done. Just not enough hands for the work while still being able to keep things secure. Even that is thin at best."

He nodded and said, "Now that the lookout posts are

done, we can head out scouting tomorrow. I think we pretty much have the boundaries sketched out. The trick will be to make contact and get people to realize that we aren't there to get their supplies or let them rob us of ours. It's going to take kid gloves and a fair bit of luck with that one." They walked on in silence for a while, picking their way through snow covered brush and undergrowth. Jimmy thought about different approaches the scouts might take when making contact. *How would I do it? How* will *I do it?* He recalled his first meeting Al and his family and hoped they were OK. Captain was on board with letting them join the group and be a point of contact in the 'northern' section of the area they mapped out to patrol. The initial plan was to contact people closest to the three main camps and then branch out from there. Getting the inner camps secured as a place of refuge was top priority so people would have a safer place to run to if needed. His thoughts whirled as he considered all of the work he needed to do to his own place to be ready.

"Ho there, Jimmy, Tanner!" Jimmy looked up, not realizing they were already back and smiled to Denise. "You done already? If so, I could sure use a hand getting these posts up for the garden fencing. The men grinned and nodded amiably, joining Denise as she walked to the marked area meant for crops. He guessed at least an acre had been cleared (as best as could be done in February, anyway). Sam's shoulder was still tender after trying to wrestle a shovel into the frozen ground to remove a rock. They moved to one edge of the clearing and he saw a muddy hole dug deep into the ground. Looking at her with a raised eyebrow, Denise said, "I figured the fire would work as good for this as it did for the stumps."

He smiled at her and replied, "It's a good thought and it will certainly help to place the posts but we will need to watch them when it thaws. They may fall over." Denise's looked crestfallen and Jimmy chuckled, "You saved us a lot of work down the road. Don't worry Denise, you did a great thing here." She smiled and the men got back to work.

Other people from the camp came by and made small talk with Tanner and Jimmy on their way to other chores. Smells of roasted meat wafted across the clearing and he heard Tanner's stomach growl. Once the last post was in place, they moved off toward the main house to clean up. Before he could get his boots off, he heard Captain's booming voice calling him. Walking into the room that had been turned into a sort of strategy area, Captain was studying some notes and a map.

"I think we have a good overall plan set. After listening to everyone – even the children – I came up with a more defined layout. Here, take a look." Captain slid the map over and pointed. "See here? Those are good bluffs that only have some scrub brush on them. You can see for miles and I know there are a few homes down there. Over here," Captain pointed to an area about 10 miles east of Jimmy's cabin location. "If I remember right, there is a cliff that runs along this smaller river. Only a few places people can cross." Jimmy nodded and asked a few questions. If they could get the roughly 250 square mile area secured as a larger group – with communications – they would be in a good position to take on Idlewild and other groups that may try to take over. They both agreed on various points regarding scout rotations, patrol measures, and patrol sizes. Jimmy would handle the 10 miles around his cabin, Al would take 5 miles to the south, west and east of his location, and Captain would work this area.

"Cap, I'm having a hard time trying to think of the best way to approach these people. You never really know who you can trust." He felt foolish asking, but it was troubling him. In the military, everything was scheduled, regulated, and had procedure. In this world they found themselves in, there were no regulations to follow. Captain didn't show any sign of judgment. He looked at him and simply nodded.

"Well, people are going to be more open if they know we are not trying to tell them how to live. Our message is only that we need to band together. They will handle their own areas and home and report in any information on threats. We will all work together to grow and gather food and other things. That is a start. It is too soon to go full on commune style here. People are scared and we need time to build trust with us and the world itself again. Use your instincts, listen to them. If something seems off, listen to that voice in your head. That will be your 'regulation' to follow. I know you're going it alone this first run but you are the only other one here with military training and that puts you at an advantage."

Jimmy listened and stood a little taller from this man's encouragement. "Thanks Cap. I needed that." Captain nodded and waved his hand as if to clear the air.

"We'll let you know what we find at Idlewild. I heard the lookout blinds are done?" Jimmy nodded and Captain stood up. "Well, no time like the present to get this going then. I'll have Denise get you some hot food and have Amie with the skis ready to get you up the hill. We should be able to get you there and back by dark. Be ready in 30." Jimmy felt an incredible urge to salute but held back. He did shake Captain's hand before turning to pack his gear, though.

****

3 hours later, Jimmy and Amie were about a mile from his cabin. He patted her shoulder and said, "Give me a minute, let me make sure everything is good before coming up." Amie nodded and turned the engine off. He left his pack behind and made his way cautiously up to the cabin. There were no fresh tracks he could see, no smoke coming from the chimney and the sheets of wood were still in place. He walked around the cabin before going up the stairs to the door. Satisfied, he turned and whistled two short bursts to Amie and unlocked the door.

As he was about to go inside, something caught his eye. His training kicked in and he dropped to the deck, shotgun aimed. He focused on the area and saw a blue tarp in the distance, nestled in the trees. About 300 yards away, he just barely saw the corner but the color contrast was plenty enough to make you notice. Amie came up on the machine just as Jimmy was standing up. He motioned her to be quiet and come up to the porch. She moved quickly, her rifle in hand and looked at him questioningly as she killed the engine. He pointed to his eyes and then in the direction of the tarp. Amie squinted and nodded.

He moved quickly down the steps, signaling her to go in the opposite direction to flank the tent and any occupants. That was unlikely since the snow machine had come all the way up. As they got closer, they could see a canvas tent under a blue tarp tied into the trees at a slope. *Well, these people at least know how to tie a tarp,* he thought to himself. When he was within 100 yards, he called out. "Ho, there in the tent. Anyone there?" There was instant movement heard from inside but no response. He moved forward, shotgun now aimed at the tent and called again, "You are trespassing on my property. Come out of the tent!"

More sounds of movement came from within the tent and then, "Wait a moment, please, Sir. We are coming!" Amie came into view on the opposite side of the tent and nodded to Jimmy. The opening of a zipper sounded loud in the quiet of the forest and a pair of hands emerged, palms up. "I am here with my sister and her husband, we were sent by Al! Please, don't shoot us!" His eyebrows shot up to his hairline but said nothing as three people came out of the tent. They all had their hands up and were staring warily at Jimmy. None had noticed Amie, who was still on the back side of the tent with her rifle up and ready. He lowered his shotgun to put the people at ease. "I am Jimmy Walker and this is my property. You say Al sent you. How did you come by him?"

The man licked his lips nervously and replied, "I am Brad and this is my sister and her husband, Jessica and Terry. We talked to him about a week ago, Sir. Got him on the hand HAM but I think we are too far away now. There were some looters and they blew up our RV. We were building a cabin

72

and it was going to be done this spring. We ran out of food and needed help…" the man trailed off. As he told his story, Jimmy looked them over more closely. Brad's claim that Jessica was his sibling was clearly true. They both had dark hair, brown eyes, and the same shape to the eyes. Mid to late 20's, he would guess. Terry looked a little older but had a city air to him. The clothes they were wearing were nice but not top dollar. Jessica's gloves were mismatched. Brad's boots showed hints of duct tape. *Interesting turn of events*, Jimmy thought.

"How long have you been here?" he asked.

"Last night was our second night. I grew up in this area, about 6 or 7 miles from here to the east. Al was real careful when he gave us the location information, Sir. We will help with whatever needs doing so long as we get some food and maybe some wood for heat. The tent has a stove, so we don't need a place to sleep." Brad fidgeted and said, "I have to be honest, Sir. We did take this from my neighbor's cabin but he hadn't been up there in a long time. If he comes around, I will make amends. We are not bad people, Sir. Al asked me lots of questions and-" Jimmy held a hand up to stop the young man's nervous babbling.

"Calm down. We can figure this all out. Any of you armed?"

The men shook their heads but Jessica spoke up. "Sir, I have a .22 rifle and a .40 caliber handgun in the tent. I have a little less than 50 rounds for each and I can think of better things to do with them than threaten, and therefore have to use, those bullets."

Amie moved around to just in sight of the 3 newcomers and said, "She has a point, Jimmy. If they were bent on looting, they would have busted into the house and taken all they could. There were no fresh tracks." Brad, Jessica, and Terry all jumped back in surprise at Amie's sudden appearance. He watched as Jessica moved her hand to her hip, reaching for a gun that wasn't there. She looked up at him and turned beet red.

"Well," he chuckled, "Now I believe you are unarmed. Come on, let's go inside and talk this out. Oh, and call me Jimmy."

The newcomers were grateful for the instant coffee they were offered, as well as some fish from Captain's freezer. Terry asked how much wood Jimmy wanted brought in, Brad asked how he could help, and Jessica offered to do the dishes afterward. Amie raised her eyebrows to him as if to say, "Is this to good to be true?" He looked back and shrugged. Within an hour, the cabin was warm and food was ready. They made small talk while doing their individual tasks and Jimmy learned that Brad was a carpenter, Jessica was a cop, and Terry was finishing law school before the day everything changed. *Explains the muscle memory of reaching for a gun*, he thought.

Jessica said, "Al asked us many questions. We were on the radio trying to get any information for 3 days before he answered. If not for Terry's penchant for gadgets, we wouldn't have been able to use it for that long. Hooray for solar chargers!"

He smiled and Amie voiced her agreement. She was very quiet, taking in everything around her. Jimmy found himself getting distracted by how she constantly amazed him with her insight and more importantly, how easily he had trusted her and knew he could rely on her. *Plus, there are those dimples*…he admitted to himself. He shook his head as if to clear it and focused back on Jessica, nodding. "Explain to me how he gave the location without telling the whole area. Honestly, we could have 100 people show up in a week if he fudged it up. It can have serious consequences to the groundwork being laid."

Jessica went into detail, telling Jimmy how people in the hills used certain words that meant different things entirely. "For example, if you hear someone say, "Head down the hill until you hit the river running north," that could mean all sorts of things. Most people would assume that meant go north until you find the river or maybe you are on a hill and you need to head down to the river. Well, down the hill means go south and 'hitting the river running north' means when you find the river, cross it. See?" Amie clapped her hands and laughed, matching Jessica's smile.

"That made perfect sense to me, actually," said Amie. "My dad taught me that! It's from the prohibition days as a way to get away from the law."

Jimmy looked between Amie and Jessica and chuckled. "Well I guess you have her stamp of approval which means you tentatively have mine. You can stay where you're at and use the wood sparingly. We will be on standard rations." He told them about the plan, though he was light on certain details. He wasn't ready to trust right away, that is what his instinct told him and he was listening to it.

"So, we need to scout the area and your timing couldn't be any better. Amie will be going back tonight and will let Captain know about you three. You are in until you decide to leave or give us reason not to trust you. Certain questions will not be answered until such a time as you need to know or are trusted enough with more information." All three nodded in agreement and looked him in the eye as he spoke. "Brad, Terry, I will want you to come scout with me. Jessica, I need you here to keep an eye and listen to the HAM in the other room. I am taking a huge risk here. So are you but I have to let you know there are checks and balances all over that keep things as safe as we can at this time. Oh, and thank you for not looting my cabin." He grinned amiably to them and everyone had a good laugh..

****

The next morning, Jimmy woke up to a light tap on the front door. Dawn was straining against the black sky and he grabbed his handgun before calling, "Yes?"

He heard the door crack open and Jessica called, "May I come in and prepare things for the rounds?" He relaxed and laid back down.

"That would be wonderful. Thank you, Jessica." He laid

there and listened to the sounds of her moving around stoking the fire, filling the kettle with water. *Many hands make light work, indeed. Today is going to be an interesting day.* He got up and pulled on some clothes. Stepping into the main room, the smell of coffee hit him and he smiled his thanks to Jessica as she handed him a cup. He turned and grabbed a pad of paper. "I have a few messages I need you to get to Al and Captain. I will write the times down as well. Your unique dialect may come in very handy."

Jessica laughed and said, "It got us here, didn't it? And now I am part of something again. I have a purpose and a goal. That is priceless to me. I will make sure it is done." The look of determination in her eyes was enough to make Jimmy feel at ease, at least about her intentions. As for the others, he would learn more about them today on the trail. They planned to make a large perimeter scout today to about 2 miles out, if the snow would let them. He was the only one with snowshoes. He realized he would have to make them some for future trips. He looked out the window as footsteps came up the stairs and on the deck. He saw Terry's face and motioned him in. In Terry's hands was a shiny foil package that had "Oats" written on the side.

"I hate to rub it in, honey, but…how crazy am I now eh?" Jessica gave her husband an eye roll for a response and took the bag from him. "Yeah, yeah.."

He watched with amusement and said, "Prepper?"

Terry shrugged and nodded, "I was just starting. If I had 5 more years well… Even now, that bag is precious and I wanted to show you good faith." He looked Jimmy square in the eyes, too. *Bet his wife taught him the importance of that one.* He nodded and told them he appreciated it and handed the messages over to Jessica. "There is some cinnamon in the cupboard for the oatmeal, if you like."

After breakfast, the men were ready to go and headed out into the weak sunshine. They each had a pack that had enough, when combined, for all three to survive overnight if they had to. None of them even questioned Jimmy when he had them repack their bags. It seemed they, too, were eager to have a purpose. They walked north roughly 2 miles, crossing a smaller stream that was frozen over. Turning east, they stopped for a break and snack. There wasn't much talking while hiking due to deeper snow causing the hike to be a calorie burner and listening for any sounds of other people. After they rested a bit, Jimmy pointed them south along a small ridge when he spotted smoke down in a valley. It was a good mile or more away but he could see what looked to be a person who was looking back at them. He pulled out his small binocular set. Looks like we have found our first person and they've seen us, too. He has a set of binoculars, a shotgun, and a frown.

Jimmy put the binoculars down and looked to Terry and Brad. He wasn't expecting to find someone so quickly. In fact, he rather hoped they would be able to get a lay of the land before they ran into other survivors. "Well? What do you guys think?"

Terry spoke up first. "I think it would be best for just one of us to go down there. The other two can give the illusion of cover fire." Brad was shaking his head and said, "They might see that as a threat, though. If we only send one down, that person is vulnerable and could be captured or killed." Terry and Brad waited for Jimmy as he was mulling his options. He knew it would have to be him going down there but that left his life potentially in the hands of two strangers.

He looked to both men meaningfully for a moment, nodded and said, "I guess this is where we start building up some trust. I will go down alone. Terry, when I get halfway there, start moving down to that boulder about a third of the way down. Brad, you stay up here with the binoculars and watch over the situation. If I think there may be trouble, I will reach up and scratch my right ear. If everything seems OK, it will be the left. If either of you see trouble, give me two sharp whistles and then get to safety. Head for the cabin as quickly as you can and get word to Captain on the radio. Everyone good?" Both men nodded and he turned back to the man down the hill who was still looking at them, shotgun in hand and while not aiming directly at them, had it pointed in their general direction.

Jimmy took a deep breath and unslung his shotgun from his back, lifting it high so the man could see it and then lowered it on the ground. The man lowered his own shotgun but did not put it down. He put his hands out to the sides, palms up and started making his way down the hill. When he was about three-quarters down, he called out.

"Hello neighbor. We mean only to talk to you." The man seemed to be in his late 50's and was dressed like a person who was well accustomed to living in the forest. He also looked extremely comfortable with the shotgun in the crook of his arm.

The man took a step forward, his face unreadable and said, "Not much to talk about. The whole world has gone to hell and soon the zombies will be crawling all over these hills." The man eyed Jimmy up and down. "'What's your story? You want to talk, so talk. I will tell you straight out that you have no less than 3 scopes lined up on you, so don't be stupid. Say your piece and get gone." The man's voice was strong but gravelly and he didn't seem to blink while talking. Jimmy kept his hands out to the sides in a non-threatening manner.

"Well Sir, my name is Jimmy Walker and you are right: it has gone to hell in a hand basket. That is why I am here. We are out patrolling to find other people in the area to band together against those zombies you were talking about." As he was talking, he let his hands go back down to his sides and gave the air of a man relaxed, in control, and unconcerned. On the inside, his heart was pounding and butterflies were boxing in his stomach. "We have an area sketched out and decent communications started. What we need is more people to help with the work, information, and shared supplies. Now, before you tell me to get lost, we are not asking for handouts. You participate as much as you feel comfortable until trust can be built and we go from there."

He watched closely to gauge the man's reaction and was still unable to read him.

The man looked up behind Jimmy and asked, "Just the three of you? Don't even think of lying—" suddenly there were two sharp whistles and he turned quickly just in time to see Brad aiming the shotgun he left behind at another person who was aiming back. Jimmy heard the shotgun click as a round went in the chamber in down the hill from his position.

He threw his hands up and hollered out, "WHOA WHOA!! Now just everyone calm down and HOLD ON! Brad, don't do anything stupid or I'll put one in you myself!" He turned back to the man and said, "Sir, only the three of us and we are not here to cause any trouble!"

The man again looked past Jimmy up the hill and called out, "Three?"

"Just the three!" came the answer.

Terry was sitting on the larger rock down the slope in what looked to be shock; not responding to anything around him, just sitting. *He may have started to prep, but he sure wasn't prepared for this*, he thought to himself. He looked back to the man and said, "May I have your name, please? At least give us a chance to show we mean what we say." The man looked over Jimmy again and made a motion to his man on the hill. Jimmy glanced over his shoulder and saw a total of 5 people making their way down the hill, including Brad and Terry. "Well," he muttered to himself. "Captain's not going to like this much." He turned back to the man who had a look of surprise on his face.

"Excuse me? Did you say Captain? As in Captain and Amie? CAQ7G?"

It was Jimmy's turn to be surprised and he nodded quickly, "Yes! I am THR4K. You have a HAM?" His mind was racing, unsure which way this was going to play out. He heard footsteps behind him but kept his eyes on the man with the shotgun in front of him.

The man eyed Jimmy again before lowering his shotgun,

fully this time, and nodded. "My name is Art but everyone calls me Pops. We have a makeshift HAM set up, but enough to get some information here and there. We have a lean-to about half a mile away where we can talk but I will ask you to give us some space. Trust takes time to build. You didn't lie about how many of you there were, so I will let you keep your weapons for now." Pops turned down a trail that was hidden from the rise. It looked well used and Pops started walking without another word. He looked at Brad and Terry and nodded. Terry still had a bit of a shocked look about him but he was following along. The other three men fell in behind them and after a quick walk, they came upon the lean-to that was placed close to a frozen stream. Tracks were everywhere and going in all directions. A fire pit had been built and looked well used. In fact, nothing about the area looked newly constructed. Jimmy tucked that piece of information away for later. He and the others moved to the fire and warmed their hands. Pops said, "I don't mince words Mr. Walker. I don't have the time so give me the highlights." Jimmy nodded and told the men about the basic goal and the plans Captain and him had come up with to reach it.

When he told them about Idlewild and the distress call from N1RL, one of the other men piped up. "I heard most of it, actually. I was scouting down that way before the sled ran out of gas. Sounded bad."

He took that in and nodded before continuing. He kept information about exact locations, numbers, and supplies to himself. Thankfully Brad and Terry kept their mouths shut. "For now, we simply want to make contact with people in the area we marked off and let them know about it. Like I said, they can participate as much or as little as they want to for now. What we are asking for outright is for you to patrol the area around your cabin and report any issues back if you have communications which it sounds like you do. We need to be prepared for those from Idlewild, larger cities, and whatever form of government there is out there before spring thaw and we are running out of time. Eventually, we will need help building and repairing cabins, planting, hunting and of course patrolling." Pops listened to everything in silence. The other men had done the same though it seemed to Jimmy that there was a spark of hope in the eyes of the one who had heard N1RL's distress call.

He was surprised to see Terry focused so intently on Pops. Before Jimmy could catch his eye, Terry said, "Sir, your area is yours. If you prefer not to be part of the group, we understand but please keep in mind that we are not the enemy. Time will prove it but this is the starting point. We will need good people before it is all over and settled but you have to understand that it will never go back to the way it was before. We are on our own to defend our own but; we cannot do it on *our own*."

Jimmy's eyebrows climbed up into his hairline. He glanced at Brad who was simply nodding agreement and then he remembered: *Terry was studying to be a lawyer. Those negotiation skills could come in very handy.* He wanted to show a unified front and schooled his face back to neutral, also nodding. Jimmy broke the momentary silence and said, "If you would like to think about it, we understand and respect that. If we have not heard a reply over the radio in 2 days, we will take it as a message that you prefer to be alone. In that case, I repeat what Terry said, "We are not your enemies." We are trying to get a foothold to protect what and who we can before the storm blows in. My cabin is about 2 miles from here as well in case you need to bug out."

A silence stretched out for what seemed like hours. Pops simply stared directly at Jimmy. Finally, the man nodded and said, "We're in. I've known who Captain is for some time now." He released the breath he didn't realize he was holding and offered his hand to Pops who grunted and shook it firmly. The tense situation eased and Jimmy learned there were 8 total people in Pops' group – 4 men, 3 women and one 8 year old boy. "We are sparse on food for right now but we will make it just fine. It is the spring I am more worried about. We have no seeds to plant."

Jimmy nodded and told him there is already land being cleared for planting. "If we can get some people to dedicate more land to staples like onions and potatoes, that will free up space for others to grow some more variety. It also gives us a better chance to be able to stockpile enough for next winter, including seeds." He remembered one vital question he needed to ask everyone they came across. "I need to ask one more thing. Do any in your group have medical training?"

A look passed between the men and one replied, "My sister is an RN but she is terrified to help others for fear of epidemics. She said the sickness will be running rampant starting any time now..." the man blushed a little and looked away.

Jimmy nodded and said, "I can't say as I blame her. We will figure it out. The first step is to get others on board and patrol the areas, get to know the land better. Speaking of, we need to be on our way." Jimmy stretched and stomped his feet to get the blood moving again. He looked at his watch and figured they could finish the circuit today though they would probably get back at dusk. Pops and the other men shook hands and said their goodbyes.

CHAPTER THIRTEEN

Jimmy, Brad, and Terry started back up the hill and continued along the ridgeline. They stopped to boil some water and heat up some food before continuing. Hours passed and they were heading back toward the cabin from the west when the CRACK! of a gun stopped them in their tracks. Jimmy dropped to the ground instinctively thanks to his military training. "Get *down*!" he hissed at them and they quickly obliged. Heart pounding in his ears, he listened to the silence of the forest. He whispered, "Too far away from the cabin to be Jessica, unless she went out. Could be a hunter after some game…"

Brad shook his head and Jimmy raised his eyebrows questioningly. Brad shrugged and whispered back, "My gut says it's a hunter, just not the kind you are thinking of." He nodded and sighed. He heard the sounds of something moving out there but couldn't tell who or what it was. He handed Brad his sidearm and whispered, "I am going to move closer but stay in sight. Cover me, but do not reveal yourself unless you have to. Remember, right ear is trouble and left is good."

Brad and Terry nodded as he stood up, slinging his

shotgun over his back like a guy who had been sitting down and decided to get up and walk. He moved as if he hadn't a care in the world in the general direction of the noise. He hadn't gone more than 150 yards when he heard the sounds of a struggle. Moving more quickly, Jimmy ducked down and made his way closer as quietly as possible. Suddenly, a man was thrown to the ground from behind a tree and immediately tackled by another man. The first was warding off the second who was covered in blood. Both looked to be in their early 30's and he could see it was a fight to the death right away. Neither one noticed him standing there, shotgun in hand. He was unsure what to do. Was it really his place to get involved? He had no idea what was going on to cause it.

Before he could make up his mind, the blood covered man cried out with his hand high in the air, the fading light sparkling off what looked to be a straight edge razor. He brought it down upon the other man and cut his throat open. He had seen death before and he had seen violence, but he had never seen anything so brutal. He scratched at his right ear and stepped back slowly. The killer was still on top of the dying man who was pitifully trying to close the slice as his lifeblood poured into the snow. The movement caught the killer's eyes who jumped to his knees, razor held to the side, and ready to strike. His eyes were wild, almost feverish and Jimmy was suddenly incredibly glad that he had two other people with him. Everything happened so fast that he forgot he had his shotgun on his back and quickly unslung it and aimed it at the crazed man.

"Well," said Jimmy, "What the heck are we going to do about this situation?" Should he try to learn the story and judge the person? Should he bring him to Captain and let him decide? They hadn't talked about what to do in this situation. *Trust your instincts*, he heard Captain's voice say but this was much different.

He stood in the snow and fading light with his shotgun aimed at the blood soaked man. He heard steps behind him but didn't dare turn and look, hoping it was Brad.

"Everyone, just calm down. Let's figure this out. Sir, what is your name? I am Jimmy and behind me is Brad and Terry. We don't want any troub–" He was cut off by the sounds of the dying man coughing and sputtering his last breaths. The man with the straight razor jerked at the sound and suddenly stood up and backed away, looking down at the body. Emotions ran across his face ranging between horror at what he had done, to anger, and back to horror. He looked over at Jimmy and then at something behind him. Jimmy risked a glance over his shoulder and saw both Brad and Terry coming behind him slowly with Brad aiming at the blood soaked stranger.

When he turned back around, the man looked angry again and was breathing heavily. Jimmy looked more closely and noticed that the blood soaked clothes were ragged, thin and torn. The man was sweating and had what looked to be some kind of medical band around his wrist. "Come on now, just breathe slowly and tell us your name."

"THIS MAN TOOK MY STUFF, MY STUFF!" hollered the man. And then, like a light switch, the man calmed down and said, "My name is Cal. This man took my stuff and I need it to keep going. I'm a scout, see?" Cal turned and went back to the dead man and started going through the pockets. Jimmy caught a glimpse of the man's arm through a tear in the sleeve and saw multiple track marks from drug use all along the forearm. He immediately moved forward with his finger on the trigger and barked, "You move away from that body NOW. Who are you scouting for?" Cal didn't pause in his search even though there was a man a mere 3 feet away from him with a shotgun pointed at his head.

"I just need to get what is mine and I will be out of your way." He felt like he was in a dream. *Is this really happening? This guy is out of his mind!* Jimmy turned to Terry and Brad and pointed them to surround the man. As they were moving, Cal took the dead man's pack and upended it into the snow. Jimmy was sickened.

"Hand over that blade, Cal. Right now!" Jimmy took another step closer. To his surprise, Cal simply tossed the blade at his feet without hesitation. "It don't matter if you kill me, there are plenty more of us than you bumpkins out here. I just went before everyone else so I could prove I am better than the others. When I bring back information, it'll be Cal's day to shine. Aha!" Cal picked up a purple Crown Royal bag triumphantly. Jimmy noticed Brad and Terry moving into place about 10 feet away on either side just as Cal did. He jumped back to his feet, clutching the bag and screamed, "It's mine! You find your own!" He opened the bag and a case for carrying glasses came out. He opened it and picked up the little vial that was next to a spoon and needles. Grinning, Cal lifted the vial to the light and shook it it. He frowned and shook it again. "NOO!" Cal screamed, and threw the vial and case at the dead man.

He began kicking the corpse and screaming at the top of his lungs. Jimmy shook his head to shake the dream-like feeling he was having and said, "You tell me right now who you are scouting for! What is your purpose here!" Cal whirled on Jimmy and screamed, "I don't have to tell you a thing, man! I will anyway because it don't matter! NONE OF IT MATTERS!" Cal turned to look at Brad who had the sidearm up and aimed at him and laughed. "You stupid country bumpkins are going to be in for a world of hurt! We gonna own this WHOLE VALLEY!" Spittle flew as he whirled on Terry and began coughing. "You are all going to serve us and grow our food. And when the U.N. dogs come, we will feed you to them!" Cal began laughing again which brought on another coughing fit.

Jimmy had heard enough. *Trust your instincts, he said. I can do that, but will I ever sleep again?* He raised his shotgun back up and took aim at Cal. "You had better make peace with whatever Gods you believe in, Cal. I can't let you run off and I will not babysit a drug addict." Cal laughed between coughs, and turned on Jimmy. "Kill someone and we kill you back? Is that the new law? Yeah well, I'll see you in hell, you stupid mother-" The sound of Jimmy's shotgun cracked and echoed across the forest floor. Cal's body jerked back and fell over, taking what seemed like hours to hit the ground. The silence afterward was deafening. Nothing moved. Cal's body twitched a couple times and then lay still. Jimmy took in a deep breath and lowered his weapon and then looked at Brad and Terry. Brad's face was a mask of shock, his eyes darting between Jimmy and the bodies in the snow. Terry's eyes locked on to his and he simply nodded.

"Jimmy, there was absolutely no getting around that one. That is the only conclusion this could have come to. Either you kill him or he would have killed you."

He jerked at the comment and scowled, "I am not one of those dumb people in the movies that lets the psycho go only to have them come right back with a mob!" Jimmy calmed himself and said, "Thing is, what to do with the bodies? We have to think about diseases. The ground is too frozen to bury them. I suppose the animals would clean them up but that could make it worse."

Brad shook his head and handed the weapon back to Jimmy. "We should burn them." He looked at Terry and Jimmy who both nodded. The men got to work with the hatchet and saw that fit into its handle. Jimmy pulled out some surgical gloves from the first aid kit he carried before going through the dead men's packs and pockets. His conscience poked at him but his logical side won. He wasn't interested in loot, he wanted information. In Cal's pocket, he fished out a piece of paper that had been folded many times with smudges of dirt and ink. He carefully unfolded it and opened what looked to be a crude map of the valley. He folded the paper and put it into a plastic bag. On the other man, he found the same map, but more detailed and on heavier stock paper. He put that into the plastic bag as well and then got up to help Brad and Terry. They piled wood high to make sure it would burn hot enough. By the time the blaze was licking 10 feet into the sky, the stars were twinkling in the velvet sky. With no lights from any cities, it was hard to tell where the Earth stopped and the sky began. By the light of the flames, Jimmy looked at Brad and Terry who nodded and grabbed their packs, turning for the cabin without a word.

****

The days began to run into one another with all of the work that needed to get done around his cabin to make it useable for more people. Brad, Terry, and Jessica were an integral part of getting things in order. Particularly Jessica. Her training as a law enforcement officer was both a blessing and a curse to the men. More often that not though, Jimmy found himself incredibly grateful for these three people. It would have been impossible for one person to make the progress the four of them did.

Days went into weeks and weeks into months. One morning, when he was on patrol, he thought he caught a whiff of spring in the air. Brad turned out to be a decent trapper and they were able to supplement their food stocks with rabbit now and then. The four of them had conversations about the little things they noticed in the woods, as if it really was waking up from a long nap. Their awareness was honed to a keen edge as spring approached.

CHAPTER FOURTEEN

The sun was shining brightly when Jimmy woke up. He could hear the sounds of people moving around outside tending fires, laughing, someone chopping wood. It was early April and spring was showing definite signs of staying. The last harsh snowstorm had been two weeks ago but the warming temperatures were quickly turning the area around the cabin into a sopping mud hole. *We should take care of that today, and get the paths done as well,* he thought to himself as he swung his legs over the edge of the bed and stretched.

He went over to the water basin on the stand and splashed some water on his face, looking into the mirror someone had given him. His beard was fully grown in and itched. As he brushed his teeth with the thinnest layer of toothpaste, he idly wondered if he should try shaving it off. As he was getting dressed, there was a tap at the door. "One moment." Jimmy strapped on his boots and opened the door to see Amie standing there with a steaming cup of coffee in hand. He found himself smiling and said, "Well there are one of two ways to take this. Either it is my lucky day or I should beware of strangers bearing gifts. Either way, I'll take the coffee" He reached for the cup as Amie laughed.

She's looking a little thin these days. Then again, I guess we all are.
Still got those cute dimples though.

He moved into the main room of the cabin with her and
nodded to Jessica who had the radio report in hand.
"Anything change out there?," asked Jimmy as he took the
piece of paper from her. She shook her head. "Nothing new
on the waves but the guys say they should have the Hall
done today. The kids are groaning about it already." Jessica
smiled and left the cabin to assign work duties for the day.
He turned to Amie who had taken a seat at the table that
used to have the HAM radio on it. The camp had grown
from 4 people to over 70 in short order and a lot had
changed with it. Thankfully, he had been really lucky in the
people he met and hadn't anymore experiences even close to
the one with Cal. There were a few out there who refused at
first but had made their way either to the camp or into the
group in general eventually.

Al was having a harder time of it, being further north and
even more remote than he was. Captain's camp was the
largest by far with over 100 people. They had already cleared
the land 50 yards out and milled the wood to build a school
house, cold frames over raised beds that were growing
greens, and the largest medical facility of the three camps.
They had even managed to find concrete for the floor. The
other camps weren't as fortunate. While Captain's camp had
the only actual Doctor, Jimmy had a nurse and Al had two
nurse's assistants, though one was also an EMT. Overall
though, they could be much worse off.

He joined Amie at the table and said, "So, to what do I
owe this pleasure?"

Amie grinned and replied, "Always the charmer. Well, I
came to see if I could lend a hand. I am here a few days to
see how things are going and get a list of what is needed. I
just left Al's and they found an old bunker under a carport.
It took them a week to get everything out but for once, there
were no troubles. We are really low on fuel and the snow is
just about melted off so it seemed the best time to get an

idea of what we have."

He took a drink of coffee and nodded. "That makes sense. How is he doing overall?"

Amie sighed, "He has it rough but I have to give him credit, he has a good attitude. He has about 40 people or so up there at the camp and another 20 who are within 3 miles. They like to keep to themselves, I guess. What about you here? You're building a Hall, eh? Fancy yourself a proper town now? Should I call you Governor Jimmy instead? That'll make Captain Iau-" Amie cut off as they both heard footsteps pounding on the stairs and an urgent knock before the door flew open.

"Sir!," said young Ryan Stephens. "You need to come to the Comm Shack now, please. It sounds bad." They got up and followed him to the smaller log cabin that had been built for communications.

"What do we have Jessica?" She turned to him and the look in her eyes was one of shock. She flipped a switch. The speaker crackled...

"This is a message from the United Nations Disaster Communications Department, North American Division. Be advised that radiation levels within 10 miles of major cities are still lethal. Anyone still in those areas are required to stay in place. No medical attention will be administered as supplies are low and must be rationed. Disease is on the rise due to lack of sanitation and basic utilities. Patrols are being sent to gather supplies and record identifying information. You are required to comply with United Nations authorities. As this is a global disaster, the United Nations is now the recognized global authority. All individual states, provinces, territories, and commonwealths have been abolished. You will now be identified with the country of where you are located. Previous citizenship is no longer recognized. Records of the current global population will be organized with where you were found and you will be recorded as a member of that country. Until further notice, crossing into another country is an offense punishable by death. This message will replay four times daily and be updated as new information becomes available."

Everyone was quiet until Amie said, "Well, at least it is a new message!" Jimmy and Jessica chuckled.

He took another drink of coffee, savoring the flavor while gathering his thoughts. "We will need to make the plan for contact with the U.N. a priority. The ground is softening up enough to turn the area into a mud pit and needs to be filled in. That is another priority." He sighed and slumped a moment before looking up and saluting Amie with his mug. "Well, at least I have had some coffee to start the day!" He had run out the week before and it had been torturous.

Jessica laughed. "We're all saved! You've been grumpy. I will get Brad to get some guys moving in rock and wood chips. If they get the last of the Hall done," Amie snickered and coughed at the comment which caused Jessica to look at her curiously before continuing. "If they can get the Hall done early enough, they can all help. After that, we will have them dig the holes for making caches. In the meantime, everyone else can get things together to be moved."

Jimmy saluted Jessica with his coffee cup and said, "You have it all under control, as always! I keep saying, soon you guys won't need me!" Jessica grimaced and waved him off as she turned back to the radio. Amie smiled and coughed again as they stepped out of the room into the cool morning. The sun was still weak but Jimmy could feel the warmth when the wind stopped blowing.

He looked around at what he now considered his home and was amazed at all the changes. It looked like they would get the main gathering building done today like Jessica said. He saw a few ladies tending the cold frames they had built with fresh boards. His victory garden seeds were coming in handy. Thanks to one of the people who had joined them, they had a mobile wood mill though fuel for the chainsaw was getting lower and lower. He would have to figure out how to best use what they had left. The men had taken to chopping trees down by hand to save the fuel for making boards. He could see tents of all colors and sizes lined up under tarps and other plastic sheeting that had been salvaged and wrapped around crude but sturdy pole frames. There was also a rock fire pit that the younger people had constructed. On the south side of the clearing, the trees had been cleared as well.

The best part was there had been no more word from Idlewild. Reports from Captain's camp, now called Main Camp, said that their wall was completed and there was always smoke coming from the area. Jimmy's area was Center Camp and Al's was North Camp.

Amie stood next to him looking around and said, "You've come a lot further than Al has."

He grunted. "It comes down to how many hands you have to help and the resources available. More abandoned cabins around here than up there." Amie nodded in agreement. She smiled and cocked her head to the side.

"You hear we have a gasifier going now?" At his incredulous look, she went on. "Yep! We have it attached to one of the trucks and had used it a few times before I left for Al's. Sure is going to make certain things easier. We plan on sending Lisa, who designed it, up after the thaw is done." Amie laughed at his look and ended up coughing again. The rattle was deep in her chest and he did not like the sound of it one bit. Suddenly he realized she wasn't only thinner, she was pale.

"Hey, are you OK? Let's go sit down and get you warm." He took her arm and led her back to the cabin. On the way he called out to Ryan who was running back across the clearing, "Get the nurse! Bring her to my tent immediately." Ryan nodded and ran off in the direction of one of the larger tents that was the makeshift medical center and where Holly, their nurse, slept. "I don't know what all the fuss is about, it's just a little cough." Jimmy kept moving her to the cabin and once inside, sat her down and then turned to stoke the fire.

Amie had started sweating by the time Holly came in with her medical pack. "Someone ask for a house call?" Holly took off her jacket and smiled. She was in her late 40's, a little thick around the waist but that was a blessing in the current reality they lived in. She checked Amie's pulse, listened to hear breathing and heartbeat, and took her temperature. "Feeling dizzy? When did the coughing start?"

Amie was visibly sweating now and had a gray pallor to her skin. "A little dizzy this morning and a couple days ago. There were some people with the sniffles at main camp when I left." Just then, Jessica walked in with a look that Jimmy was beginning to recognize as bad news.

"Let's hear it, then."

Jessica cleared her throat. "It seems Main Camp has an illness that is spreading. Some of their scouts reported seeing corpses being tossed out of Idlewild and set on fire. They went to look after the fire went out and that is where they think it started. The fire wasn't hot enough. The doctor says that this will be the first big test of our supplies and health. Seems to be a ten-day to two week gestation There may be deaths."

Jimmy sucked in a sharp breath and looked at Amie. "I am certain you are going to be fine."

Amie's eyes were huge as tears welled up and spilled down her cheeks. "You think I give a rat's ass about that? I have infected everyone! Al's camp and now here!" She leaned back in the chair and let Holly finish the examination.

"Swollen glands, clammy skin and a fever of 102. I am sorry Amie, but I can't let you travel back until you are better." She turned to Jessica. "Please let Main Camp know that Amie will be here for a bit. I have some antibiotics that should help speed her along." Holly then turned to Jimmy and said, "We will need to get the quarantine area up and ready today, not later this week."

Jimmy groaned inwardly. *Another thing that needs to be done today. More like yesterday.* He nodded and got up to get some people to help. As he was putting his jacket on he said to Holly, "She won't be in quarantine, she will stay in here. This is non-negotiable." He zipped up his jacket and walked out the door without waiting for a reply.

On his way to where the workers were finishing up the Hall, Jimmy saw another three hauling a wheelbarrow with rocks and wood chips over to add to the area they had started. "Looks great, guys! Keep it up, I will try and help you later on today!" The younger men waved and smiled. Jimmy came up to the Hall and had a look around. The roof was in place and the last of the shingles had been put up. Around back, the finishing touches on a section of wall that could be lowered like a drawbridge was being completed. He got Brad's attention and pulled him to the side.

"Hey, Brad. Excellent job on the Hall. We can have a little feast in there to celebrate."

Brad smiled and looked at Jimmy a moment before saying, "Tell me what is really going on. I saw you leading Amie to the cabin like she was going to die or something." Jimmy turned red and told Brad about what was going on. Brad took it all in and nodded. "We need to get the tent up away from the others. I think I know a spot for it, too. I will split the crew up. I'll add a few more of the younger boys to the mud detail and the rest on the tent and whatnot. Have Holly come over when she is done with Amie, please." Jimmy nodded and went to have a talk with Jessica when Brad called him back, "Hey, Jimmy!"

He turned and waited for Brad to trot over to him. "What are we going to do about this? Quarantine all the sick in there? Are we going to tell everyone about the sickness? It may turn into paranoid chaos. I need to know the plan so I know how large to try and make the sick tent."

CHAPTER FIFTEEN

Jimmy was exhausted and it was only noon. People were nervous, anxious, and he didn't blame them. With a sickness going around and no luxurious hospital available, even the common cold made people wary. Jimmy had the feeling this was no common cold though. He walked through camp and told the pockets of people about a meeting in the new "Hall" at 3pm today. Of course, everyone knew it was about the illness and new quarantine tent that was being erected about 500 yards away from the main area. The back of the pavilion-styled tent was nestled in some trees that would provide additional protection and the slope off the back side would help to keep contaminated liquids away as well. *We got lucky with that one*, thought Jimmy to himself as he was walking up to see if he could lend a hand.

He saw Brad and about half his crew moving makeshift tables and stools into the tent. He heard a loud "Riiiiippp!" and turned just in time to see one of the younger men tearing a sizable swath of canvas off of an older tent. Just as he was about to scold the youth for foolishness, another one came in with two long poles and between the two of them, were able to make a decent cot for someone sick to lay on.

They put it over a pile of evergreen branches. Jimmy nodded at the teenager and moved on to where Brad was helping to assemble a makeshift shelf for the medical supplies. Brad looked up and nodded a hello.

"Jimmy," he said. "The sick tent will be ready for patients in a couple of hours. We should have enough room for 10 people. Any more than that and we will need to shift other tents around. It will be another day or so to get some kind of rain catch going. Then, it needs to rain."

Jimmy chuckled and replied, "Spring rains will come soon enough and then we will wish for paved streets and drain systems. You know about the meeting?" Brad nodded. "Good. We will need to quarantine any newcomers, and anyone who begins to show signs of illness. Holly said she has a decent stash of antibiotics but we should reserve those for the worst cases. Children first." Though there were only a dozen or so children, most were between the ages of 6 and 15 with only one toddler as the youngest. "Patrols should be next. Fresh foods are to be split between the ill and the patrol. The healthy can last a little longer on the MREs."

Brad grimaced and Jimmy laughed, clapping him on the back. "I know, I know. Doesn't sound that good to me either but soon we will have all sorts of fresh vegetables and whatever we can forage. Hopefully the last patrol will come back in today with something good. Until then, we need to lock the camp down." Jimmy was worried about the last group that went out. Only one veteran, a man who went by the name Poncho even though he was as white as Jimmy. The rest were green boys and one younger woman new to anything like a patrol. They should have been back last night.

Brad was called away by one of the building crew and Jimmy wandered back to his cabin. As he entered, he felt a wave of heat wash over him and saw Holly the nurse applying a cool cloth on Amie's forehead. Amie looked to be sleeping but her breathing was shallow.

Holly glanced over her shoulder as he entered, "She

degraded fast Jimmy. It's like she hit a brick wall and the wall hit back. I am not really sure what it is. I thought maybe just a flu or something at first but with main camp suspecting it came from the dead that Idlewild was burning, it opens up a whole new category of possibilities. She absolutely must be quarantined. You may not like it but you cannot make all of the choices here. There has to be a balance and even in the military, a doctor can order a general to go to bed if needed. I will not back down on this one." Holly's eyes were determined and though her tone didn't suggest it, Jimmy felt almost chastised. He put his hands up in surrender.

"I give, I give! Brad says the medical tent will be ready in a couple of hours. It is kind of impressive what they were able to accomplish in such a short amount of time. I think we need to keep the medication under lock and key though. People may get desperate. At first, they were just happy to have a place to be and warm food in their bellies. Now they have settled in some and that is when things can get crazy. I will need you on hand for the meeting at the Hall in a few hours to help answer questions."

The tension slowly went out of Holly's posture as Jimmy rambled on and then sighed in relief and nodded. "I agree about the medication. I will be there for the meeting but how much are we going to tell them?" Jimmy scratched at his beard and replied, "Everything. If everyone knows it all, they can better handle it and it leaves less room for an 'us and them' situation. If we start to hold back information now, it could cost us everything later."

Holly pulled the blanket up to Amie's chin. "It could also start panic and-" Jimmy shook his head. "How can you be so sure?" she demanded. Jimmy smiled and stood up.

"Don't you think the whole place knows all about it by now? There are only 70 of us on 3-4 acres of land. How long do you think it took?" He gave her a little salute and headed for the door. "See you at the meeting. I am going to walk the perimeter."

****

Overall, people handled the news fairly well and Jimmy chalked it up to everyone knowing before the meeting. No one really complained but a few people asked some questions. "I think you really helped keep things calm. Thank you Holly."

Jimmy was helping her move some things into the medical tent. Outside, the building crew was reinforcing the roof in case it decided to dump snow again. Amie had been moved in and put in the bed closest to the area set up for Holly to work. There were a few emergency medical books but most had the same information written in different ways. A pad of paper, pen, and pencil were the only other things on the little table. A small portion of their medical supplies was in the crate Jimmy was carrying. Holly checked on Amie again and then began putting the supplies away. Jimmy sat next to Amie and looked at her. Pale and covered in a sheen of fever sweats, he felt helpless. He reached out to move a strand of hair clinging to her cheek when Holly said, "Best not Jimmy. Do you hear how quiet it is? People are scared and if you get sick, the camp could tear itself apart." His hand froze and he scoffed at Holly, pulling back.

"I won't have anyone put me on a pedestal. I'm guessing here just as much as anyone else." He got up and began to pace, running his fingers through his hair. Holly snorted and stood up, advancing on Jimmy. "That crap will not work with me, Jimmy Walker! You are the leader of this camp here whether you consider yourself one or not and people are relying on you, looking to you for guidance. So get out there and do what you do best. Go on a patrol, chop some wood, whatever it takes." Her cheeks were flushed as she came closer and poked him in the chest. "Just let me handle this here and you handle the rest so we can all handle whatever gets thrown at us next. Get it?"

Jimmy's jaw dropped open at her tirade and he grunted when she poked him. He barked a laugh in disbelief. "You are something, Miss Holly, really something. Take care of our girl, there. I apparently have somewhere else to be." He nodded to her and stepped out into the cool air. He walked to the middle of camp, looking around. People had their heads down, looking like they were just working but he could see the tension. He noticed the same group working on filling in the muddy areas and called out to them. "You guys want another hand? I can help spread." That brought smiles to them all and one handed him a shovel. Jimmy let himself get lost in the work.

"Go on a patrol, chop some wood," she says. *Well, that other patrol is late. Might be a good idea to see if anyone on the waves has seen them.* He was shaken from his reverie when he heard one of the ladies call for dinner. He looked around and was surprised to see they had almost finished the main clearing. "Wow, you guys are something else! We made some kind of record. Let's go get our reward, eh?" The others nodded in agreement and smiles, joking with each other as they made their way. Jimmy headed to the Comm Shack to see if there had been word on Poncho's group. They hadn't been heard from and Jimmy feared for the worst.

****

The next day brought more news of illness spreading and the Doctor at main camp was fairly certain that the cause was lowered immune systems and vitamin deficiencies combined with a particularly nasty flu. He had a copy of the Physician's Desk Reference available to him. Al's camp had reported no sickness yet but he was already making plans to have a place ready just in case. During their bunker discovery on patrol the week before, they were very lucky to find a hefty medical supply, some honey, and toilet paper which was a complete luxury at this point. Jimmy put out a call for any information on his patrol to the people in his area. No one reported anything and he decided two days later that he was going to lead the next one and look for the first group. Amie's fever had broken a couple of times but kept stubbornly coming back. Holly was still holding out on giving her antibiotics, instead giving her tea whenever Amie came to. A wood stove was crudely crafted and installed. It wasn't pretty but it gave off heat and kept the smoke out and that was all that mattered.

He thought of Holly's words and the way she handled him. *"You can't do it all alone, Jimmy….they look to you for guidance. Whatever it takes."* Jimmy nodded to himself and headed to his cabin, calling out in his military no-nonsense tone. "Brad, Terry, Ryan, Sheila! Patrol tomorrow at dawn. We need to find the others and get information." Four voices called back to him from various parts around camp and he went in to pack. Later, as he was getting ready for bed he stopped suddenly, ears straining. Is that an engine? He shook his head and listened again, moving to the door. As he reached for the handle, footsteps pounded up the stairs.

He opened the door to see Jessica there, hair tousled. "I hear an engine, something is coming Jimmy." He nodded and moved to the railing of his deck. A bell had been installed that had been found in an old barn under years of dead leaves and soil. He rang the bell three times and heard the camp spring to life. He moved back into the cabin and grabbed his boots, jacket, and shotgun. Reaching for his sidearm and extra shells, he heard people gathering in front and went out to meet them. "You all hear it. Until we know better, treat it as a foe."

People nodded and quickly moved off to their pre-designated places like clockwork. *Good thing we drilled,* Jimmy thought to himself as he looked up on the ridge and saw a light flash. He counted to 10 before he saw the light flash again. Only one vehicle, good. He moved toward the only road that came close to the property with his team. He saw others fanning out around the perimeter as best as they could with the amount of people they had available. Brad's team was the one closest to the road with Jimmy's a quarter mile back in reserve. It still rankled him but he was outvoted on the matter and chose his battles elsewhere. As the sound of the engine got closer, the tenser Jimmy got. His senses were on high alert. He could hear one of his team members breathing heavily and gave them a sharp look.

Suddenly the engine roared as the accelerator was pressed and voices shouted, a gun was shot, and shortly after the engine turned off with more yelling echoing through the trees. Jimmy was just about to send someone down to find out what was going on when he heard Brad yell his name. He got up and ran toward the road, loading one in the chamber of his shotgun. He flipped the safety on and before long, saw the lights from headlamps and heard someone groaning in pain. As he neared, he was shocked to see an older truck with stacked plastic totes in the back. He looked around at the people and was both relieved and angered to see Poncho's patrol. His eyes fell on Poncho who was kneeling on the ground with one of his team in his arms. Noah, his name is Noah. Son of one of the builders. Jimmy said, "What happened?"

Poncho replied, "We found this truck and some supplies about 2 hours before some people on dirt bikes came up on us and decided it was theirs. We had to convince them otherwise but they slashed a tire and it was a trick or two to change it without a lug wrench. They slashed Noah here, too. Holly around? He needs something to kill any infection."

Jimmy nodded and then stopped a moment, his eyes wide. *They have no idea about the illness. It is unlikely they have been exposed to it but we agreed all people coming back need to be quarantined. The trouble with that is it may actually make them sick, especially with being gone so long.* He shook his head and put a smile on his face. "We will get you patched up Noah. Brad, tell everyone to stand down but send Holly please. Oh, and I am making you part of the Camp Council." Brad nodded and turned then stopped in his tracks. "Camp Council? What are we, kids?"

He laughed, "What would you rather be called? Camp 2

Council? Center Camp Council? Whatever you call it, you are on it. Holly, too. I cannot and will not do this alone. We are in it together."

The supplies were brought up to the camp, inventoried and stored. Much to the delight of all, cake mixes and frosting were found along with four tins of coffee. Food was brought to the patrol team and Holly tended to everyone's hurts. When Jimmy made it back down half an hour later, Holly motioned to him. "Jimmy, this is quite a situation. I worry that if we quarantine them they will actually get sick but it was agreed on. They all live in different tents but I am just not sure about putting them in with Amie, either. There was word today that two people are sick at Al's camp, too" Jimmy nodded and looked at the ground, trying to decide the best course of action. He looked around the camp and said, "We need a tent set up for patrols to hang out in for a few days when they come back. Have Brad help you with that. I am going to check on Amie."

****

Fire was everywhere and spreading fast. The tents, tarps, trees, and even the stones were ablaze. Jimmy Walker ran through the camp, calling out for people to get buckets but no one was answering. He heard a scream and a child came running across the center of camp completely engulfed in flames. He ran toward the child but his feet felt like lead weights and the child was too fast, disappearing in the forest. Screaming more loudly for help, Jimmy looked around and saw Amie walking up to him, her eyes accusing. Her skin was blistered from the flames and she stumbled on burnt feet toward him. "This is your fault, Jimmy Walker. You didn't do enough and now we are all going to die." Jimmy was rooted to the ground as she came closer. Flames reflected brightly in her eyes as she stood before him. "There you are, unharmed, while everyone else burns. I think YOU SHOULD BURN!" Amie raised her hand, a white bone glowing bright against the blackened skin and she poked him hard enough to push him backward. As he fell, the flames began to spread across his shirt. He cried out, "I am sorry, I AM SORRY!" Just before he hit the ground -

Jimmy jerked awake, covered in sweat and twisted blankets. His breath was fast and ragged as the images from the nightmare faded and his heart started to calm down. *Another nightmare. That makes 3 this week.* He sat up in bed and shivered a little at the chilly air in the cabin. He grabbed a towel and wiped his face, taking in deep breaths to calm himself further. He wasn't too surprised that he was having nightmares, even recurring ones, given all that had happened in the last week. Amie getting sick, quarantine issues, tent movement, and implementing the best practices for keeping people from getting infected were all starting to take their toll. Not to mention the lack of certain nutrients and a lot of hard labor everyday. It was decided that people who were on patrol teams would be quarantined in the newly moved patrol tent and he couldn't help but think of them as barracks. Once they had been cleared after 72 hours, they were able to join the rest of camp. If any were found sick, they would be moved to the medical tent where Holly would look after them.

I really hate logistics, he thought to himself as he got up and went to the table to pour some water into the basin and clean up. He glanced out the window as he was getting a cloth wet and noted that it was still the better part of two hours before dawn but he knew he would get no more sleep. After he was done, he slipped on his last set of clean clothes and set the bag of dirty ones in the main room of the cabin. Going about his morning routine, he went over the day ahead of him. He was going to head out for a patrol with Brad, Terry, Ryan, and Sheila today and hoped to cover a full 10-mile patrol in 3 days. With spring coming on, the traveling was easier and they could get a better assessment of the land that had been, until recently, buried under several feet of snow.

He checked his pack one last time before he made a very

thin version of coffee, rationing the grounds Amie had brought with her. That seemed like years ago. As he took his first sip, he heard someone coming up the stairs and a light knock before the door eased open. Holly looked exhausted and he knew something was wrong. His heart clenched as he asked, "Amie?"

Holly shook her head and said, "No. It's Noah. His cut was infected which I was treating with antibiotics but I am certain he has also gotten sick. I have no way to tell if it is the same sickness as Amie or something entirely different. It's bad Jimmy. I could pump him full of antibiotics that may or may not save him but that would leave us enough for one, maybe two more prescriptions' worth. He is young and may be strong enough to fight it on his own but with the lack of vitamins and regular meals…I cannot guarantee that even if he does make it that he will not have permanent damage from fever. He may also lose the use of the arm. It was deep, like a stab and slash." Jimmy could see she was trying to be strong but her rapid blinking told him she was trying her best not to cry. He nodded and motioned her in, offering her the cup of coffee. As he turned to make himself another cup he heard Holly close the door and sit down. *Looks like that patrol may have to wait. We need to let Main Camp know about this. Can't we catch a break?*

CHAPTER SIXTEEN

The smell in the shipping container was a nasty mix of human waste, body odor, and smoke from the candles. The light they put off only made the area seem darker as shadows cast here and there across the faces of people that had been taken captive and tossed in with the rest. Their eyes were dull, clothes filthy, and spirits broken. Two corpses were in a corner covered with whatever could be found. Their bloated bodies mixed in with the overall stench that permeated everything. Most eyes of the living were fixated on the metal door, hoping that it would open if only for some fresh air. Food or clean water was sparingly given even at first and now that so many had gotten sick, it had been two days since anyone had come in. The captives knew better than to try and get the attention of anyone on the other side. The tortured screams of those who had tried were enough to keep others from attempting it. A child began to cry and no one moved to comfort or console her. The sound was feeble and did not last long. Silence washed over the space again.

There were 47 people at the highest count. Now there were only 14 alive and barely at that. Some had been taken; the younger women first and then the older ones. One time the door had opened and volunteers were asked for. Some went and tried to escape, only to be hunted down like animals. Sometimes, laughter could be heard outside. All that had changed when the sickness came.

Hours ticked by and shouting could be heard outside the metal door. Suddenly the door was thrust open and those inside cringed and covered their eyes from the sudden light pouring in. The cool, clean air rushed in and the men standing in the doorway backed away at the stench that greeted them, covering their nose and mouth. "Good god, what the hell was he thinking? They are useless, half dead and will only take food away from the rest. We should just get rid of them. What do you think Gordy?"

The captives gave no reaction to what had just been said. The man called Gordy was tall and lanky. Dressed in a leather jacket and chaps, most would have thought him a biker who was part of a criminal gang. The truth was, "Gordy" was Gordon Williams, a successful mechanic, husband, and father of three. When an accident took his family, he buried Gordon Williams that day and "Gordy" was born. Ruthless, violent, and cruel, Gordy was out to make the world pay for his loss. He looked over the people in the room, some of whom were asking for water, food, and help. "What was that? You want help? I will give you the help you really need and it ain't food or water." He nodded to his companion who grinned and raised his gun, opening fire as Gordy walked away. *Less mouths to feed, less BS to look after. Just like it should be.*

He walked about 15 feet away and turned around in time to see the metal door being shut on the building. "Seal that thing up good, I don't need any more sickness getting around. The last bout almost did us in." The other man nodded and Gordy walked back to the beat up truck that was given to him for being second in command. Gordy was one of the most trusted people to the leader of what used to be known as Idlewild. Though outsiders might still call it that, those who resided there called it the Fort. He jumped in and waited for the other man to finish, idly playing with his pocketknife. *We are going to need more supplies soon. If we have any hopes of taking over the whole area, we are going to need them sooner rather than later. But if we keep killing off everyone who won't fight for us, who will grow our food for us?* Gordy looked at the whole operation like a machine and without fuel and oil, the gears come to a halt. They needed supplies and food and they needed it yesterday. *I hope they found something on the radio,* he thought to himself. 10 days ago, a radio system had been set up. They couldn't talk out, but they could hear what others were saying and they had people listening in 24/7 as long as the batteries had enough juice. It took Gordy showing them how to rotate the systems before they got more than 10 hours at a time out of it. When they came and asked him to fix something else, he literally shot the messenger and made it clear that he was not a fix-it boy, he was a killer who got things done. Let someone else get greasy and bruised, scratched up. Machines needed fuel and that was a very limited commodity. He had a new career in a new world. He heard the other man coming up to the truck and waited for him to jump in before tearing off back to the Fort.

Coming up to the wall, he saw people walking along the top and in the lookout posts that had been built. The gate was opening up as they came closer and the guards were pointing their weapons at the truck. Gordy put his hand out of the window, then smacked the top of the cab twice and honked the horn once while still moving forward slowly. The guards lowered their weapons and the doors opened faster. One guard saluted him as he went through and he heard an order given to close the gate. Gordy drove over to 'his spot' and parked the truck. He got out and told his companion to bring him some food and drink at the old city hall building. That is where the leader of the Fort took his quarters and gave out orders. No one knew his real name but everyone called him Mister. He was reputed to have run the drug scene out of Idlewild before IT all happened but now he dealt in things other than drugs.

Walking in, Mister was seated in his large wooden chair. When Gordy had first seen him, he fit the chair much more fully but lack of steady food will make anyone lose a few pounds. Mister was listening to a person who was kneeled before him in an almost worshipful pose. "Please, Mister Sir, please! We only ask for enough rice to get through another week." The man cowed under Mister's emotionless stare. Looking up, Mister saw Gordy and nodded to the seat to his left. Gordy moved up and took a seat. The man was now laying flat on the floor, making begging sounds and crying. After a full minute, Mister said, "Give them 3 cups of dry rice. If that isn't enough to last you TWO weeks, then perhaps you should sacrifice yourself and give your portion to your children." The man sobbed his thanks and literally crawled out of the room, praising Mister for being kind and generous. Gordy shook his head and said, "You know we are low on everything, right?"

Mister turned and looked at Gordy through eyes sunk in his head but clear and calculating. He nodded and said, "I know that. There has been some interesting information over the radio the last few days. Seems the rumors were right about another group organized further north and east. We are working on figuring out their exact locations. Cal and the others who took off haven't come back which means they either died or deserted to these other people. I expect they died. I only gave maps to those who were completely hooked on heroin. I knew when it ran out along with the meth, there would be serious trouble so I sent them off to die. You get those containers cleaned up?"

Gordy nodded and said, "You are one cold son of a–" he was cut off by a gunshot outside the building.

Mister rolled his eyes and said, "Guess the guy tried to get one kernel too many. One less mouth to feed. Well, anyway, I am sending you on a scouting mission to get information about these other people. I want to know how many, how far, and what they might have. You have a week and leave in the morning. Take 3 people with you. Don't be seen." Gordy smiled as Mister laid out his plan.

****

The drizzling rain came down through a pale spring sun as people gathered around to say goodbye to one of their own. Jimmy walked with leaden feet toward the group, wishing he could be almost anywhere other than here. As the leader of Center Camp, he knew he had to say something and help to ease the grief that young Noah's death had brought. Not all gathered were mourning; some had seen so much death and violence in the last couple of months that they were beyond grief. *That does not mean they feel nothing though*, he thought to himself. He had seen and met several soldiers with the same hardened look when faced with tragedy, even when it was this close to home. 3 days ago, a missing patrol had come back with, shockingly, a truck loaded with supplies. They also had a run in with some other looters on dirt bikes which is where Noah had been cut. The looters had rushed the patrol with pipes and baseball bats, knives, and wicked looking homemade weapons. Noah had been cut deeply and an infection set in. He wanted to implement an age requirement right then and there for patrols but that was simply unrealistic in the world that had been thrust backward into the dark ages. Each day brought more use of 'modern' supplies that may never be replaced in his lifetime. *My kingdom for some real toilet paper*, he thought.

Holly, the camp nurse, walked up to him and looked him in the eyes. She put a hand on his shoulder. "Would you like me to help with this one? Sometimes it makes it easier when you state the medical facts."

He shook his head and replied, "No, everyone here already knows what happened. All of this is such a wake up call. Even a scratch could kill you now!" He laughed mirthlessly and Holly smiled at him with sympathetic eyes. He looked around at those gathered and nodded to them. After everyone had quieted down, he said, "Today we put to rest one of our own. Noah's service to the betterment of this camp and to the valley overall is the same of any serviceman doing his duty. We honor Noah and will not take lightly the lessons his passing has taught us. Life is more fragile in this world we now live in. While his wounds were grievous and infection took him, we must remember that even something as simple as a scratch can prove fatal if steps are not taken. We must pay closer attention than ever before to hygiene and sanitation. Disease is almost a larger threat to us than looters and gangs. We cannot afford to be slack on this. Holly will be taking medical histories of everyone and it is important that you do not lie. You could put the entire camp in danger. Let me be very clear on this: no one will be shunned based on medical issues. We will not lose our civility so quickly like those who have taken Noah from us." Jimmy nodded to Noah's father who stepped up to say his words.

As those who wanted to speak did so, Holly tapped him on the shoulder and they moved off a little. "I am going to need an assistant and I think it's wise that we start training immediately. Shirley has some medical knowledge from being a medical coder so at least she has some terminology. We need to have some basic first aid and CPR classes as well, Jimmy."

He nodded in agreement and said, "I will leave that to you. Get with Jessica for scheduling and have her put a priority on it. She has come up with a new system for us to prioritize all that needs to be done around here." The amount of information that needed to be taught to everyone was overwhelming. Until recently, there was no need for any of these people to know how to field dress an animal, purify water, or even start a fire. The learning curve was brutal for some.

After everyone had dispersed and went to their various jobs, he wandered to the Comm Shack to find Jessica. *We would be in a much sadder state without this woman's skills*, he thought as he entered and saw her taking notes and putting them into a makeshift filing system. The building had been slapped together hastily to make more room for communication and organization than what was available in Jimmy's cabin. Though built quickly, the structure was solid and there were plans to get a wood burning stove installed but the one meant for here was now in the medical tent. Supplies had to be found and then time carved out to assemble another one plus a thousand other details that all went through this one building, masterfully orchestrated by Jessica.

She looked up and nodded a hello. "Ryan said you are going on patrol tomorrow morning? I need you back in 5 days at the most. We had another family come in last night, they are in quarantine. No apparent sickness and the woman knows how to make all sorts of household stuff from scratch." She handed him a small stack of papers. He scanned the information sheets and saw that it was a family that had been contacted on patrol a couple weeks back. They had no communication and limited supplies but the man wanted to stay put and argued with his wife in front of the patrol. *I hope he doesn't cause trouble*, Jimmy thought. The woman claimed to know how to make detergents and other sanitation items like soap from scratch. They had not come empty handed either. In Jessica's neat print, he saw they brought two bags of lye, some corn seed, various amounts of beans meant to be planted, and the man knew animal husbandry of a fashion. He handed the lists back and asked if there was anything new on the waves.

"Much of the same. The U.N.'s message is the same, sickness running rampant, looters, fires. Ryan heard something last night about a U.N. outfit moving through major cities and fanning out in Virginia. There is some resistance here and there but most people are just looking for normal. Al's camp only had the two people who got sick, thankfully, and Main Camp has reported eight in quarantine though the first person pulled through and is in a recovery area." Jessica smiled, happy to give *some* kind of good news.

Jimmy's face brightened at the last just as Holly poked

her head in and said, "Jimmy? Amie is awake and asking for you." Her smile was huge and he turned to Jessica to say a hasty thank you before trotting over to the medical tent. When he walked in he saw Amie sitting up, looking thin but color had returned to her cheeks. She smiled weakly at him as Shirley was feeding her some broth. He came over and pulled up a chair next to the bed.

"I imagine I look as bad as I feel," she said and took his hand in her own, giving a light squeeze.

He looked down at her small hand in his and squeezed lightly back, replying, "You'd still win $10 in Monopoly, kid." Amie laughed again and started coughing. Shirley gave him a reproachful look and he put his hands up in surrender.

"Okay, okay. I just had to check on her. Keep me informed." He realized he was still holding her hand and lifted it, pressing a light kiss on the back before getting up to leave. "I will send word to Captain, he has been more than anxious." She smiled her thanks and sat back, exhausted and warm from the broth. She drifted off to sleep before Jimmy had even left the tent.

He relayed the message and went about the rest of his day. He checked his packs again and was ready for the patrol. Everyone gathered in the Hall for the evening meal. The overall style was similar to a Viking long house, complete with a fire pit in the middle set into the ground and an opening in the roof for smoke to vent through. A few crude tables had been set up with mismatched bowls, plates of food, and pouches of MREs were sitting next to a beat up pot of hot water. Putting all of it together, Jimmy was amazed to see so many things that had been scavenged or re-purposed. On one platter that looked to be made from a slab of wood, he was shocked to see greens. Small leaves and coiled fiddlehead ferns were mixed in with some of the lettuce that had been growing in the cold frames they built. Out of all of the food there, he found it amusing that it was the thought of a salad that made his mouth water.

There were not enough chairs for people to sit on. Blankets were thrown down with the odd homemade pillow or bag of clothes to lean against here and there. He moved out of the way as people came in with their bowls and utensils and sat down. He watched as people entered and noted how they shuffled in with heads down and how they would look up when the smells of all the food hit them. One girl squealed with joy at the greens on the table and he couldn't help but grin. *I know just how you feel.* The mood lightened considerably after that and soon people were sitting down with more food on their plates than had been seen in weeks. The first bite of lettuce was so good that Jimmy almost cried with joy. Later, he swore he could actually feel the nutrients working their way through his body. By the end the evening, people were laughing and Noah's father was telling stories of his son when he was younger. He made sure to speak to all of the people who worked on the meal and thank them, especially Cass who oversaw all of the meals and inventory of food supplies. He touched base with his patrol team and headed off to bed.

****

"Captain," as his friend's called him, was relieved to hear the news of his daughter's recovery progress. He knew she was in good hands but it still rankled him that he couldn't break away to go check on her. His hands were full of running Main Camp and their numbers had increased yet again but thankfully, the latest group of twelve came with two trucks loaded with supplies including medicine. They were in quarantine until this evening and places were being made for the newcomers. He looked at his watch and headed from the main house out across what people had dubbed as Town Square. The sun was shining weakly and there was a hint of rain in the air. Captain looked around and saw activity everywhere.

People called out 'hellos' and 'good mornings' as he made his way to the communications building, Comm Hub for short. A shriek of frustration and the sounds of a chicken in distress made him stop in his tracks. As he watched, a chicken came flapping and running as fast as it could away from a child that looked to be about 7 years old who was screaming. "Run away chicken! Run for your life!" Following directly behind the child was a teenage boy with a hatchet in hand hollering, "Joey, that is our *food!*" Everyone in the clearing stopped and started laughing. Captain found himself smiling and recalling his childhood on his grandparent's farm. Sometimes, like now, he felt like they had gone back to the old western days, complete with trouble always on the horizon. The main difference is there was a far greater threat from humans than wild animals.

He continued walking, waving to people when a man who looked vaguely familiar approached him. "Captain, Sir. I have a message from lookout station 5. They said there are 3-6 men prowling around, headed this way but taking a wide circle about it. I think we are being scouted."

Captain nodded and replied, "Thank you...Pete, is it?" the man smiled and nodded.

"Yes, Sir. I am real thankful you took my wife and I in. She wanted me to tell you she hopes you liked the cobbler she made." Captain remembered that cobbler and couldn't believe it had been made using long term food supplies. One of the families were Latter Day Saints and had brought with them cases of #10 tins of flour, red and white wheat, beans, dehydrated milk, berries...it was an amazing boost.

He grinned and winked at Pete. "Please tell your wife that was the best cobbler I have had in years and it is not something I'll soon forget." The man stood a little taller hearing Captain's praise and nodded before saluting and heading off on another task.

Walking into the Comm Hub, Captain looked around at the people inside. There was a definite advantage to having so many hands available for projects. This building went up in less than a week and had tables, stools, and even some shelving crafted for it. They were incredibly low on fuel to cut more boards with, let alone anything else, and work was being done on converting the engine to a gasifier since the previous truck experiment was a success. He approached Denise, his sister, and asked about the report from the lookout.

"The report says the same people have been spotted twice and maybe a third time over the last few days. The Addams off to the south reported hearing a ruckus in their chicken coop and one of the hens was missing. Could be connected, maybe not. The tracks were human though, 3-4 different sets that they could tell."

Captain nodded. "Anything else?"

She flipped through a few pages on a clipboard. "Doc says our medicine stocks are strong though he recommends we start making bandages and save the others for patrol units. Food stores are doing well enough and the gardens are starting to produce. Foraging groups will head out today. What we are lacking in is ammo. I know you can reload several thousand rounds but the fact of the matter is we need to get more primitive to save the modern stuff for when it is really needed. The boys are going to have to get creative when hunting but who knows how long that will last before it is all wiped out? Let's see…that is about it. Any orders?" Denise looked up at her brother and waited. She knew he liked to consider everything first and was not one to make quick decisions.

Captain scratched at his beard while thinking. It seemed everything was moving along; people were not going to starve and they had a good solid camp going. The news of potentially being scouted irked him and he thought about the map that had been sent to him some weeks back with a letter from Jimmy. Idlewild didn't have a good fix on their locations but they knew about the presence of another group in the area. All those kind of people knew about was taking and consuming, not producing anything. They would eventually run out and they would be coming once they did. Likely they had already exhausted any surplus they might have gotten in the weeks after IT happened. Captain needed to head them off as long as he could and since he was the closest, now seemed the best time to get some information.

"Where are we in the patrol rotations?" Denise moved to the desk and flipped through another clipboard.

"The next patrol is set to head out tomorrow morning but it is scheduled to go north, not south." She looked at her brother's expression for a moment and said, "I can see that look in your eye Cap. Who will you want to take, how long will you be gone, and what ground do you expect to cover?" She poised her pen on the paper, waiting for the information.

Captain smiled sheepishly and detailed out the plan he had rolling around in his head. He would take 5 others: 1 veteran, 3 adepts, and 1 greenie for training. They would scout out Idlewild first, including the areas marked on the map as being "supply" spots and then work their way in a sweeping motion back up to camp. It should help flush out any unfriendlies and also help him get a better assessment of the land and areas he could take advantage of for defense. They already had perimeter defenses in place at varying distances from main camp and once the ground thawed the rest of the way, they would be digging holes for various traps, snares, and hiding places. He knew they were going to come, but he wanted to control the playing field and led them where he wanted them to go.

CHAPTER SEVENTEEN

Three days later, Jimmy stopped and dropped to his knees, putting a fist up to signal those behind him to do the same. He heard what sounded like voices up ahead. They had been following some tracks for the last day that were south, about 4 miles from Center Camp. They led in an arc further south in a general direction toward Main Camp. It looked to be 4 or 5 people and they were taking pains to avoid contact with others. He made the motion for everyone to settle in. He wanted to see what they were going to do. After about 20 minutes, he heard a shout but it was hard to tell how far away they were or what exact direction. The trees that were growing closely together had a tendency to throw sound off. He waited another 10 minutes, ears straining to hear anything that might give him a hint as to what was going on. Just as he was about to signal the patrol to be ready to move, the smell of wood smoke drifted across the group. He looked at everyone and gave the motions for "keep quiet, split up and flank." Everyone nodded.

Brad and Terry moved off to the right and the others moved left. Jimmy stayed right where he was and waited. He could reach either group should they whistle the need but he

AFTERMATH: A STORY OF SURVIVAL

hated the actual waiting. 15 minutes passed and Brad and Terry made their way back around, shaking their head at seeing anything. The other two were still out there but there had been no distress signal given. Brad and Terry followed him to the left, tracking their missing people. The smell of smoke was stronger the further they went and after half a mile, they could see the plume of smoke rising into the air. He was about to move in further for a better look when Brad tapped him on the shoulder, shaking his head emphatically.

Brad leaned in and whispered, "See all the smoke? They WANT to be found. I smell a trap. We need to be care-" Brad was cut off by the sound of a scream coming from the direction of the smoke and Jimmy knew at once that it was Alison, who had taken Shirley's place on the patrol. It was only her second time out and she was a semi-city girl somewhere in her early 20's. She sounded absolutely terrified. They cautiously moved closer toward the sound. While they were worried about her well-being, they did not want to give away their position or tactical advantage. The attackers had no idea just how many people were in their group and he hoped they could get to her fast enough before any information was given in duress. He knew he had to move quickly and hoped the last of their group was OK, too. A few minutes later he heard a shot and a scream from Alison.

Everything seemed to slow down as he jumped up with shotgun in hand and ran toward the area. He came around a group of trees and saw three armed men back to back aiming outward in a defensive triangle stance. Alison was on the ground, shirt torn open with blood smeared along her arms where she held the last of their party, Kurt. She was crying hysterically and it was obvious he was dead. One of the shooters was aiming at Brad but Terry was nowhere in sight. He felt his blood boil as he lowered his shotgun and reached for his sidearm. Just before he was about to let some lead fly, starting with the guy aiming at Brad, he heard a voice behind

LEANN EDMONDSON

him say, "I wouldn't, if I were you," and felt cold steel push into the back of his neck. He dropped the weapon and raised his hands. He was pushed forward with the others and saw Terry being pushed toward the fire as well. *What a rookie mistake!* He mentally berated himself as he moved forward and took stock of their captors.

He saw 5 dangerous looking, well armed, men. The one who was obviously the leader came around from behind him, gun still pointed at his head and smiled nastily. There was a cruel light to his eye and Jimmy knew this man would not think twice about killing all of them. Especially after he got the information he was surely going to ask for.

"Well, look what we found while hunting! Got some macho men and a pretty little thing. Sport and fun to be had for everyone tonight boys!" The others laughed over Alison's crying. One of the men kicked her over and told her to shut up as the others moved to tie Brad, Terry, and Jimmy together. They tied Jimmy's hands to Brad's ankles and so on to keep them from running. He studied the others as they were searched for valuables and noted that both men were quiet, calm, and determined. *And to think that Terry was studying to be a lawyer not 6 months ago…now he is acting like a hardened soldier. We need to get out of this and get word back to camp.* They were due back in 3 days, 4 at the very most.

Once they were secured, the men turned their attention to Alison. One grabbed her by the hair and lifted her up, she shrieked in pain and began to struggle. The man laughed and said, "Ohhhh, got a lively one here boys! I say we have our fun before the sport, eh? Been awhile for me." The leader watched Jimmy, Brad, and Terry closely for their reaction at the treatment of Alison. The men ripped off her torn shirt and were dragging her off to a fallen log.

Jimmy couldn't stand it anymore and hollered out, "STOP THIS! This is barbaric! She has done nothing to any of you!" The man laughed and continued amid Alison's screams. The leader got up lightening quick and open-palm slapped him across the face, knocking him into the dirt and wrenching the rope attached to the others.

"We live in a barbaric world and only the strong survive. You will have our full attention after we have our fun. I have a feeling you will sing us a pretty song before we are done with you." The man turned and walked over to where Alison was stripped naked and being held down. "I like a good fight, she's mine first." Just as he was about to reach the others, a shot rang out in the woods and one of the men holding Alison down stiffened, blood blooming from his chest. He looked down and then back up in confusion.

"Gordy? I thought you said there were only…" he fell over and chaos erupted. The others holding Alison down let her go and reached for their weapons. Shouts rang from the trees around them and more shots were fired. The man called Gordy grabbed his weapon and pack and disappeared just before 10 armed men and women came out from hiding, guns pointed. One of the women went to Alison and helped her up. Two men moved over to the would be rapists and shot them point blank without a word. Alison was dazed and obviously in shock.

He felt the ropes being cut and looked up into the face of another man he had never seen before. The man's brown eyes were boring into his for a moment before he offered his hand to help him up. Jimmy took in the situation. All of these people hadn't said a word so far, just came in with guns blazing and for that he was most grateful. But what kind of people am I dealing with? He noticed that every one of this new group were wearing white armbands. Some had what looked to be a trumpet embroidered on them, others a cross in gold. He looked at the man who helped him up and said, "I am most grateful for your timing and assistance, sir." He offered his hand, "My name is Jimmy Walker and-" The man cut him off midsentence.

"The names you had before the Almighty judged us is not important. Only what you do to redeem yourself in His eyes before the final reckoning!" The others in the group murmured, "Final reckoning!" Jimmy's gut clenched. Ohhh boy. *Out of the frying pan and into the fire. These people are almost more dangerous than the ones they killed. Tread easy, Walker.* He looked to Brad and Terry and caught Terry's eye, nodding ever so slightly. Terry got the message.

"It is a trying time indeed, Sir," said Terry. "We were out foraging for food and then smelled smoke, heard a shot, and Alison's scream. We are all very lucky and grateful for your help."

The man went on as if Terry had not spoken to him, "The Lord decrees rape a most grievous sin and it is up to the righteous to cleanse the land for His coming!" He raised his hands, rifle still in hand and his followers cheered him on. Some had a fanatical look in their eye as if every word this man spoke was from the mouth of God Himself.

Jimmy spoke up. "We would very much like to get back to our camp and get Alison some proper clothes." He saw the lady who had helped Alison up had wrapped a thin blanket around her shoulders and was trying to get her to drink some water. Alison looked off in a daze and did not respond. "We need to get her some help."

The man looked at the dead companion sprawled on the ground and said, "We will tend the dead as is the sworn duty of the Cathars of Christ."

Jimmy nodded politely and moved to gather his stuff. Brad and Terry also moved quickly. They retrieved their items and he moved to take Alison by the hand. She moved with him as if in a fog. As they were making their way back into the forest, the man who had spoken to them called out, "Should you wish to see the light and join us as one of the chosen, meet at the river fork at the full moon and you will be accepted as a brother. All of you! Beware though, those who we find sinning against the innocent and God will be dealt with the same as these foul souls here today." Jimmy raised his hand in acknowledgement but did not look back.

As he helped Alison walk along, the going was very slow. Everyone was silent, lost in their own thoughts. If they were anything like Jimmy, their thoughts were having an all out brawl inside their head. He was caught between the people who had attacked them and almost raped Alison and the religious fanatics that had saved them. *Saved us today anyway.* He kicked at a rock in his path.

"I understand, I really do," said Brad. "Maybe one of us should head out and see if we can follow the cult or that Gordy guy. He got away, Jimmy. The religious people missed him and he ran off into the woods. We need information. If you guys give me some of your food supplies, I could scout them out. One person is easier to glance over than a group of 5." Jimmy stopped and looked at Brad, considering the suggestion.

Brad waited impatiently for him to make a choice. Terry was on edge and Alison was still mentally shut down from being assaulted. She moved easily enough when you guided her but would not speak or even look them in the eyes. *We are all still in shock but hanging around here is asking to be ambushed again.* He looked at Brad and shook his head. "I can't let you go alone Brad and if Terry were to go with you then I am the only protection Alison has and we need to get her back to camp. I am not about to risk anyone else on this patrol."

Brad pursed his lips together in dissatisfaction but nodded and said, "I just hate the thought of him getting away with it. That Gordy guy will report back everything and that could spell serious trouble for us sooner rather than later."

Jimmy nodded. "The lesser of the evils says we stick together and get back to camp. Maybe those religious people….the Cathars of Christ was it? Maybe they will be able to track him down in their wanderings."

Terry spoke up. "That main guy is a real nut job, Jimmy. They may be trouble later on, along with Gordy and the Idlewild group." He sighed and began walking with Alison again. "We will run circles if we try to meet all of the problems and potential problems we have. Right now, we get Alison back to camp and then take the next steps to meet the threats." Brad started to make his case for going after

Gordy again but Jimmy stopped him. "I know, Brad. It ticks me off, too. I want revenge or justice or both but right now, getting our own selves to safety is the top priority." Brad and Terry looked at each other and then back to him, nodding. They continued making their way back to camp in silence.

CHAPTER EIGHTEEN

Captain and his team found the trail made by the people that lookout station 5 had reported. He saw 4 distinct tracks, maybe a 5th and had followed them backwards, much to the confusion of his patrol. When finally asked, he explained. "We need to make sure we know the origins of the scouts. First of all, that is the last thing they would expect us to do and second of all, it will give us an advantage to scout them when they absolutely least expect it. So far, they have no reason to think we know anything about them or their location or plans and I mean to use that to our full advantage. Let's keep going."

At the end of that day, Captain was certain these people were from Idlewild and their 'scouts' had little to no concept about leaving signs behind. He easily followed their pattern that wound around in a semi-spiral. On the second day, he met up with the Addams who reported no further issues with their chicken coop but their eldest daughter had found a ribbon tied around a smaller sapling about 500 yards away from their home. A marker likely left by the scouts. The Addams were on high alert and Captain promised to send them a couple people to help out with some supplies. He filled them in on the other happenings that evening over dinner and the patrol bedded down in an outbuilding that had been converted to a sort of cabin. It was dry, heated with a fire and kept you off the ground with 4 old army cots inside.

The next morning, Captain and his patrol broke their fast with boiled eggs and fresh bread baked by Mrs. Addams. The patrol was very grateful and promised to bring information on their way back through. By midday, they had covered another 2 miles and found tracks of another, much larger group that had come from another direction but met up with the scouting party's tracks and crossed them. Throughout the day, Captain determined that there were two groups out there and that was cause for alarm. If they were working together, their patrol could be overtaken before they could get word back to Main Camp. He pressed on, being even more cautious. Using the crude map Jimmy had sent him, he made for one of the locations marked as supplies on the map. He let the patrol know that they were not to be seen as they fanned out. It was their job to get information and not engage in battle or conversation with anyone they met. If people wanted to talk, Captain would be the voice that spoke back.

The group came to a clearing that had 2 shipping containers. It looked to be the remnants of what could have been some kind of camp with a busted smokehouse next to the shipping container that was on its side. The door was open. The other container had what looked to be tar or something all over it. As they moved closer, Captain saw it wasn't tar. Tar doesn't move in 45-50 degree weather. One of the others kicked a rock as they approached which set the whole black cloud lifting into the air and hovering above the container for a moment before descending back and swarming it. Captain put up his fist to signal everyone to stop and then to move backward slowly.

"We do not want to have anything to do with those containers," said Captain. He pointed to the refuse around the area. There were clothes tossed here or there, food containers and other garbage littered all over the place. "My guess is they kept prisoners in there and that is a mass grave of sorts. They wouldn't have let food just rot like that. Food is power and that is all these people know or care about. Keep alert, we continue scouting." Captain knew the perceptions the valley group had of these people needed to shift if they were going to survive. Idlewild would get more and more desperate for supplies and when people were starving, things took on a new level of danger. They moved out and continued. After tonight, they would head back toward Main Camp but Captain wanted to get a bit more ground covered. With the snows melting off, traveling was much easier and what had taken 4 days just to reach the Addams' cabin a mere 2 months ago now took half the time.

Captain wasn't sure what he was looking for and ended up going further south than he meant to. He smelled smoke and garbage on the breeze long before he saw any sign of human activity but he knew they had to be close. Likely too close but Captain was never one to shy away from a thing needing doing. Right now, Captain needed information and that was that.

Leaving the rest of the patrol, he took the only other veteran with him to get closer and figure out what was going on. The other man's name was Nate. Though Captain didn't know him very well, he knew the man's type and was confident that he wouldn't react irrationally to adversity or ambush. They crossed a country road that didn't look like it had seen much use and worked their way toward the smoke they now saw, though faintly. Captain figured they were within half a mile and the stench was getting stronger. Captain was moving along as silently as he could when Nate grabbed his arm and yanked him back. Captain struggled a bit and looked at Nate angrily. Nate let go silently and simply pointed. Captain blinked and then looked where Nate indicated, not seeing anything at first. Then his eyes caught a glint of silver off the remaining light and saw the trip wire.

He had almost walked headlong into one of the oldest tricks in the book. He sheepishly smiled at Nate and nodded. Nate bent down and followed the line to the base of a tree where he found some tubes wired together crudely under some leaves. They looked to be homemade dynamite sticks. The wax that sealed it was still unmarred by being moved around or in too much heat. They both stepped over the wire and were extra cautious as they continued. Suddenly, the trees and shrubbery ended and the men were standing there, wondering what to do as they looked across a large clearing. The stench of rotting material was overpowering at times, even with a breeze, and the men had to keep from gagging. The clearing had stumps and fallen trees in a large roughly circular shape. In the center was a walled town that had to be Idlewild. Captain didn't realize they had actually made it that far and quickly dropped down so he wouldn't be as easily noticed. Nate followed suit and looked to him with a question in his eyes. "We sit tight for an hour and observe, then join the others and head home," Captain said as silently as possible. They dug in and waited to see what information they could gather.

****

Gordy was tired, bloodied, and really pissed off. *Those idiots deserved what they got and I don't feel one bit of guilt. One of us had to get away to let the others know.* He had been chased by the religious group until dusk that night when he managed to hunker down inside a rotted out root burl. He hadn't seen or heard another person since. He got up after a while and tried to put more distance between him and the ambush site. He was exhausted and the going was slow in the dark. *This is stupid, I need to sleep.* When he found a hollow to burrow into, he slept for twelve hours straight and woke to a sunshine-filled day in full swing. He was stiff and sore from sleeping on the ground, not to mention his panicked run through the forest to get away. While eating some food from his pack, he considered his options. He knew he needed to get back to

Idlewild and let Mister know what was going on out there. He was fairly certain the first group he came on was not part of the second. The man who he had backhanded was the leader of that group. Gordy recalled the man's features in as much detail as he could and tried to commit it to memory. His hollering had ruined all of Gordy's fun and that man would pay for it.

As he began to make his way back home, he thought about what he would tell Mister. He hoped that Mister was in a good mood. Those who had failed him were taken care of quickly but hopefully with the information Gordy had, Mister might be lenient.

He had to hide from other people walking through the forest since he was alone and only had a few rounds. As dusk neared again, he broke through the clearing that had gotten much larger in the last few days and picked his way across the stumps. As he walked, he tied an orange ribbon on the end of the rifle. The stench rolled across the land. He was making his way around to the area he knew to be free of traps when he heard a cough behind him at the tree line. He did not stop moving as to give himself away but his adrenaline kicked in. He kept moving as he had before but angled his path to move more closely to where he heard the noise.

****

Captain saw the man come out of the tree line into the clearing. He was in tattered clothing but armed and seemed to be methodically picking his path around stumps and brush piles.. Suddenly a breeze kicked up that brought dust and a heavy stench of rotting refuse to them, making Nate cough. Captain's eyes got wide and he quickly looked back to the man to see if he heard as well. If he hadn't been looking for it, Captain would have missed the split second pause and then semi-subtle change in his direction. He was making his way for where the two of them were hiding and trying to be nonchalant about it. He came closer and closer in an unhurried pace and Captain was faced with a decision. He couldn't risk being discovered but shooting this man would only draw attention. If either he or Nate moved backward, the motion would surely give them away. *Well, damn,* thought Captain. Nate noticed that Captain had eased his sidearm out and had it in hand, ready if needed but they were here for information, not confrontation.

Gordy smiled to himself as he looked up, eyes searching the tree line. *Mister sure knows how to sow some fear,* he thought to himself. Nothing moved, not even a twitching branch from a breeze and the forest was silent, too. It was kind of eerie. As suddenly as that breeze had come, it left again. He continued to pick his way. Nate felt, more than saw, Captain tensing up and spared a glance to his side. He noted Captain had the sidearm ready and pointed in the general direction of the man. Suddenly, a bird burst out of the bushes and the man jumped, startled. When he realized it was just a bird, he swore and turned around and walked away muttering under his breath. Captain and Nate watched, unmoving, as he got further away. Captain let out the breath he had been holding and Nate silently slumped in relief. When the man had gotten within shouting distance of the wall, they moved backward slowly and made their way to where the others were waiting.

"That was too close, Cap," said Nate as they met the rest of the patrol. Captain nodded and filled the rest of the group in on what had happened. "I am certain that this gang of people mean to spread out into the valley and take whatever they can. We need to get back. Prepare for a hard march, I want to get back there as soon as possible. No one speaks to each other about this, we don't know who may be watching us out there as we pass by." The others nodded and followed Captain as he made way for home.

CHAPTER NINETEEN

Jimmy sat back in his chair, exhausted, and it was only 9am. He had called Holly, Brad, and Jessica to a meeting at his cabin, not wanting to discuss everything at the Hall with so many people constantly moving in and out of the building. Though everyone knew the patrol had gone bad, they did not know all the details yet which was why he called the council in. Alison had been seen to the evening before and was talking again but her sobs could be heard around the camp. All of the women had gone in after Holly had checked her over to help comfort her.

Holly said, "To be blunt, there was a long conversation about rape and assault. In this world, the chance of being raped is higher than at any other time in our lives. It is something that must be mentally prepared for as best as possible but these ladies need some self-defense training." Jimmy nodded and watched as Jessica recorded everything. When she looked up, she was met with three sets of eyes intent on her.

"What?" she asked.

"You are the only person here who has that type of training," said Holly. "Other than Jimmy and maybe a couple others but as a woman on the force, you had to have had some kind of training on it. Right?" Jessica nodded and wrote her name next to the note. "I will work it in the schedule. I want girls as young as 8 to attend this. Yes, I know that means some scary conversations with very young girls but there is no luxury of innocence right now. Knowledge and practice will serve them better than keeping them in the dark and being taught about sex in a violent and traumatizing way. I will not budge on this." Holly's jaw had clenched in determination.

The men shifted in their chairs uncomfortably. It was just one more slap in the face of the realities of the world they now lived in. Silence stretched on a few minutes as each person was considering the implications and effects this may have on not only their camp, but the whole valley group. Holly spoke up. "As horrifying as the thought is, we cannot turn away from the ugly truths because they are uncomfortable to deal with. We will be stronger by meeting them head on. I will help as best as I can, Jessica."

Jessica smiled and nodded. "We will need to send someone to the other camps about this one, I dare not put this one over the waves. Speaking of, Al reports that the religious group you met have also made their presence known at North Camp. No issues or problems between the groups but 4 people left and joined the cult." Jimmy's eyebrows drew down at this new development.

He sighed and nodded, "Well, people are allowed to leave if they wish. My only concern is how much information they will give over about supplies and schedules as their loyalties shift. Perhaps we should get some kind of fortifications built around camp."

He looked at Brad who said, "We have a lot of pit traps dug already but it will need to warm up a bit more before we can get the spikes driven in. There are some trip wires and other booby traps that will alert us when people are sneaking in. We should focus on ways to drive people where we want them to go, just like Captain did. I think that will serve us better than a wall. A wall will just give outsiders something to attack and put off the message that we have something worth taking."

Jimmy, Holly, and Jessica agreed. They moved on to discuss food and medical supplies, general state of the camp, and what had gone on over the radio during the days he was on patrol. "Captain went out on a patrol the day after you did, Jimmy. No word back yet. Al is asking for more people to be relocated up at his camp to make up for those who left. He needs someone who can help with building and gardening," said Jessica.

Brad replied, "Maybe Captain could send some people. I don't have a soul to spare for all that needs done around here as it is." He nodded and asked Jessica to put the call out.

It was lunch before they were ready to end the meeting. Everyone got up and stretched and headed for the Hall. Jessica caught his eye and they both hung back. Jessica moved close to him and said in a lowered voice, "I wanted to let you know that there are several radios out there that have gone silent over the last week. A couple of them we know were sick, others were close to where U.N. groups have been reported moving through. Whether they are now in some U.N. camp or dead, I do not know. The two in Virginia are silent, one in southern Indiana hasn't been heard from in 4 days and they were the closest station reporting U.N. activity. They are making their way north pretty quickly now. We need to think about the plans we have made and when we should implement them." The communications set up at Main Camp had a much longer range than his did. He listened to her in silence and simply nodded, lips pursed. Jessica knew when a man needed to be alone and think. She walked away without another word.

Instead of going to the Hall for food, he found his steps leading him to the medical tent where Amie was making excellent progress and had even gained back a little weight. When he moved the curtain aside, he saw her up and folding linens with Shirley and laughing about something. Those dimples will be the death of me, he thought as he watched the sparkle in her eyes and the easy way she moved at whatever task she put her mind to.

Amie saw him standing in the entryway and said, "Jimmy! Did you hear? They are cutting me loose tomorrow and I can head back to Main Camp!"

Jimmy's heart lurched a little but he forced a smile as he walked inside the tent toward them. He tried to sound happy about it when he replied, "That's great!"

Amie's eyed him and she moved closer, putting her hand on his arm. He barely noticed Shirley quietly go out of the tent as Amie said, "I know how many nights you stayed by the bed. I am also not so blind or unfeeling as to not see what is going on here."

His mouth was suddenly very dry and he realized he was standing there like a dolt and tried to reply, "What? I was just….uh, it was normal concern for…oh damn I sound like a moron." Amie's low laughter made his heart clench in his chest just before she raised up on her toes and kissed him firmly. When she pulled back, they were both a little breathless and he found himself feeling like he did at 13, being kissed for the first time by Christine Ross. He was as able to speak now as he was then, which was to say not at all. Amie's cheeks were flushed as she pulled back.

"The time will come and when it does, we will be ready and won't look back but things are too fragile just now. I need to get packed for tomorrow and I am sure you have some things needing your attention." He realized she had walked him back to the entryway of the tent and jumped when she pinched him before ducking back in to finish folding linens. *What just happened?* he thought to himself and jumped at Shirley coming around the corner.

"Whoa! I didn't uh…see you there Shirley. I was just…uhh…" Shirley laughed and went in, leaving Jimmy with a blush that went to the tops of his ears. He cleared his throat and went off to see where he could help with today's projects.

****

Two weeks went by without any issues or major catastrophes and that was worrying the camp leaders more than anything else. Idlewild was quiet, the United Nation groups had stopped moving north as quickly once they hit the major cities that had not been attacked by nuclear bombs, and the U.N message hadn't changed. No one new came in, no one left, and no one was sick. The sprouts were doing well under cold frames and in containers and people were shifted around to North Camp to help out. Patrols did not report anything overly alarming other than the religious group being reported as larger than initially thought. That could be trouble down the road but for now, all was quiet.

A location for trade and larger group meetings had been scouted, marked and partially cleared out about a mile away from one of the two state highways that ran through 'their' area. In 4 days, there would be a gathering of people from all three camps to trade information, techniques for various work, and socializing. Holly and Amie had thought up the idea as a way to help solidify their bonds as a group even though they were spaced out miles apart. They picked May 15th to be the first of such gatherings and there were lists upon lists of details to be taken care of. When the announcement was made to the Hall at Middle Camp, the cheer was deafening and morale went to the moon and back. With the weather warming and spring flowers coming up, it was hard to believe that only a few months ago, the whole world as humanity knew it had changed. Jimmy enjoyed it as much as the little voice warning him it was far from over would allow. He couldn't shake the feeling that this was all the calm before the storm and he didn't like not knowing which direction or what kind of storm was coming. Every fiber of his being was warning him that trouble was headed his way. He did his best not to show it.

****

"I'm telling you Mister, those people got food and ammo and everything else we need in a cozy spot just ripe for the taking." Gordy was in the Fort and this was the first time he had had a chance to talk to Mister since he got back 10 days ago. Mister had been working on something at another location that Gordy didn't know much about. Just as he was finishing his story, a man walked in and sat next to Mister. He looked to be about 35 or so but it was hard to tell. The man had no expression whatsoever. His hair was buzz cut and he was clean shaven. If Gordy were to guess, he had military background but *there is something off about this guy,* he thought to himself. Mister listened to the story in silence and remained silent for a full five minutes before replying. Gordy was sweating and certain he was going to be killed for failing to get more information and everyone else being killed in his group. He tensed up when Mister stood up.

Mister said, "I had given you up for dead or deserted. While you were gone, some things have....*changed.*" There was an ominous tone to the last word, changed. Gordy schooled his emotions and forced himself to calm down and pay attention. He noted the man had not moved more than an inch since he sat down. He just listened with eyes that bored holes in whatever he gazed upon. Gordy noticed there was a white armband around the man's bicep with something sewn onto it but he couldn't get a good look without being obvious.

Mister turned to the man and said, "This is Seth, a member of a group that has been patrolling the area. He told me of some other camps out there. There is more than one and more people than we thought before. Seems they are led by some military men."

At that, Seth stood up and declared loudly, "The military of the old world is a dying product of that world. We must cleanse the land of the old and make way for the new and the coming of the Lord!" Gordy's mouth dropped open and he didn't care. He looked at Mister quickly and then back to

Seth.

Mister snapped his fingers in front of Gordy's face and said, "Perhaps I should explain so you can understand. Seth, please allow me some time to help him see how things are now." The man nodded once and marched out of the room. Mister turned and slapped Gordy across the face and growled, "You idiot, don't you see what we can do here? What the hell happened to you out there eh? You lose your marbles? You forget what's going on, you forget the plan?"

Gordy refused to raise his hand to the stinging cheek and glared at Mister. "I went through the mission and almost died doing it. I remember the plan perfectly and I don't recall there being some religious nut-job cult in there."

Mister raised his hand as if to slap him again and Gordy stood up slowly saying, "I wouldn't if I were you." He eyed Gordy a moment and said, "Tell me what the hell is going on. And where have you been?"

Mister turned and sat back down, turning to light a cigarette. After exhaling he said, "You know the United Nations is only about 80 miles away? That is where I've been, checking it out which you should have been here to handle for me. They got tanks, trucks filled with troops, machine guns and grenade launchers. They even got dogs to sniff people out. We barely got back here ourselves but on the way, we run into a group of those people," he gestured to where Seth had been sitting and took another drag of his smoke. "We have gotten a lot of information from them and we have similar goals. Cleanse the world of the old authorities." He lowered his voice. "You think I buy into that whole second coming crap? This disaster is all man-made here, all of it. I mean to use these people as the front line and once the U.N. is taken care of, all we have to do is clean up the rest of them freaks. Then we move on the group in that valley, then out further. One of them radio guys was saying that the death toll is in the billions now. I been thinking, we will need to keep some people alive who have skills we need like growing food and animals and stuff.

137

Then we just sit back like fat cats. Now what do you think of those 'nut-jobs,' eh?"

Gordy was grinning by the time Mister was done. He cleared his throat and said, "Sounds like they may have a vision after all."

CHAPTER TWENTY

A small tent city had sprung up literally overnight in the trees at the edge of a large, recently cleared area. Trees that had been felled were used as posts for a covered area in the general center of the 3 acre space. A rough path had been made to the structure that was just large enough for a 4 wheeler to travel on, if there was fuel to be had for them. The mid-spring morning was filled with the smell of wood smoke of a dozen or more fires. People could be heard laughing and the scent of food cooking woke those who were still asleep. Most groups had foraged greens and early berries along the way to what was dubbed The Market. Captain, Jimmy, and Al were all enjoying some of the precious coffee that was available and no one complained that it was weakly brewed. Denise was cooking some oats in a pot over the fire.

"So," said Jimmy, " What do we have on the agenda today?" He smiled and saluted Denise for the coffee. Just as she was about to answer, Jessica came running - literally running - up to them and was out of breath.

"The United Nations," she said, gasping. "Reports just came in that they are about 80-90 miles from here. They have stopped for the time being, maybe they hit a pocket of resistance or something but they are closer than we thought!" She coughed and tried to slow her breathing. Jimmy stood up and guided her to the folding camp chair he was sitting in. He had never seen Jessica so shaken before and that made him nervous.

"Well, this changes everything." His mind reeled with all the implications the news brought with it.

Captain grunted his agreement and said, "Yup, helluva pickle we're in. On the one hand, we may need to deal with Idlewild which means we need access to our supplies. On the other hand, we have the United Nations who will take our guns, our ammo, all of the 'excess' food and whatever else they think we can live without. I, for one, am not willing to allow that to happen. That means we need to put the plan into place for stashes and whatnot. You can bet they will have some dogs or something and if they think we are hiding anything which they usually do in warfare - you better believe it is warfare and population control - they will rip it all to the studs in the walls to find it."

"So the question is," said Jimmy, "What is the balance here? Do we focus more on keeping supplies stashed from the U.N. or being ready to handle Idlewild?"

They all stood around, lost in their thoughts. There was also the religious group to be mindful of. Captain reached into his pocket and pulled out a pouch of pipe tobacco and an old, well used wooden pipe. Denise's eyebrows climbed up into her hairline as she said, "Cap, are you ok? You only smoke at night!"

Captain took his time puffing to get the ember going before he exhaled and replied, "It helps me think and we need to try and get this right the first time. The coming confrontation will either make or break us in the valley." The mood grew somber as Denise was handing out bowls of oatmeal, the sweet smell of pipe tobacco mixing with the wood smoke. After everyone had eaten, Captain said, "I think the best course of action is to meet all threats as best as we can. The trick - the balance - will be to make sure we are not spread too thinly." Jessica and Denise both nodded. "We should make cache spots like we had talked about. Each camp puts back enough supplies as they can for 1 month in three locations. Keep enough around for about 2-3 weeks. With summer coming on, we will be able to forage and use less of the long term supplies, save them for winter."

Jimmy shook his head, "That is all well and good but what about the firearms. Didn't I hear they were disarming everyone they came in contact with?"

Denise nodded and replied, "They are letting people keep smaller caliber guns, knives, even bows and arrows but they are taking all handguns and large rifles. The HAM in Kentucky said they left him with his .22 rifle but only one box of ammo. They took everything else. He went silent afterward. Not sure if they took his radio, too. He may have gotten sick or bugged out. Who knows? We may need to be careful about using them and might want to think about stashing them or moving them to a better spot."

Captain piped up, "Have you talked to anyone who still had their radio after the troops left?" Denise said, "Yes, in Tennessee. That is the only one I have heard of though."

Silence came over the group again as they considered it all. Al slapped his leg suddenly, making everyone jump. "I am not about to give up now. We can outsmart these people. Why don't we work *with* the United Nations. Feed them some information about Idlewild and the status here. Of course, we still need to-"

Denise jumped up and said, "No! I will NOT go to one of their camps! I have had a bad feeling about it since I first heard about them and I Will.Not.Go!" Everyone looked surprised at the outburst and Denise's face began to turn red. She lowered her voice and said, "What I mean to say is, once people go to those camps, there is absolutely no word from them again." Captain cleared his throat and Denise sat back down, in control of her emotions again.

"We need to deal with one thing at a time. The first thing

is to let people enjoy themselves a few days. We will need the morale boost and the memories in the weeks and months to come. In the meantime, we have some details to iron out and perhaps get some people shifted around. I would like to get more people up at Al's and will be asking for volunteers at the end of Market. Caches will be made as suggested and planned for. I think it would be prudent to have all non-essential ammo and firearms stashed as well but close at hand so if there is an hour's warning, each camp can get to their weapons and defend. We need to take this slow and easy while still being proactive instead of simply reacting to what others do. Denise, for our camp, I need..." he rattled off various plans against surprise attacks, hostage situations, and coordinating with the other camps.

Al spoke up. "Not everyone knows what everyone from all the camps look like. We need a way to easily identify each other. I think armbands would be too obvious and make us targets." The others nodded and he went on. "We could have some kind of gesture that is casual looking or maybe carry some kind of trinket."

Jessica exclaimed, "We can paint our faces!" She giggled and that broke the tension.

Everyone laughed and relaxed with Captain saying, "We have a little time to figure things out. For now, let's just try to have some fun and get to know one another. We will be relying on these people and they will be relying on us. It is important to bind the community together." There were noises of agreement and everyone dispersed off to their areas.

Jimmy headed back to his fire and tent, calling hellos to people and smiling at some children playing and chasing each other. He sat down on a stump and sipped at the last of the coffee in his cup. He was thankful that he didn't get headaches from the lack of caffeine any more. He sat back and simply watched the people around him. He used to enjoy people watching but he noticed some real differences between what he was seeing today and what he used to see before IT happened. Over at the next fire, a man was teaching a young girl of about 8 or 9 how to stack the wood so you could cook right on top of it. Then he showed her how to stack the wood so it would burn longer and put off heat without burning up the wood too fast. At the A Frame, people were laughing and ladies were looking at what was for sale. He watched with interest as one lady bartered a hairbrush for 2 sewing needles and a spool of thread. *No, this is certainly nothing like it was before*, he thought to himself.

The day passed and everyone enjoyed the downtime. Ideas and methods are discussed, gardening tricks and cycles are shared and even though there were patrols around the area at all times, people are able to relax. Just for a while, they are able to forget the world around them and act like this is simply some camping adventure and new friends are being made. A lot of laughter and playing children were heard all day long.

That evening, people began showing off their skills for everyone's entertainment under the A Frame. Jimmy's jaw dropped open when he walked through and saw Jessica juggling cups. He laughed and cheered with everyone else, clapping when she finished with a flourish. She bowed and blew kisses at the audience as she moved out of the way for the next person in line. She came over to him, a little out of breath from her performance.

"So, I just have to ask myself, "What would make a city cop learn how to juggle?"

She laughed and took a drink of water before replying. "Whew! It has been awhile. I learned to juggle from my Uncle. He used to be a carnie and would come through every August for about a week. He had dinner with us most of the week and taught me how after. You wouldn't believe how many times it has helped me save a falling vase or drink. Really helps with coordination."

Jimmy nodded and smiled. "Well, you haven't lost your touch. The tough lady cop reputation may be shattered after that performance, though." He grinned when she playfully punched him in the arm. Jimmy looked up to see a man walk up, smiling at Jessica. He nodded to Jimmy and offered his hand. "I'm Derrick. I'm with Al's group at North Camp."

Jimmy smiled amiably and shook his hand. "Well, as far as I am concerned, all of the camps are just part of one big valley. Like 3 large families living close enough to keep in touch but far enough to spread out. I'm Jimmy Walker, Center Camp." Derrick nodded but he could see the man was more interested in Jessica.

She smiled at him and shook his hand. "Hi. I'm Jessica, also of Center Camp."

Derrick looked surprised and he said, "Jessica on the waves? The Coordinator?"

He could hear the capital on the word and his eyebrows rose up questioningly. She blushed as she started to explain the nickname.

"Uh, well we are in the center so it makes the most sense to use it as the hub between all of us, right? I set up a system so we know the status of each camp and can move stuff around as needed. I wanted to wait until it was really going before I brought it to you…" she trailed off.

He laughed and put a hand on her shoulder reassuringly. "How did I get so lucky to have you on my team, eh? I trust your judgment Jessica." He turned to leave. "I keep saying, some day you will realize you really don't need me!" He laughed when she replied, "Stop saying that!"

It has been a great day, he thought to himself as he went back to his tent. He settled in to get some sleep before his shift on patrol and he thought about the next day. There would be a meeting between the camp leaders including those who oversaw key areas such as communications, patrols, and building. Then, after lunch, there would be a meeting with everyone together where Captain would address issues and questions people had as well as let them know what is going on and ask for volunteers to be shifted around as needed. There was a lot to decide. Jimmy was not looking forward to a bunch of drama and hoped people kept their heads. The morning after that, people would disperse and head back to their camps to put plans into action. It was going to be a busy. The upside to it all though was Amie would be there. As he drifted off, he thought of all the things that needed to be decided.

****

The next morning, Jimmy woke up feeling better than he had in months. The patrol he went on in the middle of the night was unremarkable and that was more than fine with him. The sun was well past the dawn and all manner of birds could be heard in the trees. He had become used to listening for the birds as a sign of everything being OK around him. He knew today would be busy and stressful but Amie would be here and that seemed to make it all worth it.

He got up and stretched, shrugging into some cleaner clothes and pulled on his boots. *We are going to have to figure something out for footwear before next winter,* he thought to himself as he walked out of the tent. He saw some people stoking fires and getting water on to boil for the morning meal. A few people waved to him as he made his way to the ramshackle outhouses that had been hastily dug out and built. The plan was to have better structures in place before the end of summer and the whole gathering place a bit larger and more secured. As he stepped out, he went to the bucket of water with a thick bar of homemade soap that had been placed there. He washed his hands and splashed some water on his face. As he shook his hands dry, his stomach grumbled its protest. Turning to get some food, Brad fell in step next to him.

"G'morning, Jimmy. Sleep well?"

He found himself smiling at this man he regarded as a friend and vital asset to his camp. He clapped Brad on the shoulder amiably. "Good morning! I slept better than I have in a long time. You?" Brad nodded and returned the smile. They walked to the area that had been set up for cooking. There were men hauling some water in buckets with the ladies preparing food and kids running around. The normalcy of it struck him as a precious thing and he laughed loudest when a girl had run into the back of his legs, knocking him down. She had a bit of dirt on her face but clear green eyes that did not turn from his when she said she was sorry.

He nodded and laughed as he dusted himself off and told her that she couldn't help how strong she was. Her beaming smile before running off after some other children warmed his heart and loosened the knot of worry a little more.

Brad laughed. "And here we thought the threat was all 'out there.' Looks like we have some heavy hitters in here, too." He winked at Jimmy playfully and everyone around them chuckled. One of the ladies came up and asked for their bowls, filling them quickly before going back to her work. She smiled at him widely when handing him his bowl. She was middle age, gaunt from sudden weight loss but still pretty. He nodded respectfully and moved out of the way for the next people waiting for food.

Brad and Jimmy sat down to what they believed was more plain oatmeal but this time there was a hint of honey sweetness that made both men's eyes close in pure pleasure. Not another word was spoken while they ate. When they had finished, Brad said, "You know one upside to this new world we live in…it forces you to enjoy and cherish the little things. It makes you live in the now more than I have ever had to before."

He nodded his agreement and they sat in silence, watching the camp around them. A patrol came in and the peaceful morning was shattered when the leader came marching up to Jimmy, his face all business. The men stood up and Jimmy nodded a hello.

The man stopped and said, "Name is Max, Sir. We have just come back from the south route. There is something going on out there… all sorts of people in the woods but it doesn't look like they know where they are going. They look like they're in a hurry, though. We didn't get close or engage them, only observed."

Jimmy listened closely. "Are they armed? Do they look sick? Wait, we need to get Captain and Al in on this one."

****

Once everyone was settled, Jimmy nodded at Max to tell the story. "We were patrolling the south route. We noticed the birds stopped making noise so we hunkered down to see what was coming. Thankfully, we were on a rise and could see them first... dozens of people in the woods. I didn't see any guns and no one looked sick but they looked lost. They also looked terrified and kept moving even when it was obvious they were exhausted. Some of them had a kind of smock on. Brown or dark blue, almost like they used to work in a hospital or something. We followed them to a cave where they built a fire and settled down. Most of them seem to be loosely together but whether that is by circumstance or choice, I am not sure. No one really talked but they did put someone on a watch. I think they are just wanderers trying to find a place to be. We headed back to report. It is likely they are smelling the food right now."

Max said to Captain, "They are in that cave about two miles from your camp. In daylight, it would only take an hour to get there. We should keep patrols on for the rest of the gathering or it might be best to just head out. A gathering draws attention." The men nodded in agreement, but there was a troubled look on Al's face.

"Wait," he said. "We cannot go through the rest of this life afraid of every other human being we run across. Eventually we will have to stand our ground and fight to stay on it. These people are not armed you said? What about organization?"

Max shook his head. "The only thing that seems to tie these people together is to keep moving. It was eerie."

Captain and Jimmy looked at each other. "It's the wave before the United Nations people. I'd bet my last bullet on it." Jimmy agreed.

Max looked surprised. "United Nations are close? Why didn't you tell any-" he stopped when Captain put up a hand. "The reports say they are about 80-90 miles from here. There is much that can be accomplished at this gathering and there are more of us than there are of these wandering people. Speaking of, we need to get the meeting going. All of your questions will be answered then."

CHAPTER TWENTY-ONE

That afternoon, Jimmy was eating some exceptionally good rabbit when a familiar voice came out of the woods. He smiled when he heard, "Pardon me, Sir. Is there a place a girl could sit and warm up?" He turned and his smile broadened when he saw Amie there. He had hoped to see her earlier that day but the meetings took longer than expected. Thankfully, they didn't go as bad as he had worried about, and better than he had hoped. There were some people who were upset about being left in the dark about the military being so close. Captain explained why they felt the gathering was worth the risk and most calmed down. A few people grumbled and protested about being treated like the peasants in the Dark Ages but quickly shut-up once Captain reminded them that they were not bound to stay in the group if they did not like the way it was being handled.

"This is not a democracy, people. Yes, we listen to everyone and we take viewpoints into consideration but this is a survival situation of not only us but humanity itself. The luxury of voting and worrying about being politically correct is long gone. About 4 months ago and it isn't coming back here. There will be civility and common courtesy but the popular idea of never hurting someone's feelings or offending others is a luxury that existed in the last world. Not this one and certainly not in this valley. The summer is coming on and that means more people moving around. We have far more to worry about than someone's 'feelers' being hurt because they didn't get what they wanted. I do not have the time or the patience." By the end of his speech, most people were nodding agreement.

Calling it like it is...amazing how much easier it is to do that now, he thought as he listened in.

Jimmy was pretty pleased with all they had gotten accomplished that day. People volunteered to be shifted to other camps to help out. It was decided that the women would choose for themselves whether to run or stay and fight. Any children who showed the desire and skill to help with the supplies would be trained. In fact, it was agreed upon that all camps would have reading, writing, and math in the mornings and survival training in the evening for anyone of any age who needed it. The ladies had formed their own sort of council to handle female matters and that suited him just fine. All camps unanimously agreed about the education and defense training for all able-bodied people, especially the young girls who had all heard the story of what happened to Alison.

The discussion about identifying each other from camps was lively and good humored; there was more than one comment about shields and crests and castles in days of old. It was agreed that there would be a word that all used followed by a gesture that identified which camp. Each camp was to decide what their gesture was and share with the others but the word used by everyone to initially identify themselves as friend was to mention something about apples.

"Even under stress, you can still work it into a sentence such as, 'I just wish I had one more apple,' or you could say you were trying to get to the apple orchard," Captain explained to the group. There were many nodding heads and it was decided upon that there would be a gathering like these twice a year. The first would be in early May and again in mid to late September. The word and/or gesture would change at those meetings.

He shook his head to clear his thoughts and scooted over to make room for Amie on the log set close to the fire. He returned her smile as she sat down and said, "Quite the day huh? I think the plan is working." She nodded to a group of people laughing by the A Frame. "There are people from all three camps over there, laughing and having a good time. Creating bonds, trust, friendships. Maybe even love. So long as we hold on to that, there is still hope." She turned back to Jimmy with such a smile on her face that made him move before his brain kicked in. He kissed her firmly and wouldn't let go when she squirmed half-heartedly.

When he pulled back, they were both breathless and had flushed cheeks. Amie grinned after a moment of surprise and said, "My father is going to tan your hide, Jimmy Walker."

He grinned boyishly back and said, "Worth it."

She laughed and punched him in the arm before looping hers through his and holding his hand. He looked down at her small hand in his and then looked up around them. People were trying not to stare which of course only made it more obvious. He turned to look at Amie again and saw she was holding back a laugh. When their eyes met, they both burst and didn't care if everyone was looking or not. Let the rumor mill have their fun.

They sat there talking hand in hand for a good hour before another patrol came in, this time carrying a small girl. There was a commotion and a group of people following as the child was carried to the medical tent that had been set up by the doctor from Main Camp. Jimmy and Amie looked at each other and got up to see what they could learn. Amie kissed his cheek and went off to find her father. He nodded to the patrol that was waiting outside the tent and was about to get the report when Holly and the doctor from Captain's camp running.

"Make a hole!," he shouted and everyone moved aside to let them in. The man who was carrying the child came out and Jimmy put his hand up. "I'm sorry but you will need to stay in there until you have been cleared of any infection or parasites." The man's face stiffened but he nodded and said, "I understand, Sir. They can tell you what happened. When you hear it, my vote is to help these people." Jimmy's eyebrows shot up to his hairline and he turned to the rest of the patrol. "This way, please."

People moved aside to let them pass. Captain, Al, Brad, Jessica, and Denise came from the tree line and Captain motioned them to follow. They walked to a tent that had been set up away from the others for just such a situation. Once inside, the patrol sat down gratefully and one of the women, Robin from Al's camp, began to tell the story.

"We were west of here and had already finished the south side. We were making the last of the loop when we heard what sounded like a kitten or some small animal. We found that girl there with a dead woman, I am assuming her mother." Jessica gasped and put her hand over her mouth. "I know, sickness risk but I will not leave a child alone to die. She was delirious. I think starved and dehydrated. not sick from infection or disease. She didn't even struggle when we picked her up. There were tracks everywhere though. Dozens. It looks like they went around us, avoided us. I sent a couple of people to scout while we started back here. They are slow moving so it was easy to catch up to them. They just look lost, scared, and like they are running from something. One of them saw a scout, hollered out and they all tried to move faster." She stopped and looked to one of the others in the patrol. He was in his early 20's, thin but toned. "One person raised a gun and screamed to leave them alone but never fired. I imagine there was no ammo. His hand was shaking as he pointed it at me. I just backed away and came back to report." Everyone was silent, taking in this new information.

Footsteps could be heard approaching the quarantine

tent and Holly entered. She looked around to everyone and said, "No infection or disease that I can see. She has some lice but that is easily taken care of. We had to give her an IV. She is badly dehydrated and may suffer some long term effects from it. If she was healthy before, she should pull through." There was an palpable release of tension. "She is delirious and was mumbling a lot while we got her cleaned up and into a cot. She kept calling for her mother but there was something else. Something about getting away from the bad men. I would guess her age about 6 or 7 at most." Holly sat down on a stump that had been moved in for a seat. She looked pointedly at each of the camp leaders.

"We must put the plans into place immediately upon return to camps. There is a group of people who know some things about booby traps and other ways to warn us and slow down the wave that is coming. We have no idea how much time we really have but there isn't much between us and their last known location and it has been 3 days. We need to get moving now. We need another meeting. Now." Her tone brooked no argument and Captain chuckled.

"Well who am I to argue with such logic? I agree. Let's gather everyone and let them know that once they get back to camp, they are to implement the plans. Remember what we discussed though." He looked meaningfully at Jimmy and Al who nodded.

The meeting did not take long to gather because everyone was already outside, milling and speculating about what was going on. They quieted down when they saw the camp leaders emerge from the tent. The patrol stayed with Holly to be checked out. Captain stood on a large stump so everyone could see him and gave an abbreviated version of the U.N. location and the group of people who had gone around.

"The storm is coming, faster than we expected. Tomorrow, when we break camp it is important that everyone makes haste to their homes to prepare. We do not know much about the other people, only that they have avoided us. They are running from something and we need to be prepared for it."

Someone shouted from the crowd. "Are we going to go after them or leave them be? If they are running, shouldn't we know what they are running from?" Others murmured agreement and Captain shook his head, "No, we are not going to go after them, that is their own choice and as far as running, it is likely they are the first wave of people running from the military. We need to think of our own." There was a low rumble amongst the crowd.

Well, this is an interesting turn. He watched with interest to see how things would play out. Jimmy knew without a doubt that overall, they had had it easy. *REAL* easy. No one had starved to death, no murders, no sexual assaults within camps, or other criminal activity within their groups. He knew that most people who were part of the valley had escaped the worst of it but they could no longer hide in their little areas away from everything. The new world was coming to them and most people feared the unknown. Horror stories had trickled across the waves from HAM radio to HAM radio and the fact that it was only snippets of information here and there made things seem all the more sinister and threatening.

A voice rose above the crowd, "I say we let them have their peace but maybe send a small patrol to get some information from them? Trade some supplies for information? We need to know what they are running from!"

There were mutters of agreement and heads nodding. Jimmy watched Captain's reaction carefully. He liked to think he was a fair judge of character but this was the first time the group as a whole had voiced their feelings on something. Captain was standing comfortably, taking it all in. There was no hint of negative emotion; he simply stood and listened to people's ideas. When the group seemed to be in agreement, Captain cleared his throat to get their attention.

"I agree. That is sound thinking there but we will need people with experience to handle this situation. These people are hungry and hurting and took steps to avoid us. That tells me they are more afraid of what is behind them than seeking food and assistance. That means they are panicked and unpredictable so this needs a firm but gentle hand." Captain let that sink in a bit.

People talked amongst themselves and Terry from Jimmy's camp raised his hand and declared, "I volunteer to go! If these people are running from the military, that means they are likely on the same side as us. Has anyone considered that we may need them? What if there is another doctor in there? Or a chemist? Or a proper teacher? We need people with skills and I for one think we need to help them. If we do not help them, we are no better than those at Idlewild!"

Jimmy grinned widely and nodded his agreement. He walked up to stand next to Captain and said, "I agree and I will lead this patrol. I need two more people." Hands shot up amongst the group and he picked one person from Al's camp and one from Captain's camp. He was just about to turn things back over to Captain when Amie called out, "That is all men! You need a woman on this patrol, too!" She walked up to the stump her father was standing on, hands on her hips just daring him to say something to the contrary. He looked down at her a moment, then gave the barest of nods. Amie relaxed and smiled at Jimmy as she stepped back.

Captain looked over the crowd and said, "This is going to be the biggest test of our plans, our strength, and commitment to each other. This situation moving toward us will either bind us together and make us strong or it will rip us apart and destroy what we have worked hard on for the last several months. We have been lucky, very lucky. If we look out for each other and stand firm, we will have something better than luck. We will have a true community. We must weather this together otherwise we all fall. Everyone be ready to leave at dawn. Information will be shared on the waves and runners between camps." He stepped down and the crowd silently parted to let him pass.

Jimmy's eyebrows knit together and he could tell that Captain was not happy about Amie coming. He sighed heavily.

He caught up to Captain after talking to his patrol team about logistics and agreed that they would head out this evening to catch up and locate the group. It also gave them the ability to scout ahead and report any trouble back to the groups leaving in the morning. Captain turned to him and grunted as he continued walking. He knew better than to say anything and just followed. Once they reached the tent, Captain went in and Jimmy hesitated. He felt like a teenage kid, nervously waiting for his girlfriend's father to decide whether or not he was acceptable. It both amused and upset him. He was about to turn away and leave it be when he heard, "Well are you coming in or what?" He lifted the flap and went in.

Captain was sitting on a round of wood with a flask in his hand. As Jimmy entered, he was offered the flask and given an order to "Have one with the old man." He did as he was told, enjoying the burn of the scotch as it went down his throat. He capped it and handed it back. Captain took it and set it down next to him saying, "Being the father of a daughter is rough from day one. She seems so small, helpless, and your instinct is to protect her from everything. Then they get older and you are their whole world, their only man. Before you know it, she is grown into a woman and making her own choices but the instinct to protect never goes away."

He didn't know what to say so he kept his mouth shut. Captain eyed him a moment and grunted again. "I suppose she could have chosen worse men to fall in love with but no matter how much I try to be mad, I can't help but like you, Jimmy. You take care of my girl out there." Jimmy was stunned into silence and realized his mouth was hanging open. He closed it so quickly, his teeth clicked and then began to stammer. "I, uh..Sir, I would never disrespect...I mean if you don't-" he was cut off by Captain putting a hand up.

"We aren't kids here and I am not deluded into thinking that she will listen to me even if I tried. You just take care of my girl and make sure she doesn't do anything stupid. Sometimes she gets tunnel vision on her goal and doesn't see what is around her." Jimmy nodded silently, still feeling like a teenager and stumbled out of the tent when Captain waved him off.

Jessica was standing outside with a barely concealed grin on her face and he smiled sheepishly at her. "Heard that, did you?" She laughed quietly and nodded before getting serious.

"I have something I would like you to see. I thought of different scenarios and wrote some procedures up based on police training. They aren't a handbook, mind you, but they will give a jumping off place." His eyebrows shot up in the air, the embarrassment from a moment before gone. They walked together and began making plans.

CHAPTER TWENTY-TWO

Mister put on a face of concern, even though he could care less about the "Cathars of Christ" beyond their role in his plans to take out the military. Thankfully, he really only had to deal with one, but sometimes Seth was a bigger pain in the ass than it was worth. They claimed it was their duty to rid the world of all the past corruption and society to make way for the second coming. Mister played the part well and had even closed his eyes during their prayers when it served his purpose.

They were in Mister's 'office' discussing details. The plan was for the Cathars to infiltrate the military group while giving the impression of being helpful and law-abiding. Many of the group had served in the military when they were younger and would be able to blend in easily. Mister was surprised to learn that they had already gathered intel this way. The information brought back had been shocking to say the least. There were areas all over the world where the United Nations had gathered people and kept them 'for their safety' but most who were being held were young and healthy. Mister grinned inwardly, thinking about 'saving' a group of young and healthy women. The men could do the grunt work for them, too. They would likely be so happy to be rescued, they would throw themselves at his feet and offering anything he wanted.

He was smacked on the shoulder, which brought him back to the present. "Hey, are you paying attention? I said we will need a signal for when your people are in position. We will have explosives set in key places by those on the inside. We must time this perfectly for maximum damage."

Mister nodded and fantasized about snapping the man's neck. Seth continued.

"Most of the force will be on patrol but with the runners in place to guide them to the ambush spot, we can make quick work of it. Then, we follow the military's path right back to their deployment camp. Once we take that, we head to the main camp in this sector and so on. We will need to winter over in the deployment camp before we head out to take the next location. It is 500 miles away."

Mister nodded again and tried not to smile. *You won't live to see that day. Once I have the supplies from the deployment camp, we won't need you anymore.* He schooled his face to reveal nothing. Talking to cops and thugs had honed that skill at an early age. Mister put part of his plan into play. "We will need to keep one or two alive for information. We will need 6 uniforms for our scouting group, ammo, and grenades. My group will handle the questioning," said Mister.

Seth nodded and replied, "There are caches with supplies that are being emptied and brought to key locations now."

Mister's temper spiked into overdrive. "You never thought to tell me about that?"

Seth lips curved into what would be a smile, if it ever reached his eyes. "You are told vital information on an as-needed basis. You are a means to an end, nothing more. Some of you may be redeemable. Time will tell." He rolled up the map on the table and walked away without looking back, leaving Mister to seethe with fury.

****

Jimmy, Amie, Terry and the rest of the patrol headed out 2 hours before dusk. That would give them enough time to pick up the trail and follow it for a bit before it got too dark. They would sleep out under the stars tonight. Jimmy wanted everyone light on their feet even though they carried extra food to be traded and an empty milk jug to fill with water for the refugees. He glanced at the sky and wished, once again, for a weather report. Even at the end of May, the rains were cold in northern Michigan.

They found the area where the girl had been located. One of the previous patrol had tied a small knot of pink plastic ribbon around a branch. They fanned out and walked in a line side by side to look for tracks and try to get an idea of how many people there were.

He felt a tickle at the back of his neck and turned to look down the line. He saw Jake from Al's camp with his fist up and was staring at the ground. Terry and Amie kept a look out while he moved over to Jake as quietly as he could. When he looked down, his heart lurched at the sight of a tiny hand poking out of a rock pile. It looked like the child had been buried in a rock-cairn style. Likely, they did not have anything to dig with and this was their best option. It was obvious animals had tried to get under the rocks but only one side had come loose. He motioned everyone to come help rebuild the grave. Amie gasped quietly at the small hand and even though Jimmy could see the tears welling up, she immediately bent over and began stacking more rocks while Terry unfolded a camp shovel and filled in the spaces between rocks with dirt. It took all of 15 minutes before they continued on their way. It did not take long to figure there were maybe 8-10 people fleeing in this direction and 1 of them looked to be a child.

They continued on at a steady pace until it was getting hard to see. Jimmy stopped and gave the signal to do a perimeter search to make sure this was a good spot to make camp. Everyone began spiraling out as he watched from the center, ready to assist wherever a call came from. He couldn't help but feel a little pride at the cohesion of the group. They moved quietly and thanks to the hand signals, were able to keep talking to a minimum. *We need to step up the training to make sure everyone knows these signals, even if they do not patrol.* The forest could do funny things and make sound either travel long distances or snuff it out 20 feet away. In the coming weeks and months, everyone would be called upon to defend their homes for that is what this valley now was. Home. The thought both disturbed and comforted him. He didn't choose this new community and family, but he was damn thankful for them.

A sharp whistle indicated someone found something. He quickly moved toward the sound and saw Terry holding a water bottle to a man's lips. The man was filthy, in ragged clothing and the rattle in his chest as he breathed heavily was so loud that Jimmy was surprised they hadn't heard him when they stopped.

"He is badly dehydrated and burning a fever. I don't know Jimmy…." Terry trailed off. Amie was about to bend down and comfort the man when she stopped and straightened, looking around the area they were standing in. He reacted to her sudden movement instantly and unslung his rifle whispering, "What?"

Amie turned a slow circle, weapon raised and ready before she replied. "I was just thinking he may be some trap or something." He nodded and felt foolish for not thinking of it first.

The man said, "Please, kill me so I don't have to fade away. Just one mercy shot, please." His face hardened at the request but he also understood. He looked to the rest of the group and Terry said quietly, "He is too far gone, Jimmy. He knows it and we know it." Terry looked at the man and said in a kind tone, "Your suffering will end, friend, and you can be at peace but before you go, we need your help."

The man's eyes went wide as if he was seeing everyone for the first time with their weapons and gear. He cried out, "Nooooo! Just let me die, let me die!" he began to struggle

161

against Terry who stood up and backed away with his hands out unthreateningly.

"We are not your enemy! We are trying to help. Please, calm down and help us understand those you are running from. We need to know about what made you avoid us when it is obvious you needed help!"

The man looked at Terry with feverish eyes and said, "Not all people who wear the uniforms are military. You are just like them!" He struggled to stand up and ended up slumping back down, exhausted. Between heaving breaths he muttered, "Please....just grant me mercy. Make it all end. I am tired, so tired."

The group stood in stunned silence. Jimmy slung his rifle over his back and kneeled down in front of the man. "Sir, there were others with you and they need our help. We mean to save them from the same people you are running from. There are others out there who would also do them harm for no other reason than they like it. Please, help us understand why you are running so hard."

The man looked up at Jimmy with fever shot eyes and swallowed before replying. "Those military people kill you unless you are young and healthy. They take all your supplies and round up the young, kill the rest. The others that dress like military do worse than kill first. But those, they kill everyone. 40 of us got away but now there are only a dozen left. Maybe less." He slumped back from the effort of speaking so much, the rattling in his chest even louder. The man looked at him hard and nodded once, then leaned back and shut his eyes. He knew better than to press this man further. He pulled his handgun out of its holster, took aim and whispered, "Thank you. Thank you for helping us." The man gave a small smile with eyes still shut and Jimmy pulled the trigger, granting mercy and ending his suffering.

****

In the early morning two days later, Jimmy and his patrol came upon the group. There were 9 of them, 2 were toddlers. The patrol dropped down into the bush to observe them. A fire had been built and it looked like a couple had packs. One man had a hatchet in his belt and another had a knife strapped to his thigh. No one spoke, they barely moved. They looked utterly defeated. Their clothes were filthy, torn and no one had any real jacket to speak of. The children were wrapped in what looked to be wool blankets. Their eyes were dull and it was eerie and heartbreaking to see them so obviously malnourished. Amie put her hand on his arm and gave him a pleading look. He sighed and nodded, motioning them all to move back.

When they were about a quarter mile away from the group, they laid out the plan again. Amie would go in with only a concealed handgun on her person. The others would fan out and give cover if needed. She would explain they meant no harm and had supplies to trade for information on why the group was running. The rest would be played by her signal or unless he felt she was in danger. Everyone moved into position and Amie smiled at Jimmy reassuringly before she stepped into the clearing with her hands up.

She called out in a voice that would carry. "Hello? Please, do not be alarmed. I am not here to chase you or cause any trouble!" The people instantly sprang into action and Amie was so surprised she stepped backward a few paces, hands outward. The men pulled their weapons and the rest got behind them and started to move away. Amie's heart broke seeing some hobbling and obviously in pain. She put her hands out imploringly. "Please! There are still good people in this world! Please believe I mean you no harm or want any trouble!"

One of the men screamed, "But you have been chasing us!"

Amie shook her head, "No! We have been following you to try and learn what you are running from! We will trade water and food for information!"

One of the children began to cry as the woman holding it was helping another get into the woods. She stopped and turned. The man who spoke eyed Amie and demanded, "How many are there of you! Don't you lie to me, I may not have anything to my name but I will go down fighting and I swear i will take you WITH ME!"

Amie could see he was on the verge of cracking and took a risk. "There are 4 more of us. We come from one of three camps in this valley. We have a community here. You avoided the first gathering the camps have had. Please, we only need information and have supplies to trade for it. We will not make you go anywhere you do not want to. We are not part of the military."

The man lowered his hatchet and scoffed, "Well I know that, who do you think we were running from? There is some information, now show me what you got. We don't need to get all friendly but we haven't eaten more than leaves, berries, and dirt in days."

Amie nodded and gave two sharp whistles without looking away. She knew in her gut that they were meant to help these people. The man with the hatchet held her gaze without flinching which confirmed her suspicions that he was a leader of sorts. His eyes darted away as the others came into view. Amie said, "Please do not think of doing anything foolish here. We are sincere and I hope you are, too." The man's eyes flickered a moment and Amie thought she might have seen a chink in his armor. *Progress.*

"My name is Ross. I speak for these people and will negotiate. Water for the first question I already answered. Keep them back there. You bring it and set it by that stump alone." He gestured to the stump of a fallen tree about 100 feet away from him.

Amie nodded and said, "My name is Amie. The leader of our group is Jimmy back there. We also have Terry, Jake, and Mark." She nodded, looking him square in the eye and turned to get water from the packs that they had gotten last night. She came back with a gallon of water and a beat up plastic cup, placing them on the stump and backed away. Ross moved forward as she backed up and she noticed his hand shake as he reached for the water. He moved back quickly and whistled a perfect imitation of a tree swallow's call. He poured a few swallows of water into the cup and offered it to the man who was still holding the knife. Amie heard the Ross say quietly, "Drink it slow, you don't want water sickness." The man nodded and sipped slow but steadily. The other people came back out of the woods. Ross took a drink for himself and then passed off the water and cup to the others. One woman began crying and said, "Please! Do you have something my baby can eat? She is only two and so hungry!" Ross whirled on her and said, "Be quiet woman! What if they are like the others who only pretend? Do you want to have it happen again?" She cried out and sat on the ground defeated and began sobbing.

Jimmy stepped up and said in a clear voice, "Absolutely no harm will come to any of you unless you try to harm us. That is an absolute whether you choose to believe us or not. Everything Amie said is true. Especially the part about there still being good people in this world." He moved deliberately so they could see the he was only putting his weapon down and taking his pack off. The others followed suit and Jimmy waited to see what the man would do.

Ross's face reflected that of a conflicted man and a mental war with himself. He had spent so much time over the last few weeks running and fighting, starving, and watching people fall behind and die that it all blended together. He wasn't even sure if this was really happening. The water tasted real enough, it was cool and refreshing. The thought of real food seemed like a dream, though. Finally, he just exhaled, slumped and said, "Ask your questions, we have nothing more to lose." Ross walked back to the stump and sat down, his face a broken mask of defeat and anguish.

Jimmy made to move forward but Amie paused him with a look that spoke volumes. She turned and walked to Ross saying in a kind voice, "Ross, let's sit by the fire to keep warmer, ok?" He nodded and got up without looking at her. Jimmy and the rest stayed back with the firearms and packs of supplies.

The group looked at her warily as she moved behind Ross to the fire. She was nervous but schooled her face not to show it. She moved confidently and made sure to stay back a little further from everyone. "Please, tell us what you are running from. The military you said? What other people? Why didn't you try to contact us when you needed help?"

Ross looked at the people around him and it seemed to make him focus. "That is three questions. That will cost you food for the children." Amie nodded and turned to Jimmy. "I need the pot, cinnamon, and oatmeal. Oh, and the can of pineapple." The people in the group gasped and more than one started crying with relief, muttering prayers of thanks.

Ross's look was half suspicion and half shock. "You cannot be serious. Pineapple?" Amie nodded and replied, "Yes, you need the vitamin C to keep from getting scurvy and curing it if you already have it. Not to mention your overall immune systems. I will pour the juice into the water jug after you answer some more questions." Ross gulped and watched as Jimmy handed over the supplies, stepping back. Amie asked for the water jug to be passed and was pleased to see that no one had overdone it. She nodded to Ross and went about making a large pot of oatmeal, hoping her actions looked confident instead of showing the nausea caused by the butterflies duking it out in her stomach. She turned and caught Ross's eyes and said, "You see the food, you smell the cinnamon, now it is your turn." Ross licked his lips again and nodded.

"We were all in a condo in Bay City when everything went crazy. We ended up going to the government shelter areas when we ran out of food. There were bombs being launched all over the world with each country thinking the others had done this to them. The virus was bad enough but when militaries from all over the world are mobilized…. we were taken in a truck to another location because there were so many of us. Then people started to get sick and supplies ran out. Before we knew it, the soldiers stopped coming and riots started big time. We fled, only to get caught by U.N. military. They said they were gathering survivors and taking them to places to rebuild at. Some people wanted to go be with their family in other states but they said, 'There are no states anymore." Can you believe that?"

It all came out so fast that Amie jerked when a stick popped in the fire. She stirred the oatmeal and added a little more water to thin it out. These people could not handle anything heavy right now plus, it would make it stretch. There was no way she was only feeding the children and she hoped Jimmy noticed the man, though broken, had the clarity of mind to put others first still. "Ross, I am thinning this out so there is enough for everyone to eat this meal. After so little food, you can't handle anything full strength. I am showing good faith and need you to do the same. We want and need to hear your story as much as you need and want this food. Let my group check the perimeter to make sure we are safe, ok?" Ross immediately stiffened up and looked around in fear, like he had completely forgotten to look over his shoulder. Amie hid her smile. *Again, progress.* Once he scanned the area, he nodded and the patrol slung their firearms and packs on and began the sweep. He never let her get out of his sight though.

Ross continued. "The place we were taken was attacked but we were safe in a shipping container that was buried. When we came back out, there were some new soldiers but we just thought it was reinforcements. We were wrong, very wrong. When the real military did come, more fighting broke out and then they tried to separate us into those with certain skills and ages. Anyone who was sick was taken and never seen again. All those 7 years old to early twenties started disappearing. And then, the shootings. We managed to get away during another attack by some people from the bigger cities like Detroit and Lansing. Neither group was better than the other. To the U.N., we were merely a resource to be picked through and used up." He swallowed hard and paused a moment before going on. "To the others who managed to put the uniforms on, we were there to be tortured and do all the work. The women had it the worst but the men weren't immune to torture and even rape." Ross's eyes had glazed over as he was reliving the horrors the group had endured.

Amie didn't say anything as she took the food off the heat to let it cool down. She called out for spoons and bowls to be brought. She turned to Ross and said, "Thank you for telling me the story, Ross. The food is ready though you will have to share bowls. We only have 4 but there should be enough spoons and you can keep them. We have a person who whittles wood all day and is teaching others how to do it, too." One of the other ladies in the group whispered, "Bless you for helping us. Thank you so much for this food." Amie's heart broke at the sound of pure gratitude in her voice and she nodded but had to look away for fear of crying.

Eventually, the rest of the patrol came back and oatmeal was served to everyone. Jimmy asked some more questions which were answered almost immediately by Ross and then others started talking, sharing their stories. Hours went by and Amie had moved to sit next to Jimmy. She had poured the pineapple juice into the jug of water after it was refilled and made sure everyone got some of it. She had to keep cautioning people to eat and drink more slowly so it wouldn't come back up. Thankfully, only one person was sick and had cried over the bits of oats on the ground. Amie comforted them and gave them the last in the pot. After everyone had eaten she noticed Ross eyeing her. "So, now what? We go on our way and you on yours? Do you have more food we can take with us?"

Jimmy decided it was his turn to do the talking and spoke up. "Where are you going to? There are others in the valley that are not so helpful; plus the wildlife." Ross shrugged his shoulders and said, "We keep going until we think they cannot find us." He felt Amie's nudge and nodded to her.

"I agree, Amie." Ross looked at them curiously. "Ross, I

think that if you continue what you are doing, death is a certainty and you do not get to really choose how it happens, as much as any of us do. There is room for you and yours, should you wish it. The closest camp is only a day or two away and we can take the time needed for your wounded. We need hands to prepare for what is coming and your group has firsthand knowledge of the enemies we face. I personally don't give a rat's ass what the United Nations says about states. I am an American and I live in Michigan and we were not founded by those who would be lorded over. Are you with us?"

Amie looked at Ross and the group with imploring eyes. Ross was shocked at the offer and his face showed it. He looked to the others in his group. Some looked hopeful, but others showed the same fear that had landed in his gut. It was hard to trust anything in this new world. He looked back to Amie and the rest of the patrol and shook his head. "No, I am sorry. I cannot take that kind of risk. We agreed at the beginning." Amie hung her head. Jimmy nodded and gave him a look of respect that let Ross know he understood.

"Well," he said. "You can keep the pot, the water jug and here." He reached into his pack and pulled out a beat up plastic container and passed it over to Ross. "In there is 3 cups of beans, 3 cups of rice and 3 more cups of oatmeal." Amie looked up and handed over the can of forgotten pineapple. "Eat that slowly. A ring for each of you today and one split between the children. Trust me, it will help. You may feel incredibly energized from the nutrients but be careful not to over exert yourselves." Ross nodded and took the items, handing them off to one of the men with a pack who stuffed it inside so fast it was as if he was afraid they would ask for it back.

Jimmy and the rest stood and stretched. He was saddened they were not joining the valley camps but he respected their choice. The information they gave answered a lot of questions and of course created even more. If they had joined up, they likely would know more than they think when it came to what strategies were used by both the military and the 'others' he mentioned. That sure would have been useful. Maybe he should tell them where his camp and Captain's were just in case they changed their mind? Then again, if they were captured, they might tell the wrong people and jeopardize everyone and everything. Sure, they had told other people the locations but those people had already lived in the valley.

His group was ready to head out and the people in Ross's group looked better for having had a meal, some hydration, and rest. Jimmy slung his pack on and took a couple steps forward, hand extended. Ross met his eyes and moved forward to meet him, returning the handshake and nod.

Jimmy said, "If you change your mind, come back to the gathering place and leave a ribbon tied to a post of the A Frame. It is patrolled and we will know what it means. Hunker down in the tree line near the A Frame until you make contact."

Ross gave him a confused look and said, "That is an awful risk you take."

He nodded and replied, "It is. But I believe it is the right thing to do. Once we stop doing what is right, we lose everything. Best of luck, Ross. We all hope you change your minds and thank you for the information you gave us. It will help us to be better prepared for what is coming." The two groups went their separate ways.

He turned to his patrol and smiled ruefully. "Well, that could have all gone much worse and before you say anything Amie, let me say that you were right. Having a female in the group made the difference." Amie beamed a sassy grin and nodded. The patrol headed toward main camp where they would check in and report, then head to their respective camps with any stragglers. The late spring sun was shining warm and bright and for a while, Jimmy could believe he was just on a nice hike with some friends. The birds chirped and squirrels scampered from tree to tree, chattering at the humans walking through their area. For a little while, things seemed normal and Jimmy let himself relax a little.

CHAPTER TWENTY-THREE

A week later, everyone was back at their respective camps and preparations were in full swing for an invasion. Word had come across the waves that six of the people that Jimmy's patrol had talked to came back and were now in quarantine at Main Camp. Four of them had useful skills and would be going to Jimmy's camp once they had been cleared. Amie had also moved to Center Camp which had caused some good old-fashioned gossiping. Amie laughed it off when Jimmy expressed concerns about it.

"Let them talk, Jimmy. It gives a sense of normalcy and it is nicer to talk about that than trying to figure out what will happen next." He sighed, knowing she was right. He just didn't like to be the topic of household gossip as a rule.

They were walking out of the Hall when Brad came walking up. "Jimmy! I need you to come take a look at what we have come up with. Amie, you should come too." They both nodded to Brad and held hands as they followed him to the outer perimeter. He could see people everywhere, busy working on this or that project.

There were three levels to the security lines at this camp. The first was to give them warning of people coming by way of lookouts and patrols. Some brush had been cleared and rocks moved around to make visitors funnel a particular direction. The second level was the trails that went through the bushes and trees that they had not cleared out. Trails that had been worn over the last few months were being booby trapped and new trails had been hacked out that everyone had been shown to start using. Only those who were not from the camp would use the obvious trails and there would be people in place to watch them and act as bait to lure enemies. Off the sides of the trails, there had been pit traps dug in with spikes made from the saplings that had been cut while clearing the new trails and a perimeter. There were line traps attached to various noisemakers such as bells or glassware that would break if tripped. Around the 'back' side of the camp, two of their six grenades had been rigged to blow but also had some fishing line looped and wound through the forest floor and bushes to a location where someone could pull the pin out from a safe distance.

The third line was if enemies made it inside the camp. A few hand held blow horns had been scavenged and were set up in key locations to alert the camp if there were people trying to get into the food stores, ammo stores, and there was one located in the Hall. If anyone got into The Hall, instructions were clearly given to everyone in the camp that whoever could get to it would blow the horn until it ran out or help came. Jimmy was impressed and offered some suggestions on making sure the grenades had enough slack to avoid the pins being pulled by someone simply stepping on the line.

All in all, the beginnings of their defenses were solidifying nicely. He took comfort in the knowledge that starting tonight, they had a much better chance of being warned of approaching enemies than they did before. They could not stop these people from coming, but they could give themselves a fighting chance by being alerted and slowing them down. He was surprised something hadn't already happened but was grateful for being able to get this far.

Amie was called away to help Jessica with some communications and he watched her go.

Brad chuckled and said, "Close your mouth, you'll start attracting flies and drooling." Jimmy closed his mouth with a click of the teeth and grinned back to Brad.

"Well, can you blame me?" Brad shook his head and the two of them walked back to camp to see where they could help.

****

Thunk! "It's been a week already, man! I'm getting sick of sitting around doing nothing." Gordy tossed his boot knife into the wooden table, yanked it out and tossed it again. *Thunk*! "When are we going to move in on these guys? I need some fresh food, fresh women, and am sick of those whack jobs always looking at me, judging me." *Thunk*!

Mister turned and snatched the knife out of the table and threw it into the wall behind Gordy's head. Gordy didn't flinch, just looked at Mister with barely concealed anger. "We move in a few days. They needed to wait to get the explosives built and in place. Then again, you keep runnin' your mouth like that and you might just not get to see any of it happen. They judge you because you make such an ass out of yourself. You're a grown man, chill out or be chilled out."

Mister turned his back and looked at the map on the wall. Someone had found one of the Huron-Manistee National Forest in large scale and it was the main one used. There were others that showed locations of other United Nations deployment camps and the "rebuilding" camps that were more permanent, but only in a few other states. Mister had no intention of going to other states. All he needed was the supplies and set up at the nearest deployment camp to get his claim on this whole valley going. He thought about all the extra baggage he could get rid of once it was done; the Cathars, the thugs, the lingering addicts. He looked back over at Gordy who was still staring at him. Maybe Gordy needs to go, too.

Just then, the door opened to Mister's cabin and Seth walked in. He scowled at Gordy a moment and then looked at Mister. "Looks like we have had some divine intervention. A new U.N. message just came across the waves. We will be leaving tomorrow morning. Come with me." Mister raised his eyebrows and both he and Gordy followed Seth out to the radio room.

****

Jessica scrambled out of her chair and was immediately jerked back by the headphones she forgot to take off. She tossed them down and ran out of the room. "Someone go find Jimmy and bring him here!" One of the men took off out the door of the communications building. Marsha, who was on duty to help in the office today, looked at Jessica with wide, fearful eyes. Jessica shook her head and said, "No, everything is ok with the camps but there is a new U.N. message." She went back to the radio and put the headphones back on. Within a few minutes, Jimmy, Amie, and Brad were all in the small room. Jessica had written the message down and gave it to Jimmy to read, her face again registering shock but this time there was something more. Determination.

He looked down to the page and began reading, noting that there were certain words underlined.

"This is a message from the United Nations <u>Global Communications Center for North America</u>. Global death tolls continues to rise in the billions. <u>Individual countries within continents are no longer recognized</u> and all previously registered people within those countries have been reclassified by continent. Any attempts to relocate to another continent is an offense punishable by death. No medical aid will be administered to anyone who is ill or suffers from debilitating diseases. It has been agreed upon that the survival of our species is priority one. Agents have been given the authority to use <u>whatever means necessary</u> to ensure this goal is achieved.

175

All remaining healthy and able-bodied humans are required to comply with authorities and relocate where directed. Resistance will be met with <u>necessary force</u>."

He read it aloud and sat down in a chair with a thump. He stared at Jessica's neat and precise handwriting but did not really see the words. His head swam with emotions ranging from disbelief to outrage. He never imagined this kind of thing would ever happen. The species? How have we been so lucky? How do we face what is coming and make it if they have been given a free hand?

"It has been my experience to never question your luck," said Jessica. Jimmy jumped, not realizing he had voiced his thoughts. Amie laid a hand on his shoulder and sat down next to him.

"We keep going until we can't anymore. That is all that has been left for us and we aren't the type to just lay down and die. Those people did not make it this far. The people who are here are not without their faults but we are all survivors. That has to count for more than two bits, don't you think?"

He looked into Amie's eyes and smiled. He loved the way she just threw it out there without being snooty or overly emotional. Straightforward and to the point. He leaned over and kissed her on her nose before turning to Jessica. "We need to up our defenses and coordinate as best as we can. We need to know if the military has made it to Idlewild yet. Get on the horn and have Main Camp send out a patrol."

Jessica nodded and started taking notes. She looked up when he mentioned Idlewild and shook her head. "No military yet but a patrol did mention seeing some of those religious people around there. I doubt they have joined up with those kind though. Likely one of Idlewild's people shot one of the other guys and took their armband."

Jimmy nodded in agreement. "Also, news from the group you helped has given us valuable information. Most deployment camps have no more than 150 people, though well armed. They use large patrols, "scavenger hunts" as the troops call it," her face twisted in disgust, "are about 100 or so people with trucks, lots of ammo, tents, fuel and room to pack whatever, and whoever, they find." His eyebrows shot up. He nodded for her to go on. "They also say that the soldiers are a mix of men and women and they cycle through them once every 3 months. So, every 3 months there is an entirely new set of soldiers in place. They usually keep a few who are from the area to help with strategy."

It was his turn to look disgusted. The thought of people willingly selling out and assisting the military in taking over people's home, supplies, splitting families up and committing unspeakable acts without fear of punishment made him angry. Amie squeezed his arm as if she could read his thoughts. "When you have nothing left to lose and are hungry enough….remember, we have been lucky and should be thankful."

He looked down, feeling ashamed but still replied, "Yes but when you have lost all honor, what do you have left to live for? You have sold everything you are or would be." Jessica nodded her agreement and the room was silent, everyone lost in their thoughts for a moment.

Brad, who had been quiet through all of this said quietly, "We need to prepare for a full scale invasion Jimmy. And we have no idea how much time we have before it hits. What can we do to increase our chances in such a short time with limited supplies? At least some of these people will have proper military training and can spot traps a mile away."

Jimmy looked at Brad and then at Jessica and Amie and just shrugged. "I never said I had all the answers. Perhaps we should put this to the older teens and adults. We are all in this together and if we discuss it at a meeting, we will save time making sure everyone knows what the plan is and then building it." Jessica grinned at him, nodding her agreement.

"Efficient diplomacy. I like it," she said.

****

That night after dinner at Center Camp, everyone who

was 16 and older stayed in the Hall to discuss different tactics they could use to help deter and defend against the coming military force. With a group of less than 120 people, it did not take long before everyone had known that the message from the United Nations had changed and that a threat to their home was imminent. While Jimmy and Jessica were explaining some of the plans that were to be executed between camps when the time came, Amie watched the people. She was amazed at how long they had been lucky. Over the top lucky. She noted that when Jimmy started talking about the plans for evacuating the smaller children and whatnot, there was more than one thin-lipped frown.

I don't think he realizes it yet. He just doesn't see that this camp, all of the camps in the valley are a family now and this is our home. A home that all of us are ready to defend to the death. She was shaken from her musings when her very thoughts were voiced by one of the first people to join this camp, Kory. He was ex-military and Jimmy had been on several patrols with him. He was liked by all though kept to himself a lot.

"Mr. Jimmy? There is no way in hell I am going to evacuate. Look around us, Sir. This is our home. We have good foundations here. I say we up the game and use some serious deception, draw the line in the dirt. I am sick of thinking defense all the time. That is what they expect! Well, I for one am not going to hide in a hole and wait for them to come to me!" There were some clear voices agreeing with him and Jimmy let the conversation play out a little before replying.

"I agree with you Kory." The room fell silent, all eyes looking at him. Amie was shocked about the turn of the conversation. She recalled her Dad talking with some of the patrols at main camp about making false trails, noise-making booby traps and other warfare tactics that would hopefully make the enemies paranoid and prone to mistakes. She hadn't paid much attention at the time because she knew she was going to be coming up to Center Camp with Jimmy. She did not realize that the plans she overheard were in preparation for being attacked at all camps. She wondered what other plans were in place she wasn't aware of.

Jimmy said in a clear voice, "We have thought about the possibility of the U.N. coming in and made some plans for this situation. Some of it uses deception, like the false trails and spiked pit traps. The thing is, we don't want them to get that close to the camps and that is where ideas from all of you come in. So far, I have heard ideas for sniper tactics to lead the military to Idlewild, making sure roads are impassable by car or truck as well as ambushing them, and using the people from all three camps to confuse and misdirect them. I agree with most of them but there will have to be some serious details worked out, especially on the last one. If we take it too far, they could just drop a bomb on the whole valley and be done with it." He let that sink in before going on. He wanted to make sure that everyone realized this was no game. They were trying to go against a well armed and armored force.

"We are one of the last pockets untouched by military force and I mean to keep it that way." There were murmurs of agreement and some conversation before Jimmy went on. "We need information which means high risk patrols. Let's not delude ourselves here folks, there will be deaths. Maybe lots of them. It is in the realm of possibility that we all fall. It is worth it. It is worth the risk, the chance to live freely. They say the death toll is in the billions and I believe it. The United Nation's priority is to protect the continuation of the species which means they want young and healthy only." He went on to give them details on what they had learned from the people who had escaped from the U.N. deployment camp. The reactions ranged from shock to fury.

Amie, who already knew about it, watched people's reactions closely. She saw pursed lips here, wide fearful eyes there, and then a strength came over the group. A determination to live and make it through this. It was her turn to look surprised and she glanced at Jimmy. *He may think he doesn't have a way with words, bah! 'Just a soldier' my ass!*

She appreciated the way he just put it out there without too much emotion. It simply was what it was; A problem that they needed to work through so they could move on. Amie idly wondered if all people felt this way when faced with no other choice. The job before them was grim and they may die doing it but when there was no way to avoid it, you simply get going.

The   discussion   went   long   into   the   night.

CHAPTER TWENTY-FOUR

3 days later dawned with the promise of warm temperatures but in these early morning hours, Gordy could see his breath as he moved through the brush. Next to him was Mister, geared up like he was with nicer stuff than he had ever had, especially the AR15s. He couldn't believe the religious nuts even had them! They were told it was just a loan but he knew better. Mister had told him all about the plan to let the cult do the dirty work and then when they were sure of victory, start taking them out and claim their prize. First, they had to ambush the U.N. patrol and take their trucks, ammo and weapons. Gordy grinned inwardly at the thought and glanced up ahead at Seth, hoping he was the one who got to put a bullet in that ugly face.

They moved with their group up the west side of the road, while another team was on the east side and there was a third, larger group already in place, hidden back from the main ambush area. The larger group was made up of local people who had gotten caught up with the cultists, but the majority were devout faithful that believed they were paving the way for the second coming. What they didn't know was Mister had some boys in reserve, too.

Seth put his fist up and dropped to a knee. Everyone in

the group followed suit. He turned and motioned two people to move away from the road and circle back around both ahead and behind. There was absolutely no speaking, not so much as a fart while everyone waited for the report for fear of Seth's temper. They started walking in about 7 miles from the deployment camp. Their agents on the inside told them they only had detection 3 miles around the camp. Every half of a mile, they paused and did a check ahead and behind to make sure they were not detected too early. Their ambush location was at mile 4. The silence in the forest was eerie and Gordy wished he was just about anywhere other than in the forest. He hated the smell, the dirt, and the bugs.

Soon enough, the scouts came back and reported all clear. Everyone slipped packs back on and adjusted gear before heading out. Seth reached up, pressing a button that was on a cord to an earpiece and reported their location, "Cat is on the fence." He then took the earpiece out and the transmitter it was connected to, tossing it on the ground and crushing it under his boot heel. One of the directives of the cult was to only use technology to see their goals fulfilled and to destroy it once it had served its purpose. Gordy shook his head at the waste but said nothing.

They continued on at a slower pace now. At the next half-mile mark, Gordy could see the ground ahead sloping upward, trees thicker on either side of the road than most places. He could see how the road had been blasted in to one side of the small rise years ago. It was grown over nicely but there were some larger areas of exposed rock. Suddenly, the sound of a bird shrilled loudly across the road and down a ways. Seth returned a different birdcall then motioned for everyone to stand down and wait. The sun had fully come up and was shining down through the leaves and brush where the group waited.

Mister caught Gordy's eye and raised an eyebrow as if to ask, "You good?" Gordy nodded and then leaned back against his pack, slipping his hat over his eyes. He wasn't really going to sleep, but he didn't want to be bothered right now, either. After about half an hour, another bird call was heard and returned. Gordy pushed his hat back and looked up in time to see a man in a military uniform come up to Seth. He pulled his shirt aside to show a white piece of cloth with a golden symbol embroidered on it and quietly spoke a word. Seth spoke a word back and the two of them moved off into the woods further back from the road and, more importantly, away from anyone else. Gordy scowled and looked at Mister who was doing the same. After a couple of minutes the pair came back. The soldier left and Seth came up to the group.

"The military will be moving on a patrol down this road tomorrow late or early the following day. Their target is Idlewild and anything in between. They have intercepted multiple radio transmissions from others in the area. The plan is for them to finish sweeping this state for healthy and *good* people to take back to the main gathering areas." Gordy gritted his teeth at the emphasis on good. He knew it was a jibe at Mister and his people, especially Gordy, to behave and they might get to go to their fairy wonderland in the sky. "This is our only shot to take over and get in to ruin the whole organization. If we fail, the whole world will fail."

Mister coughed into his hand and quickly said, "Excuse me, I need some water. All the walking."

Seth glared at him before continuing on. "We are to wait here, way back from the roads and send scouts every 3 hours to move ahead no more than 1.5 miles, wait 30 minutes and then move back to report. Further orders will be given when it is time." Gordy sighed. He really hated waiting.

****

The day after the meeting, Jimmy and a few others including Amie, made a hard march to Main Camp and Captain with their ideas and plans. They were not about to risk any of it getting intercepted.

"Agreed. We will begin with gathering intel from Idlewild and then the military camp. We need to send two full patrols for this one I think. And use the truck." Captain, Jimmy, Denise, and Richard - Captain's head of patrolling - were sitting around in Captain's main room. "We need them to leave immediately. I have some fuel for the truck that we managed to salvage with a hand pump. It was a pain to get hose long enough down in that hole though." Captain chuckled. "Never seen anything like it. It was like a quilt made of hose, all different colors and sizes somehow fit together. Worked though." He got up and moved to another room for a moment before coming out with a map. He unrolled it on the coffee table and everyone moved items onto it to keep it flat. Captain pointed.

"I would stop the truck here and then let the first group get out to check Idlewild. The other group goes on down to here." He slid his finger across the paper as he spoke. " I would walk in from there. If you time it right, you could be walking close to the deployment camp. At least, the last known location. They may have moved it. There is less and less information out there." Captain got a sad look on his face before saying quietly, "The waves are getting pretty quiet out there, and not just in North America." No one said much of anything for a few minutes. The weight of all that had happened on a global scale suddenly made what they were planning to do seem all the more important. They were fighting to live the way they wanted to, not just survive the disasters that had brought them all to this point. Not to be some puppets in a 'world government' controlled facility. Not to be bred, if they were deemed worthy enough to be chosen for the facility in the first place, like some common livestock.

Jimmy cleared his throat and said, "My people have things well in hand at our camp but we will be hard pressed to have things in place for both a direct attack on the camps or us being ready to move out and attack them overall. I'm not much of a praying man, but I am thinking of taking it up because we are going to need a miracle to pull this off." There were a couple of forced chuckles at his sally and then silence.

Finally, Captain said, "Richard, get your crew together to bolster Jimmy's numbers and see they have whatever they may be missing if we have it to give." Richard nodded and got up. He looked at Jimmy and said, "Leave in six hours?"

"Make it four."

****

Up at the Northern Camp, Al was shoring up a rock wall with a group of people when their communications guru, Stewart, walked up. "Al! That late patrol just reported in. Justin is over getting some water at the pump and told me why they are late. They are about a mile out and need some help. I guess they found something and it is a lot to carry so they have been leapfrogging the stuff along. Some crates or something."

Al's eyebrows raised up higher and higher as Stewart went on. He smiled and clapped the man on the back saying, "Well, let's go help them! C'mon boys, let's go take a load off that patrol." The 2 others that Al was working with happily grabbed up their tools and went to put them away. Al called out, "Meet in 10 minutes!" The two waved and nodded as Al turned back to Stewart. "They have no idea what is in them? That doesn't make much sense." Stewart glanced around to make sure no one was within earshot and said in a low tone, "The crates have military markings on them. They were worried it was some kind of trap and didn't want to risk it." Al's mouth dropped open and he began to walk faster.

About half an hour later, the group came upon the late patrol who was sitting on stumps and Al's gaze fell upon 3 medium to large size crates. Sure enough, there were military markings but nothing a civilian would understand beyond that. Al knew right away what they meant, thanks to a book he had borrowed from Captain at the gathering. His grin split his face almost in two and he walked up to the patrol and shook all of their hands. There was more than one confused look as he went around to them all. Al stepped back and said, "Before I tell you what it is, or at least is marked to be, tell me how you found it."

Justin had come back with them and spoke up. "We were further north and slightly west about 7 miles. We smelled smoke but couldn't see any so we had Larry there use his bloodhound skills and went in the general direction of the scent." Justin grinned at Larry who chuckled and gave him a one finger salute. "We came upon a burned out cabin and there was evidence of a fight. There were a couple bodies but nothing identifiable from the char." Justin looked down, "One was so small." The men were all quiet a moment before Al shifted his feet and Justin continued.

"We were looking around the area to see who and what when we came across an older man who was dying. He had a shotgun and raised it to shoot at us but it clicked and the poor guy just kind of gave up. He told us to just be done with it and shoot him. We told him we were not his enemy and tried to give him some water but he said not to bother wasting good water on a dying man. Long story short, he ended up telling us about these crates and said he hoped we really were the good guys. He went unconscious and passed on shortly after. We found these buried where he said and then we buried him and the small one before making it back here. He had some canned stuff and some medical supplies in a dive bag buried there, too."

Al nodded and said, "No sign of who did it?"

Justin shook his head and replied, "Either they took off or the old man got them. We checked our six often but with as slow as we were moving, anyone who wanted to take stuff from us would have had an easy time of it."

Al nodded, satisfied and then said, "Well gents, the karma from offering that man water was paid back instantly, and many times over. If I am right, that crate contains munitions." He pointed. "That crate has 5 firearms with cleaning kits, but that one I am not sure about." The stunned looks on their faces made Al chuckle. "Good job boys! Let's get these goodies back to camp."

CHAPTER TWENTY-FIVE

Jimmy waved to the patrol they dropped off to go scout Idlewild, taking it easy over the potholes. The truck had done some serious duty in its life before and the tires weren't all that great. The last thing they needed was a flat out here. In the cab was Amie and Brad with Terry and Kory in the back. They had several miles to go before they got to the spot where they would stash the truck and head out on foot and make way to the last known location of the United Nations deployment camp. They needed to go wide around Idlewild and that put miles on their journey. Jimmy hoped nothing would delay them. He wanted to get information and get out and back as soon as he could.

There wasn't much conversation in the cab. Amie had a radio rigged to the power system and was scanning frequencies. They thought about bringing a handheld HAM but decided against it. The military could be intercepting transmissions and they did not want to risk giving their position away at any time during this mission.

He glanced over at Brad who was studying a map and asked, "We on track Brad? Be sure to give me plenty of notice on when the turns are coming up. I never traveled the back roads around here much."

Brad nodded and replied, "Yeah, yeah. Just keep driving, next turn is in a couple miles." Amie reached over and patted his leg but whether it was to make him be quiet or show affection, he wasn't sure. He really didn't care, he was still a little shocked at having a woman like Amie interested in a man like him. He reached down and squeezed her hand.

Jimmy turned where he was told to and they continued on without any incident. About 5 miles down that road, they headed right across a paved state highway. They could see cars here and there but nothing moved. The hair raised on the back of his neck as if someone was watching him and he put his foot into the floor. Once they were a few miles away, he was able to relax a little and asked Brad how much further it was.

"We head down here another couple miles and then pull off to the right but I am not sure what kind of road it may be." He peered closer at the map. "It's drawn onto it. Could be an old logging road or an unused driveway or something. May be harder to find."

Jimmy nodded and slowed down a little so they could more easily see what they were passing. There was a thump on the back window and Amie turned to open it, telling the guys what they were looking for. Sure enough, they came upon a part of the road where the side sloped down and overgrown ruts could be seen going into the bushes. If they had been going a normal speed they would have never seen it. Turning down the side of the road, He eased the truck slowly across the ditch area and into the brush. Once he had gone about a third of a mile, he stopped the truck and turned it off.

Everyone piled out and stretched. He took a drink fromhis water jug and said, "We need to cover the tracks and get some cover over the truck. Amie, Kory, you're with me. Brad, Terry, you guys get some cover for the truck." Everyone nodded and moved to their tasks. Once they were done, Jimmy noticed a wind had picked up and looked at the sky. It was a few hours until dark and it looked like it might rain. Good for covering their tracks, bad for camping in. The group decided to get some space between them and the truck before making camp. About an hour later, they found a good place and settled in. They would start a little before first light.

****

Richard from Main Camp and his group watched as the truck pulled away. He checked his pack and gear to make sure everything was secure before moving out. The group had worked together several times before, and Richard was a little perturbed that Jimmy's group was sent off to check on the military instead of his. He trusted Captain and swore to follow orders but sometimes it really grated on him. Pushing the thoughts to the back of his mind, he focused on the task at hand. They should be able to make it within sight of Idlewild before dark if they put a little hustle on it but Richard was not the kind to rush things if it didn't feel right.

He turned and looked at Tori, a tough as nails career military woman. She was raised in a military family moving from base to base and was able to pass the physical tests to join by the time she was 14 years old. She didn't put up with any crap but was also the most generous person he had ever met. Behind him about 15 feet was Bret who used to be a video game junkie. Particularly those with strategy and combat, those were his specialty. He toured gaming competitions and actually earned money playing - and winning - tournaments of video game play. Richard would have never believed that a kid like him would be so valuable on patrols. He didn't weigh but a buck-twenty with boots on but that boy's brain was a tactical computer that could adapt to just about any situation. Not to mention he was one helluva shot.

Rounding out his team was an old salty sailor who everyone just called Swabbie though rumor had it before he retired, Swabbie had been a Lieutenant Commander.

Because of that, whenever Swabbie made a suggestion, it was usually followed and Richard had never been steered wrong by listening.

They made good time and stopped a few hours short of dusk to make something to eat. Bret pulled out a map and studied it, muttering to himself as he slid his finger across the paper. He looked up, "We should make it in about an hour. Might be a good idea to go silent about 15 minutes in. How do you want to split?" He bent over to grab a stick and made a sketch in the dirt. He pointed. "If we keep going fairly straight, we will end up here and the entrance is over here." Richard nodded and looked at the sketch, considering his options. Swabbie cleared his throat and everyone looked at him expectantly.

"If the main entrance is twelve o'clock, I would say we are no more than 3 hours away from each other. That way, you can provide cover if needed and still see so you don't end up shooting your buddy's head off." He had a gravelly voice that came from too many cigars before everything changed but was solid as a rock. Richard glanced to everyone else and saw them nodding in agreement.

"Done. Thank you Swabbie," he said and chuckled at Swabbie's typical response to praise which usually included insults and self-depreciation.

Before long, everyone was finished and cleaned up, ready to go. They moved out and split up. Swabbie and Tori were going to approach from the 6 o'clock position with Bret and Richard at the 9 o'clock position. They wanted to make sure to avoid the road as best as they could. As they neared the area, Richard could see the trees had been cleared and looked over to Bret with a raised eyebrow. They kneeled down and Bret glassed the area with the scope on his .308 while he did the same behind and around them, looking for any sign of patrols.

Something was wrong though, this was not what he was expecting. As was his nature, he slowed everything down and paid attention to the details. The sounds of the forest didn't give any indication there was something off but Richard just couldn't shake the feeling and told Bret so in low, quiet tones. Bret nodded his head but said he didn't see anything. There were no patrols, no sounds of humans carrying through the brush and trees, no movement. They stood up and kept going. A few dozen yards from the cleared area around Idlewild, they kneeled down and glassed the area again. It was quiet, not like the reports had been before at all.

They could see some smoke rising here and there behind the ramshackle wall that had been built. From their vantage, they couldn't quite tell if the gate was open or not. Bret clicked his tongue and Richard looked at him. Bret pointed to his eyes and held up four fingers, then looked back through his scope. Richard quickly looked in the same direction and saw the four men who were armed, walking along the top of the wall. Oddly, that made Richard feel a little better but it still wasn't the same as he had been told and seen with his own eyes on a previous patrol. Something was off. He could feel it in his bones.

There was a whistle off to their right and Richard whistled back first one birdcall, and then like a crow. That was the signal for them to make their way to his location. While they waited for the others to show up, Richard tried to decide what to do. This could be an indication of a major attack already on the move toward their homes or it was something else entirely. He couldn't be sure unless he was able to get inside but Captain said to only check it out and report back. The trouble is, the report he would give would only cause more questions than it would answer. He wasn't sure which way to go with this one.

Tori and Swabbie heard the whistle and responded back. Before they began moving though, Swabbie watched to see if any of the guards on top of the wall noticed the sound of a bird that was not indigenous to the area. No one so much as twitched and Swabbie shook his head in disgust. Tori hid her grin and they made their way through the tree line toward Richard and Bret's location. Swabbie whistled again when they got closer and moved in the direction of the reply. They dropped down next to Richard and Bret with expectant looks. Richard nodded a hello to them and then started talking in low tones about the plan. They all agreed that something was off. It was too quiet and there were too few people around compared to previous patrols of the area. Something was up and they needed to find out what was going on. They would gather intel for 24 hours, patrolling the perimeter and staying out of sight before returning to Main Camp.

****

Jimmy was enjoying the silence of the forest during the last part of his watch. He wondered how the other patrol was faring and hoped that everything went well for them. He knew Richard was not happy about his patrol being sent to check the military out but the bottom line was he had more experience in dealing with and deciphering military movements than Richard did. The man had great instincts but they needed a finer touch than gut reaction for this mission. He looked over those in his group, still sleeping under the tarp he had put up. Amie had complained about being stuck in the middle but the men were hearing none of it and she finally gave in, muttering until she had fallen asleep. The thought brought a smile to Jimmy's face and he savored the moment of happiness, when all the worry of surviving melted away. In the new world they lived in, happy moments were more precious than ever.

After another hour, with the sky giving definite signs of dawn approaching, he nudged everyone awake. While they stretched and cleaned the grit out of their eyes, he stoked up a small fire and got some water boiling. They were given a small jar of instant coffee and Jimmy was drooling over the very thought of the taste. He chuckled to himself wryly. *Not so long ago, I would have turned my nose up at this stuff. Now, I would hike for miles to get enough for one cup!*

In a twisted way, he was starting to like this more basic

way of living. He could certainly do without people trying to shoot him or take his supplies but he enjoyed the simplicity of it all. The whole focus of everyone's lives had gone from incredibly complex to incredibly basic. Warmth, shelter, water, food….these were what mattered most at the end of the day along with those you could trust. Your family, friends, and hopefully community. He felt as close to these people and those of his camp as he had his blood family and brothers in arms. Maybe even closer. Each life was precious and each person brought their skills and ideas to help the whole. He could really get used to that aspect of living like this. He just wished it didn't have to claim as many lives as it had, not to mention putting the whole globe in survival mode. As he shook some coffee flakes into the water, he wondered just how the rest of the world fared with everything. The waves had reported some numbers saying 50% of the world's population was dead from various causes. With the latest message from the U.N. abolishing individual countries though, he supposed it was possible.

Once they had gotten their breakfast and some coffee in them, they packed up the gear and checked their firearms before heading out. Kory was checking the map and said, "If we walk in a south by southwest direction and don't have any troubles, we should make it by this evening. Maybe early afternoon." Jimmy nodded and they began walking. He disliked not knowing what they would find but it felt good to be proactive. He felt stronger for being out there *doing* something other than just reacting to what had happened to them. They were taking more of an offensive and to him, that was just fine and dandy.

****

Gordy and Mister were with their 'troop' of people on the edges of the ambush area. Last night had gone by without any issues. As they were breaking their fast on some MRE eggs, Mister glanced around to make sure no one was close enough to listen. "I have word from our boys," he said in low tones. "They are in place and there is a group that will hold back until we have overtaken the military. Their priority is to get the vehicles and supplies out during the chaos while we make sure they can get away. Once that is done, it is open season on the military and those whack jobs. They don't know it but today is their second coming. Only difference is it'll be us sending them along the way, haha!" Gordy chuckled and nodded, eager to be rid of these self-righteous morons. If there was a God, he would have washed his hands clean of the mess humans made a long time ago.

Every three hours, a couple people were sent down to the road to scout for the U.N. troops on the move. When the signal was given, everyone would get into place, letting them pass into the ambush area. When the U.N. was in the kill zone, some of the cult members would run toward the road with arms out, pleading for help to get the convoy to stop in the right place where claymores and other munitions had been set up. After the initial explosions, the wave of people Seth had in the forest would know it was time to come in and take advantage of the chaos to remove threats and take over the military supplies and vehicles. A few would stay in the forest to take out any soldiers who tried to get away and warn others. No one would be allowed to escape. Of course, that is the plan that everyone knew about. Only Gordy, Mister, and those loyal to him knew about the next part. Gordy smiled and nodded while he listened to Mister go over it again. Anything was better than waiting in this damned forest, trying to sleep with tree roots digging in your ribs.

Since the patrol had not gone out last night, it was figured they would be coming sometime today. The intel from the cult members posing inside said the U.N. preferred to go at dawn or dusk to take advantage of the odd light at those times for short-range missions. There was also word that the majority of the people from the deployment camp would be on this mission because they wanted to get it over with and back to the main relocation camps. Mister smiled after telling Gordy about the final details. Today was going to be a profitable and good day. He sat back, daydreaming about a good meal and some young soldier warming his bed that night. They tucked in for the long day of waiting.

CHAPTER TWENTY-SIX

The night proved to be uneventful but informative. Richard was pleased with the intel they were able to gather. As far as he could tell, Idlewild had been cleared out for the most part. There were maybe 30-40 people left inside which would make this area easy to take over but it was the why that gave Richard pause. These kind of people did not just abandon their safe areas without another one to go to. Where did they go? There were no vehicles seen or heard coming or going to the area. The one road in and out of the compound still had barricades in place but it was not manned much. The people they had seen making patrols both along the wall and twice around the immediate perimeter of the tree line did not act like they had been abandoned. They were also loud and careless. It would have been easy to take one hostage and get information but the risk was too much. Right now they had the advantage.

One thing that the kept going through Richard's mind was something he overheard a couple of people saying as they passed by. "I hope those boys come back fast, Roy needs those meds and I could use a drink!" Medicine and alcohol? Were the people on a supply run, en masse? They wouldn't be stupid enough to attack the military camp would they? Or perhaps these people were abandoned and just didn't know it yet.

He had taken a small risk by getting all the way to the wall around 3am. It was like taking candy from a baby. What he was able to see through a slit in the wall between boards confirmed it had been mostly cleared out. There wasn't much in the way of fortifications on the inside with trash and materials all over the place. It reminded him of a ghetto in a third world country. He almost walked normally back to the tree line in the shadows. There was no noise coming from the compound other than some snoring. Richard knew there would be more questions posed with his report but as the sun peeked over the ridgeline, his patrol strapped their gear on and headed back to Main Camp.

****

As Richard and his group were heading north, Jimmy and his patrol were going in a southerly direction. They were making excellent time, too. By noon, they had cut almost an hour off their schedule. They stopped by a happily gurgling creek to have something to eat and wash up a little. The sun warmed their backs as they relaxed, talking about what they may find, contingency plans for the 'what-if' situations and going back over the main plan. It was their job to locate and gather intel on what the military was doing, where they were located, how many and what supplies they were bringing. "The gear in the wagon always tells the best tale," one of Jimmy's old Sergeants used to say and he was right. On the outside, a group of soldiers could look like they were just out on a march but if you checked their gear, you will know what they are *really* up to.

The had located the road that led to the last known location of the deployment camp and had made sure to be far enough back to still see it now and then but hoped no one saw them hiking around. They could not afford to be seen or captured, especially if they wanted to have a chance to strike first and get rid of this threat. Kory looked at his map again and then the location of the sun and muttered under his breath before saying, " If we keep pace the way we have been, we will be about a mile away from the location 1-2 hours before dusk. Considering who we are dealing with, we may want to take the last few miles nice and easy. You can be sure they are monitoring any activity within a few miles of the camp. We need to be mindful of tripwires, pits, and other traps that will alert them. And you can be certain that they will have night vision capabilities so night recon is not a good idea." Jimmy and the others nodded their agreement.

Amie asked, "So, what's the best plan?"

He replied, "I want us to split up. Brad and Kory, you guys take the other side of the road while Amie, Terry and I keep on this one. We start going in and stop every 30 minutes or so to do a double check of the surround. Do not use the radio unless you absolutely have to, there is no doubt that they will be listening in this close to their camp." With everyone on the same page, they moved out.

After the first 40 minutes had gone by, Amie gave a whistle and nodded when the reply came back. Jimmy went ahead a bit while Terry went deeper into the forest and Amie checked behind. She whistled again with the same reply and they headed out again. His adrenaline began to pump through his body, making his blood hum a little and sharpen his senses. He figured they were about 6 miles or so away from their mark. He was watching where he was walking but not really seeing what was in front of him and yelped when Terry pulled him backward. Jimmy almost fell over but managed to stay up and turned on Terry with a look that said, "What the hell?" Terry silently pointed to where Jimmy had been standing and he barely saw the sun shining off of a low lying wire.

Jimmy's breath came out in a rush and he turned back to Terry, nodding his thanks. Being very careful, Jimmy traced the line to a crude, but effective trap that fired off a shotgun shell. It would, at the very least, wound whoever set it off. His eyebrows raised and he looked up at Amie and Terry. Letting out a deep breath, he stood up slowly and was just about to give the signal to keep going when he heard an insistent whistle from somewhere across the road that was the signal for *come here*! Jimmy counted to five and then heard it again. They all sprang into action. Spreading out about 20 feet from each other and staying low, they made their way to the road and over it into the bushes and trees on the other side. Amie whistled a little chirp and turned in the direction of the answer.

They came upon Kory and Brad standing next to a large mound, Brad leaning up against it with a little grin on his face. As they got closer, he could see it was a large truck with a homemade camo paint job. It had been covered in an old camo net with branches woven in. He looked at the ground and was impressed with how well the tracks had been covered. He caught Terry's eye and raised a finger, making a circular motion.

"It's clear. We already checked. Had to disarm a shotgun shell trap but otherwise, we are good."

Jimmy nodded and told him about the tripwire trap they had found. "Well, let's check it out. Brad, you and Kory keep watch while we see what we have here." He moved around to the back of the truck and moved netting and branches aside to find the latch. There was no lock so he tested it and it came free without much effort. Before opening it, he poked his head around the side and called Kory over. "No idea what is in there and I prefer having someone covering me." Kory nodded and raised his weapon at the ready. He turned and moved the netting aside again, grasped the handle and lifted. The door came open about 3/4's of the way before stopping with a screech. Jimmy winced at the sound and sighed.

"Well, that made things more interesting. Let's be quick about it!" He moved the netting up and back, shining his flashlight into an empty cargo area. There had been crude benches installed on the sides, otherwise it was empty.

"Jimmy, I found something!" Amie called from inside the cab. He walked around as she was climbing out with a duffle bag in hand. She reached in and pulled out a white cloth with gold embroidering on it. Jimmy took it from her hands and ran his thumb across the stitches.

"Well, this just got interesting. Everyone spread out, look for tracks." As they began a spiral pattern out from the truck, Jimmy checked the rest of the duffle bag. He found a crude map, a worn Bible, more of the arm bands with the religious cult symbols, and a bottle of water half full. He took the water and one of the armbands and stuffed them in his pack. The map went into his pocket and then he joined the others to help search. It didn't take long before they picked up the trail. When Jimmy caught up to Brad, it was obvious the tracks had only been covered up to so far away from the truck before the people just walked on. He moved around the area one way and noted Amie moving around the other, her face a mask of concentration. They crossed each other's path and met around the other side again. Jimmy grinned mischievously at Amie and said, "Well Ms. Huntress? What is your assessment?"

Amie gave him a long, cool look and replied, "I would say there are about 20 of them, maybe as many as 25. The shoe tracks are too varied in pattern to be military plus, there was no formation to their march. They just loped along which is a little confusing. I mean, there are two sets of what could be combat boots and those tracks had been covered so well back there. If there was military training involved, they would have been in some kind of uniformed walking pattern to minimize risk of being seen." Jimmy watched the emotions play across her face going from confidence to confusion and grinned. "What?," she asked haughtily, putting a hand on her hip. "You think you know better, then tell us O' Mighty Tracker of the Woods." She gave a mock bow to Jimmy and the others chuckled.

He laughed quietly along with the rest and said, "I agree

with you about the numbers and I saw the two sets of boots. What I don't agree with is the walking formation assumption. You assume that the combat boots and the others were together but there is no evidence of that anywhere. It looks like the forest is full of activity today! Must be all the sunshine." He grinned at Amie who again winked. He turned to Kory and handed over the crude map saying, "Here, I also found this in there. Not sure how much use it will be."

Kory took it and looked it over, nodding. "If this is accurate, the camp is in the same place. We are about 6 miles out give or take. I think it would be best if we stuck together for the remainder." Jimmy nodded and called everyone to move out. They went at a slower pace now, listening to the forest noises, checking tracks. They decided that unless the tracks led too close to the road, they would just add their own to the ones already in place.

****

The day had grown warm enough to make Gordy take his outer jacket off. He had snoozed off and on while waiting for something to happen. It was later afternoon when he was nudged awake. Gordy bolted upright, reaching for his gun and looked around quickly then relaxed when he saw Mister standing there. Mister grinned at him and sat down, leaning against the fallen tree.

"I just got word that our boys are about half a mile further into the woods around the ambush site than the rest. Here." He passed a flare gun over to Gordy down low and made it look like he was just shifting around to get a better spot to sit. Gordy quickly took it and hid it away with a questioning look.

"This is how this will go down. Once the military are blown sky high I will go left and you go right. Get up high on that hillside where they blasted the road through. You hang back and let the Bible thumpers rush in and get shot up. Once you see they have the upper hand, light off the flare. I will do the same on the other side. When two flares have gone up, our boys will come in and help mop everything up. Remember that overgrown field back before we made that last turn in the truck?" Gordy nodded. "That is the rally point. We wait no more than 2 hours there before heading back to Idlewild." Mister sat back with a smug grin on his face.

Gordy just looked at him with open surprise. He licked his lips and said, "How the hell you come up with that plan?" Mister grinned and said, "If you weren't such an ass and listened now and then, you might learn something."

Gordy snorted but truthfully, he was impressed. "What if only one flare goes up?"

Mister replied, again with that smug look, "When the flare goes up, they will move forward to be in position and stop anyone from trying to run."

Gordy grinned and nodded. "Alright, I give. That is a good plan, man. This just might work really well."

Footsteps could be heard moving quickly toward where they were sitting and they both looked up over the log to see what was going on. One of the guys who had come earlier dressed in U.N. uniforms was speaking with Seth, pointing down the way to the ambush spot. Seth nodded and turned as the man took off again and whistled sharply. The group grabbed their gear and moved closer to hear the report. When everyone was accounted for ("Desertion is death in this life and the next" according to the cultists), the large man began speaking.

"We have word that the U.N. are on the move and will be here in about an hour. They take it slowly with troops fanned out in four lines; two in the front, two in the back. Each line has about 20 soldiers. There are two trucks for those they are taking back to the camp and assumed empty. There is also a jeep with a 50 caliber gun on the back along with 4 ATVs that have guns mounted to the front of them. There will be some casualties but if we can get them into the right area all together, they will have it much worse than us.

High end count is 100 soldiers, all armed. Everyone knows the plan. We lure them in, fire the trap and then clean up. I want this clean and precise. Remember, God is watching our actions and we must prove worthy of His gaze." There was silence for a moment and then Seth said a little prayer before they all headed out to their positions.

****

Jimmy and the patrol kept making progress but started to notice more signs of recent traffic through the area. The group agreed the tracks were no more than two days old. At one point they spread out far and Terry found another set of tracks about a quarter mile further away from the road than the ones they had been following. They stopped at this point and went backward about a mile. From that they could tell, it looked like something was about to go down and there were multiple parties involved. Whether or not they were working together was not clear. Jimmy asked Kory how far out and he said, "4 miles, maybe a little more." He checked his watch. It was a little before 4. The sun would be setting soon but he wasn't about to try and camp out here with all these tracks. He said as much and everyone agreed. They checked their firearms and moved out, moving back to the original tracks they had followed. Something was about to happen out there, Jimmy could smell it.

CHAPTER TWENTY-SEVEN

It seemed like an eternity of waiting once they got into position. The sun was going to go down soon and Gordy was so jacked up on adrenaline, he was sweating. He sat with the others on top of the little hillside where the road had been blasted through. From his vantage point, he could see down the road both directions and across it into the sloped area where others were waiting. He wasn't sure just how many were over there as they were in place before he was. He tried to calm himself down but his heart kept jumping in his throat at the slightest noise. When he first heard the sound of the engines, he thought his mind was playing tricks on him. It wasn't until he saw those around him looking down the road that he realized he had heard the sound of trucks moving. He flipped the safety off his gun and muttered, "About time."

When the convoy got closer, Gordy could see that the reports were accurate and he started to panic. If those troops combed either side of the road, they were done for. He turned quickly to look behind him and plan an escape route, then he remembered there were others in the woods who were on his side. Just as the the soldiers were about to get close enough to see those hiding, a wailing could be heard on the road down the other direction. He turned and saw a group of 2 men and 3 women in torn and dirty rags with their arms raised toward them in supplication. He couldn't make out the words but he did see the troops go into instant action. The front lines reformed and began marching down the road to the distraction while the back lines moved forward around the convoy. The trucks stopped in the road. "Shit," Gordy muttered under his breath.

The soldiers made it to the people with guns raised, screaming at them to lay down and spread their arms out to the sides. The cultists complied without hesitation and once they were down, the trucks moved again. Gordy wiped sweat off his brow as he watched the troop movement. They went up on the road where the hill began to rise and stood to the sides as the vehicles passed, then brought up the rear. Their focus was more on the people who had come running onto the road ahead. Gordy held his breath and waited for the explosion and was not disappointed. The trucks had stopped again as the cultists were tied by the wrists one to another and were being led toward them when the first claymore went off.

Everything slowed down. The ground shook and his ears were ringing from the first explosion. Gordy watched as each charge down the sides of that patch of road exploded in order, like a beautifully orchestrated fireworks show. The only problem was the body parts that were flung everywhere. He watched as the upper half of a soldier flew high in the air, his arms still moving and face contorted in a way that Gordy would never forget. He glanced down at the troops that were behind the trucks and saw a few were shooting in his direction but not aiming at him. When a bullet hit a branch next to his head, all the sound and the smell, the chaos and terrible screaming rushed in on him so fast he almost passed out from it. Through sheer will he held on and began shooting into the fray, a primal scream tearing from his throat. Sweeping side to side, the targets began falling below.

****

Jimmy stood up from a fallen tree where it was obvious that people had been over very recently. He counted at least 30 different sets of tracks. He returned the whistle from Amie who had gone with Brad and Terry across to the other side of the road. They were a little less than 4 miles out from the deployment camp location and everyone was on high alert. Amie and the others came up and she confirmed there were similar tracks on the other side. Just then, all of their heads snapped around when they heard the faint sound of engines coming their way. He quickly moved everyone further back away from the road. They split into two groups again and put some distance between them. They pressed on and made their way closer, communicating only in hand signals now.

They were about 300 yards away from where the trees thinned out and could see the road ahead. On the right side of the road was an overgrown rock face where the road had been blasted through and on the left was some thin trees and high bushes. Jimmy put his fist up and took a knee. They all watched as a group of 5 people went up onto the road and began pleading with the soldiers. He was disgusted at the way they were tied up like animals and led to the back of the truck. He did a quick count and was surprised to see such a small contingency. There was only 100, maybe 140 total if there were any troops inside those trucks. He guessed the larger ones were only for transporting people back to the camp.

He was about to signal everyone to move around when all hell broke loose. His head whipped around at the first explosion alongside the road. Then, one by one, more explosions erupted in lines down either side of the trucks, blowing troops everywhere. One of the ATVs exploded into flames and the riders on the others were blown clean off their machines from the concussive waves. Jimmy raised his weapon over the log and watched through the scope as a scene from some kind of B rated medieval movie unfolded. People from either side of the road jumped up and opened fire on the troops in the middle. "Watch our six!" he barked out as he focused in. He saw more than one white armband but not everyone had one on. He mentally tucked that away for later, gathering as much intel as he could.

****

Gordy's voice was hoarse from yelling as he slammed the last magazine into his gun, breathing heavily. There weren't many troops left alive down below but there were enough to have taken out more than a few on both sides of the road. He risked a look down the side. There wasn't much moving other than those who were dying and Gordy wasn't going to waste his last bullets on them. He wanted Seth. It was time.

He reached into his jacket and pulled out the flare gun and raised it overhead, firing it off. There were a few shots fired in his direction but not enough to make him worry. He waited, holding his breath and then laughed when he saw the second one go up. He looked around him and met the eyes of the people left in his group. Seth wasn't in sight but some of his cronies were. Some of Gordy's boys were here too. He looked further into the trees behind them and saw movement, which made him grin and laugh again. The religious zealots looked at him with confusion but his boys grinned back at him. "Well gents, I would say it is time to help these people meet their maker, what do ya say?" said Gordy. He raised his weapon and started firing. Those who tried to run ended up getting sandwiched in as Mister's reserves came in.

Gordy went hunting for Seth and found him wounded and screaming into another microphone attached by a cord that went to his ear. "It's a trap! Those godless assholes turned on us, we need people here NOW!" He yanked the earpiece out and was about to toss it when he noticed Gordy there, looking down the barrel of a gun pointed right at him. The AR was slung across his back. Seth began to pray out loud. He did not show any emotion whatsoever. Gordy grinned and said, "I really hoped it would be me who got to send you to your fairytale in the sky. How does it feel to know it was all a waste?" Seth didn't respond, just kept praying. Gordy shrugged and pulled the trigger.

****

Jimmy spared a glance down the line at the rest of his group. Kory was watching the surround and everyone else was looking through their scopes or binoculars at the scene before them. He turned back just as the first flare went up and heard Amie say, "What the hell?" He looked through his scope again and saw it had come from on top of the rise. A moment later, another flare went up from the other side of the road. He wasn't sure what to make of it and called out for Brad and Terry to split off and check their surround a little deeper to make sure there wouldn't be any surprises.

"Those flares are either a sign of victory or a sign for backup and I don't need any more to raise my blood pressure today." They both nodded with a grin and set out. Kory was still watching their immediate area from behind a large stump.

"Maybe we should move around the side a bit eh? See-," he was cut off by renewed gunfire and raised his scope. This time, the shots weren't at the road, they were on either side. Kory said, "Looks like the flares called in some new players." Jimmy nodded and remembered not everyone was wearing an armband. He mentioned it when Brad and Terry came back reporting all clear. They said they noted it, too but had no idea who the others might be. It was all confusing.

Amie exclaimed, "Look!"

He turned and saw people coming up on the road whooping and hollering as they crawled all over the vehicles, killing any survivors. He noted that not a one had on a white armband. As they watched, bodies were dragged off to the side of the road after being picked through, guns gathered and the area cleaned of anything valuable. It was done with surprising speed and efficiency. Those left numbered between 50 and 60 but more than one was wounded. Everyone piled into the trucks and started them up. It took them a bit to make it over the enormous holes blown out but they looked like they would manage it.

As the first large truck made it over and stopped to help the others, Jimmy said, "Time to go! No way we can keep up with them tonight but we need to put some serious miles between us and this area. We have a couple night vision sets but now so do some of those people and you know the military has more." Everyone agreed and they took an eastern route. It was a good 45-degree turn from the location of the camp which would gain them the most space away since they couldn't go back the direction they came from.

As they began to march, everything that had just happened started processing in his head. They knew about the U.N. coming but he was surprised at how small a force they sent. Perhaps they weren't expecting much resistance since it was so long after IT had all happened? He kind of felt bad for all the death today but he wasn't sure what to make of it. It was obvious those troops were outnumbered or perhaps just overly confident and got taken with their pants down. All of that aside, who was the group of people that took out the cultists? He knew he needed to get the intel to Captain and everyone else but he also wanted to get more information. He had a radio to call in if needed but that was only in an emergency. As he moved along, he heard the trucks open up and go flying down the road behind them. Not back to the deployment camp.

Was it all just a raid of some kind? He needed to know if there was a direct threat to the valley but radio contact could give them away. He wasn't sure what to do so he turned to his group and asked for their opinions.

****

Jimmy, Amie, Kory, Terry, and Brad were all still trying to process what they had just seen. Jimmy was worried the people who took the trucks may be heading to the valley and be a threat to the camps there.

"Jimmy," said Amie, "I know you want to protect everyone but we have done as much as we can for now for the camps. They have early warning systems in place and will be on the lookout. Right now, we need more information. I say we go down there and check the bodies to see what we can learn. Then we continue on and find the military camp." He looked at her a moment and then the others. He knew it was the best decision but he couldn't help feel like he was letting the 'bad guys' get away and pose a threat to the camps. Amie saw the internal struggle in his eyes and put a hand on his arm saying, "Jimmy, there is always a threat these days and they have done the best they could to be ready for now. They are adding to it every day. We need to finish this patrol and bring back intel. The sooner we get it, the sooner we can head back." Everyone else was nodding in agreement and he knew the voice of wisdom when he heard it. He nodded and told everyone to be ready to move out in 10 minutes. They needed to use caution; not everyone out there may be dead and there may be other people around, too.

Everyone moved forward carefully with Kory and Brad in the lead. When they were 50 yards into the clearing, a shot rang out and everyone hit the ground. A few more shots were fired off and they heard someone yelling down the road. In the stillness of the area, it was easy to make out the words, "Take that and go straight to hell, you sons a bitches!" There were some more shots and then silence. Jimmy's face registered shock, he knew that voice! Amie looked at him questioningly and then jumped back when Jimmy stood up quickly and hollered out "Raspberry lemonade rules!" He waited, ears straining. His knees went wobbly when he heard, "Blasphemy! Sweet tea rules them all!"

"Jimmy?" said Amie, standing next to him with a concerned look on her face. He smiled down at her and said,

"It's ok, I know that person. That is Bill Allen. I worked with him back in Chicago. What the hell is he doing here?" He turned to the others. "Spread out, go careful and cover each other's backs. We leapfrog it to his location." He looked across the field and couldn't pinpoint where Bill was until he saw a rifle barrel pointed up in the air with a red bandanna over the top of it. Bill always carried his red bandana. The patrol moved forward carefully; two moved up with the other three covering and so on until they had reached Bill. Jimmy could see he had been shot and it did not look good at first glance. He dropped to the ground, pulling out water and offering it to Bill while Kory and Amie checked the gunshot wound. Brad and Terry watched the surround.

"What in the heck are you DOING here, Bill? Please tell me you aren't with the U.N. troops or those religious people!"

Bill took a long pull of water off the container and replied, "No way. Me and some boys were part of a militia group. We took it upon ourselves to hound the military to keep them from hurting innocent people or dragging them away to one of the death camps. Today was the last deployment run before the U.N. pulls everyone back to the main containment areas. Holy crap Jimmy, I can't believe I'm talking to you!" He hissed in pain as Amie cut the cloth back to reveal a gut wound where the bullet went in. They helped him roll over to find the exit wound but did not locate one. Amie caught his eye and shook her head ever so slightly.

"Oh, I know I am a goner darlin' and I am OK with that. Honestly, I should have been done for long ago but perhaps God kept me around to rack up a nice number of notches." He lifted his rifle and on the stock were hundreds and hundreds of little notches scratched into it.

Jimmy gave a low whistle and said, "You been busy, that's for sure." Bill winced in pain as Amie kept tending the wound, his breath coming harder. Jimmy asked, "Where's the rest of your group?"

Bill laughed mirthlessly and said, "Looks like I am it. There were only 8 of us left at this point. Craig and Hollis were with me to scout around the perimeter while the others paced the U.N. bastards and then all hell broke loose. I lost track of them. They were caught in crossfire and half of then were killed by a surprise attack that came out of the bushes. We were tracking that troop from their camp and were planning on something similar to the ambush your people set--"

Jimmy put up a hand to stop him and shook his head. "That was not us. There was a group of religious zealots with some others mixed in, I think. Not everyone wore the arm bands. We were hoping to figure out what happened here, who was involved and maybe their plan and then get back to our area." Bill nodded and said, "Well I might be able to help with that before I…"

Bill's skin went pale white and his eyes rolled back in his head as Amie came up with a lead bullet between some tweezers triumphantly. She looked at Bill and then back to Jimmy, shrugged, and said, "It didn't go as deep as it looked. He has lost a fair amount of blood but I don't think he will need a transfusion or anything. Trouble is, how do we get him back with us? We can't leave him here."

He nodded and replied, "I know but first we need information. Patch him up as best as you can. Brad, Terry, spiral out. Kory, you're with me." Everyone nodded and moved out in their search pattern. Jimmy kept stopping, ears straining to hear any hint of someone coming to check on things. It had only been about 15 minutes since the trucks had taken off but it seemed an eternity. He was going through the pockets of one of the U.N. soldiers when he heard Kory whistle behind him. He turned and walked over to see what Kory was looking at.

"This guy is from Idlewild," he said, kicking the corpse. "I saw him patrolling the wall several times."

Jimmy's face registered shock and said, "Are you sure?"

Kory nodded once and replied, " I am positive. What I

can't figure is why they would cast themselves in with the zealots, or why the zealots let them."

Brad came up with some papers in his hand and said, "I think I can answer that. Seems these Cathars of Christ people have a mission to 'Rid the land of all former corruption to pave the way for God's return.' First on the list is anything former government related, especially military."

Brad handed the paper over to Jimmy who scanned it quickly, nodding. His eyes caught the paragraph regarding "The use of the wicked for the Glory of God's work." It detailed that using evil men to do good works in the name of God were acceptable and if, by the time their usefulness was over, they had repented and lived in accordance with the cult's rules--they would be spared. He read it to the others. "This explains one part of the mystery. The Cathars were using the Idlewild people to attack the military." He looked around and said, "Looks like Idlewild people turned the tables." They walked back over to Amie who had Bill stabilized and conscious again. Jimmy looked at her and asked if he could be moved.

"Not far, he needs time to regain some lost blood and the food to produce it." Bill looked around at the group, his eyes going wide when he saw something behind Terry. Terry turned immediately, weapon drawn, and jumped when Bill hollered, "Hollis, over here! You are never going to believe this!" A man was walking with a limp down the road toward them.

CHAPTER TWENTY-EIGHT

Gordy got out of the truck when they reached the rally point and started doing a headcount, looking for Mister. Two of the ATVs made the trip, the jeep, and one of the transport trucks. He actually felt some relief when he saw Mister climb out of the jeep and waved him over, a grin splitting his face in two. "We did it brother! We outsmarted all those bastards!" Mister gestured over to a growing pile of weapons including extra magazines, grenades, ammo, radios, night vision equipment, and even a couple Taser guns that had been looted off the dead troops and cultists. Gordy felt himself grinning back and said, "Yeah, we sure as hell did. I got my prize, too. Put one right between Seth's eyes. He didn't do anything other than sit there praying. He was communicating with someone on the radio when I came on him. He was shouting about how we "Godless bastards" turned on them. I assume he called his people inside the U.N. camp."

Mister nodded and replied, "Yeah, there were others talking, or trying to. We took care of it and with all this here plus some other stashes we got, we will be able to take out that camp and claim it for our own. The last I heard, there aren't many people left. What's the count?"

Gordy replied, "Looks like we lost about a dozen or so. Not bad really, I figured there would be more but those military were caught with their pants down and we spanked em good!" They both laughed and clapped each other on the back. Gordy asked, "What's the plan now?"

Mister looked around at the people with him and the now huge pile of firepower, grinning. "Well now, now we head back to Idlewild, strip it bare, grab up the rest there and make our move on the U.N. camp. We need to do it fast, too. Just in case they decide to send in more troops and make an example of us or something. We need to make sure we have the upper hand here. A week at most. Then we move in, clean it out, and claim it!" Gordy and Mister joined in when the group of people started to cheer their victory.

****

Richard looked up at the sun's location. He turned to Swabbie and said, "We're making great time." Swabbie grunted and kept going. It was a perfect early summer day and the going was easy. The forest was full of birds and squirrels chattering away at each other. They came on a small creek and decided to stop for a few and refill their water bottles. Tori filtered the water before handing the bottle to each person. They decided to have something to eat before heading out again.

A few hours later, they came upon the new trail that led to the camp and Richard whistled long and loud before they walked in. They heard three whistles in reply and knew all was well. Walking into the main square, Captain met them and smiled when he saw everyone had returned. Richard smiled back and after everyone had said their hellos, began to tell Captain what they found. As he gave his report, Captain's face didn't change much. He grunted when Richard told him about what he saw through the slits in the wall of Idlewild's walls, a twitch of the corners of his mouth and a sparkle in his eyes. "Just had to see, didn't ya?"

Richard felt the heat rise in his cheeks and replied, "It was a calculated risk, Cap. It was incredibly easy and besides, I had Swabbie with me. He could kill a man with his breath alone. I was covered."

The patrol group laughed as Swabbie began to sputter. "Oh and you smell like a bed of roses, too. Or maybe you just burned out your sense of smell, eh?"

Captain chuckled at the banter and was happy to see it. While he didn't give much away, his thoughts were going in five directions at once. He didn't know which way this was going. On the one hand, those people could be abandoned and not know it. They would get desperate and come looking for food but their numbers were so small, they could easily be dealt with and the threat erased. If they went out on a supply run...well that just didn't make much sense. Why take so many for a supply run? *Unless...*

"They are going for the military base! That could work in our favor. The U.N. troops may never make it this far if Idlewild is keeping them busy. The waves said they are going to be pulling out soon. This is their last run. This just might work."

The patrol nodded and Richard said, "Maybe we will get one last shot of good luck."

Captain hoped.

****

Terry lowered his weapon and looked to Jimmy questioningly. Jimmy nodded and Terry relaxed, slinging the gun over his back and moving to help Hollis. Bill was getting sleepy again after spending the energy to yell. He tried to shift for a better spot to sit and hissed at the pain in his middle.

"Boss, you gonna make it?" Hollis was a shorter man but built like a barrel with a wide chest and almost no neck from all the muscle. Blood had soaked through the cloth tied over his wound and Jimmy moved to help him sit so Amie could take a look. Hollis whistled quietly when he looked at her and turned to Bill asking, "Are we dead? Cause this lady here looks like a bonafide angel to me."

Jimmy stiffened at the remark and Bill chuckled. "Looks like she may already be spoken for, Don Juan."

Bill said to Amie, "Never mind him, he thinks he is some kind of ladies man. Harmless though, unless you are on the wrong side of course."

Amie nodded and smiled as she cut away the fabric knotted over Hollis' leg wound. "Well, thing is, I am only an angel if you are on the right side." That comment brought chuckles around the group.

It was decided that Hollis and Bill would be relocated to a safer spot to rest and recover while the patrol finished their mission. On the way back, they would join up and make way back to Main Camp. Jimmy knew it would be a longer journey back with the injuries but it was agreed that no one would come looking for them from any camps unless they were more than 3 days late. He hoped the truck was where they had left it.

By the time they had gotten Bill and Hollis moved to a safer spot, it was too late to keep going so they all decided to just camp together for the night. Brad went off into the woods with Kory to see if they could get any small game. Kory had surprised them all when he pulled out a little pellet rifle. It was made for a child but still fully functional and made barely any noise when shot. Jimmy declared him a genius for thinking to bring something like that.

They came back about half an hour later with three squirrels and a rabbit, which surprised everyone. Brad explained, "I was walking along and flushed him out. It about scared me to death! It only moved a few yards away then turned and looked at us. Didn't even twitch when Kory shot it." They set a fire in a deep hole to keep the light and smoke from giving them away. Their position was located under a slight overhang. He felt better having something solid behind him. Amie pulled out a small box and opened it, taking out vials with different spices in it. She grinned as she pinched out some salt and sprinkled it over the food as it cooked. While they waited, Jimmy took the time to ask Bill about what went on after he had left the plant the day IT all happened.

"Oh boy, now there is a story. I never would have believed it all to unravel as fast as it did. I saw you tear out of the parking lot and knew exactly what you were doing. I sure wish I had talked to you about my suspicions long ago. I just knew you were some kind of prepper."

Jimmy smiled and shook his head, saying, "It isn't 'prepping' when you are a military man, Bill. Just good sense. Typical military tactics: if you need one, you buy three." There were some chuckles before Bill continued.

"Well, like I said, I saw you pulling out of the parking lot and wasn't far behind. The militia group I am part of had a spot about 300 miles into Wisconsin but we never made it. They closed it down so fast; I never knew the government could move like that! We got turned around but then ran out of gas and had to walk back. Thankfully, we had all trained together twice a month for the last 3 years or so and made it without losing any of our own." Jimmy noted he didn't say how many they had had to take out on the way. Bill went on with his story after a drink of water.

"It is all a jumble but basically some guy named Khalid was taking credit for single handedly taking the entire communications networks down not only in the U.S. but all of the Americas, the UK, Russia, parts of China and God knows what else. No one had heard of this person before and didn't believe it not to mention his message can't get far when he takes out communications! Talk about a prime Darwin Award Nominee. Anyway, governments started to go crazy and bombs were set off all over the globe. All trade has come to a grinding halt on a global scale and even those with 'money' are now living like the rest of us or are in some government death camp. Jimmy, those places are hell. I would rather be stuck in a big city with drug addicts than go to one of the camps. The stories...." Bill trailed off, his eyes looking lost as if remembering.

He swallowed hard and continued in a voice thick with emotion, "We met a girl in the forest who was cut up badly. She had been horribly, horrifically abused in every way imaginable. The last thing she did before dying was handing me a patch she had torn off one of her attackers. A DHS patch. I made a vow that day and have been following it every single day since. Sure am tired though."

A quiet fell over the group. They had heard some horror stories over the waves, of course, but nothing like this. Jimmy once again could not believe how lucky they had been. Bill cleared his throat and said, "So, because of all the bombs flying, electronics and communications down for the first world countries and then illnesses and viruses getting out, the United Nations stepped in to take global power." Jimmy nodded and explained how they had been listening and trying to keep up but there weren't many HAMs still operational out there and there was the fear of being tracked and attacked.

Hollis laughed and said, "They thought they would be able to just comb over each continent and scoop up the people. As if we would just go along like sheep. We heard Japan ousted them off shore and closed all traffic coming in and out. A lot of other countries tried to do the same but on the main continents it was easier. Once people started getting hungry, there were a good number who sought the camps out on their own. Didn't take but a couple of weeks before word broke out about anyone who spoke so much as one word against them, and many who never did, were assaulted and killed. They were worked like slaves and fed less than the trained dogs."

Bill nodded. "That is when the tide turned in our favor. Thing is, the global population death toll is huge. Over 50% of the world's population is dead. The last projection I heard was maybe as much as 80% but the virus that broke loose in India happened early on and has mostly run itself out. Be thankful for those strong winds up here." He took another drink of water.

"So now the U.N. is claiming to want to 'save the human race' but what they really want to do is control and steer how the future generations of humanity act, think, speak-everything! We have a fighting chance though. They will not be sending any more troops out to gather the masses, at least not for a while. They need time to establish their main hubs, train more troops, gather supplies and build infrastructure. Cleaning the cities will be the first priority after that, not country folk. That will give us time, too. I hope you don't let that camp go to waste though, Jimmy. They sent the majority of the crew out on that patrol. Can't be more than 50 or so of them. Mind you, they have more fortification and firepower but if you could disorient them or lure them out, you might be able to overwhelm them. I assume you have more people than this?" He looked around expectantly.

Jimmy laughed and nodded, saying, "Oh yes, we have many times more than this." He told his side of the story from that last day at work to present. Bill and Hollis had incredible knowledge of the inner workings and procedures of how the U.N... camps functioned. "Cattle-Drive Camps" is what Bill and Hollis called them. Round up the survivors like cattle, slaughter the bad ones and take the rest back to the barn for breeding and conditioning. The conversation lasted until Bill and Hollis passed out from exhaustion.

CHAPTER TWENTY-NINE

"U.N. Camp North A5, this is Central Hub 7. Go ahead for sitrep."

"Heavy losses sustained, requesting backup be routed to finish our sweep of this sector before returning to Hub. Several vehicles were lost but we believe the area simply needs cleaned out. Recommend and request air strike. Over."

"Request acknowledged and denied. The area is too resourceful to destroy. Hold one."

The radio went silent and the United Nations soldier manning it grinded his teeth while waiting for orders. *They better send us some back up. We aren't treated much better than the civilians we gather up.* The radio crackled. "U.N. Camp North A5, orders are to sit tight and await the arrival of additional troops and supplies. Should you fail to complete your mission before the week is out, consider it a loss and head back. We need to focus on the rebuild. Current numbers show enough labor to handle most of the hard work."

"Copy. U.N. North Camp 5A out."

****

Jimmy and his patrol were able to get within a mile from

the U.N. Deployment Camp and what they saw told him they were on high alert. The fort that they had erected was impressive. The walls were manned and there were even a couple of lookout platforms at the corners. He used his binoculars to get a closer look and gather intel. Everyone settled in. After a few hours, he was pretty sure that the majority of the troops had been lost in the battle on the road. He wondered about the gang of people who had taken the equipment and worried they were heading to the camps while he was stuck here, watching people walk around on top of a wall. *Stay on mission soldier*, he thought to himself.

Amie always seemed to know when he was getting really tense and shifted her weight so she was touching him. She felt him relax and smiled to herself, happy that they had 'that kind' of communication. Sometimes words just got in the way of what you wanted to say. Brad and Terry had gone around the perimeter and weren't expected back for another hour or so. Jimmy had been very clear about them taking their time so as not to be seen. Kory was trying to find really tall trees to climb to get a better lay of the land and come up with ways they could use it to their advantage. He knew there would end up being a battle with these people but he wondered who he would have to deal with first. Idlewild or the U.N. Maybe he would get lucky and the U.N. and Idlewild people would take care of each other. He knew that was too much to ask for, though.

Suddenly, there was a lot of activity and faint shouts could be heard from inside. The troops on the walls were turned, looking in and several had their weapons aimed. "Something is going on in there," he said to Amie in quiet tones. Gun fire could be heard, POP POP POP! and Jimmy watched as a man fell off the wall while the others disappeared out of site as they hit the deck. He scanned the perimeter, looking for Terry and Brad. He asked Amie to whistle for them as her skills with local bird calls was much better than his. They received one reply only and his heart rate began to rise. He watched the camp but didn't see anything. It had gone silent and he didn't see anyone on the walls. After a few more minutes, Terry whistled and Amie replied. He came up to them and dropped down. Jimmy's eyes never left the binos as he quietly said, "Report?"

Terry took a long pull off his water container and said, "Not much to report. They have an area cleared all the way around it. There was a fuel truck around the other side with 4 guards. There is only one way in and out as far as I can tell. They have the perimeter trapped here and there with noisemakers but nothing too bad. Where's Brad? We passed each other on the back side."

Amie shook her head and shrugged, replying, "Haven't heard from him yet." She whistled out again but still did not get a reply.

Jimmy said, "Doors are opening. 2 ATVs...they are bringing people out under guard. Looks like they might have had some kind of mutiny attempt inside?" Amie and Terry turned to see what looked to be 7 people under guard being led out the doors. The ATVs turned and went opposite directions around the perimeter, toward the tree line.

Amie said, "That could be trouble for us. What about Kory and Brad? Should we fall back?" He didn't reply right away as he watched the vehicles speed around, noting how they avoided going over certain areas. "Jimmy?" said Amie again, a hint of panic in her voice.

He finally turned and looked at her and Terry, saying, "Fall back 100 yards and reposition. I need to stay here and see what is going on down there and you can provide cover if I am spotted. Kory is climbing trees but I imagine he will be heading this way after those gun shots. Brad will just have to use his skills to get back to us. If he is in trouble, there is not much we can do for him right now without putting ourselves in the same stewpot. Move out." His tone was not mean, but it was brisk and businesslike. Amie had never seen the military side of Jimmy before but she recognized it and knew that he was all soldier right now. She nodded once and moved back with Terry to a new position as the ATVs came closer, the noise almost deafening in the quiet that was becoming normal in this new world they lived in.

****

Captain couldn't stop pacing when his nerves were like this and his sister Denise knew better than to badger him about it. Even when they were kids, Captain wouldn't sit still until he had figured out a problem but when he was missing key information it was torture. The patrol had come back from Idlewild the day before but there was no word from Jimmy and his group even though they weren't due back until later today. Captain knew better than to get overly worried unless it had been more than 48 hours but with the information on Idlewild, he just knew in his gut that things in the valley were coming to a head and he wanted all hands on deck. He stopped suddenly in the middle of his pacing and turned sharply to the door, yanked it open and hollered out, "Richard and team! Report in 15 minutes, ready to head out!" He slammed the door shut and then went over to the table covered in maps. He wanted more information and was going to have it one way or another. He would not be caught with his pants down on this one. He would be ready.

10 minutes later, boots were heard on the porch and the door opened to reveal Richard, Swabbie, Tori, and of course Bret. Captain glanced up at them and motioned them over to the map he was looking at. "I need information. I need a team to head back to Idlewild and watch it. Take one of the quads. I want information back here fast without using radios. With U.N. troops around, you can be sure they are listening. The other team needs to move hard and fast with the other quad to see what they can find out about Jimmy's group." Richard raised an eyebrow at the last.

Captain noticed and said, "I know he isn't due back until tonight but if Idlewild is stupid enough to raise hell with the U.N. camp, they are caught in the crossfire. They walked right into it. Not much I can do about that, I know. What I don't know is if any of the threats are heading to us. Can I count on you to do this for me?" He looked to each of the team members who all nodded and stood a little taller.

Richard cleared his throat and said, "I want to bring one of the younger guys on the Idlewild scouting. We need to train them up and I need someone fast just in case." Captain nodded and told him to get whatever was needed to ensure information was gotten back to him quickly. Radios were to be used only as a last resort and Denise handed each of them a 3x5 card with a list of cipher codes.

Bret looked it over a moment and said, "To help with not being found if you have to transmit, move at least 500 yards away from the area of transmission as quickly as possible. The further, the better and at a 45 degree angle."

Richard grinned and clapped the small man on the back. "I will never doubt the value in video games again, my friend." Captain gave them all some last minute instructions and the group headed out.

****

Mister woke up with a 5 alarm hangover but grinned when the memories of their victory flooded his mind. That was the cause for the celebration and oh man, had he celebrated! He disentangled his limbs from the two ladies in the bed with him and went to relieve himself. The sun was shining and while it hurt, it almost felt like an affirmation that he had done the right thing. He was taking care of *his* group of people now. Making sure the common people were safe and all. He liked the idea of that, a lot. He went to get some aspirin or something for the pain because he had plans to get done.

After he cleaned up and someone brought him some ibuprofen, he went back to his room and kicked the girls out. He called for some food and someone to bring Gordy to him. While he waited, Mister looked around his room and was disgusted with what he saw. *No leader should live like some slumlord.* Once they took over the military camp, shit was going to change. His food came in the form of an MRE breakfast, but it was served on a plate so that was something, he guessed. As he sat down to eat, Gordy came through the door, eyes bloodshot but alert. He nodded his hello and called for some food to be brought.

"We need to talk plans, man. This place needs to be stripped down and a list made of what we got to use. We need to do it fast, too. I don't want to have to face another full force like that at their camp. It would be suicide but right now, we have a good chance of taking it and living high on the hog! Everything has changed man, but some things stay the same. To have power, you have to take it. Look around you, this place is ghetto. We deserve better. We are gonna take that camp, build up and then take more. It's time to stake the claim. You with me? I need a right hand man."

Gordy listened and then sat back. "What like warlords? Those bastards always end up dead."

Mister shook his head and replied, "Pfft, you're still thinking ghetto. I am thinking kingdom like the old times. You think other countries aren't gonna do the same. NOW is our chance to start something that turns into our own kingdom." The door opened and Gordy was given his food, also on a plate. He looked up at Mister and grinned. "I think I follow where you're going. I'm in."

As they finished their breakfast, Mister laid out the plan that he had been working on for a couple weeks now. They would get all valuables from this place and then torch it, which would put a little desperation into the people who had called it home these last few months. It would make them fight harder and risk more since they would be fighting for a new home that could get them through the next winter much better than Idlewild had. There would be 4 teams and women were expected to fight, too. There weren't any young kids to speak of or worry about. Not many moms would allow their kids to be around the kind of people that were there. A couple of teenagers here and there, the youngest was 14. Times changed everything, though, and the upside was all the hardcore druggies or other out of control people were either dead or had wandered off looking for their next fix. The people that were left were real survivors and though not the brightest, could ruthlessly fight when cornered. They would stage from the spot they had rallied at just after the attack on the patrol unit and then send scouts forward to get intel. If it looked like reinforcements had arrived, they would reassess but if it didn't - the attack would go as planned.

Each of the four teams would split into two, positioned at the corners. The first would attack a corner of the camp to get their attention and the second would sniper off guards on the walls. Once the main doors were opened, the teams on the back would move forward to the sides and the teams in front would focus on keeping the door open and gaining access.

"We should rig a truck up to ram it," said Gordy.

Mister grinned and said, "That is why you are second in command. I want to move out in 3 days. Call a meeting of absolutely everyone for an hour from now. If anyone resists, shoot them. I ain't got time for any crap today."

Gordy nodded and left to spread the word. He was starting to like the new world a bit. At least, he liked the possibilities.

CHAPTER THIRTY

The ATV came closer and closer to Jimmy's location. He put down the binos in case the light reflecting off the lenses gave away his position and just waited. His eyes darted between the ATVs and the people being led out on the road. Just as the closest ATV was within 60 yards of him, the driver jerked around and avoided the 50 feet or so in front of his location. His eyebrows went up and waited until it was safe before poking his head up and looking over the brush in front of him. He could barely make out the tip of a landmine and grinned, nodding to himself. Settling back down, he picked up the binoculars and watched as the people were forced to their knees and executed. He sighed as the bodies were set up on the road as a clear sign to any who were thinking of attacking. He heard a whistle to his left and then Amie's reply. He watched until the troops had finished their gruesome task and went back into their camp. He stretched and got ready to head out. He had seen enough.

He made his way back to where Amie, Terry, and now Brad had stayed to provide cover. Brad explained that he had stayed and watched the movement of the guards on the fuel truck since it could be an amazing asset or a superb weapon against the camp. As he approached, he asked if any had seen Kory. None had and Amie whistled sharply. There was no reply. Jimmy shrugged his shoulders and kneeled down to bend a few saplings in the direction they were headed.

They were about halfway to where they had Bill and Hollis set up when a sharp bird call came from ahead and above them. They looked up and Amie laughed when Kory came climbing down a particularly large tree.

He said, smiling, "Interesting stuff to see up there. It always amazes me how few people look up! Saw the whole thing at the camp. I could see the place the attack happened yesterday, and could make out the clearing we passed but not into it. Just where the trees were opened up. It is clear around here. Didn't see any activity at all and I am sorry I didn't answer your calls." Kory turned to Amie. "I didn't want to give away my position. Getting shot out of a tree is just too much like a squirrel or something. Not really the way I want to go out."

Amie grinned and called him a monkey. Jimmy ordered everyone to move out and jog back to Bill and Hollis. Once they made it, he sent Kory ahead to see if that truck they found was still there and if he could get it going. It would make up for some time and they would be able to make it back tonight instead of tomorrow night with the wounded. Bill tried to talk to him about just leaving him there and Jimmy finally turned and said, "It is not happening. There are too few good guys and that is final. Hollis too. This is the way it is for now and we can hash it out later if you insist but this conversation is currently over."

Amie turned to hide her grin. The look on Bill's face was a cross between shock at Jimmy's change of mood and a little anger at being spoken to like that. He had told her that Bill was his boss before IT happened.

After a couple hours, Jimmy heard a double click on the radio and grinned, clicking twice back. He sat back and said, "Wheels are coming! We'll be home tonight, or at least a good deal closer in a much faster fashion." Terry asked about being tracked by the radio transmissions since they were still within 4 miles of the U.N. camp. Jimmy shook his head and explained that with such limited manpower, a few clicks on the radio was not enough to send anyone out. They were likely tucking in until either reinforcements were sent or an airlift came to fish them out.

"Then again," said Jimmy, "They could be left to forage for themselves since they lost so many. It's all speculation right now. All I know is that Idlewild people have U.N. military equipment and that is more of a threat than those soldiers behind their walls." Everyone agreed and Amie got up to check Hollis and Bill's wounds. She gave them an antibiotic pill and Hollis choked on his when he saw a fish on the front of the bottle.

"Hey! What are you doing feeding us *fish* drugs?" Amie sighed and turned the bottle so he could read the ingredients. "Amoxicillin? Are you kidding me?"

Amie replied, "Nope. Same stuff that we are prescribed only, you can buy it over the counter *without* a prescription. Or could buy, anyway. Be careful though. You still need to know what helps with which infection or issue. You can't just chomp down Amoxicillin all the time and think it is a cure all. It is a precautionary measure right now. When we get back to camp, the Doc can take a look at you."

Bill's eyes got large as he asked, "You have an actual doctor in your camp? Wow Hollis, we hit the jackpot! Someone sure was looking out for us!" There was a good natured chuckle around the group. Not long after, the sound of a vehicle could be heard headed their way and everyone got their gear ready to go. Jimmy clicked the mic once and received one in return. He nodded to everyone to let them know it was Kory and helped to get their wounded loaded quickly. They moved out within minutes and sped down the road. He told them they may have to camp it one more night but wanted to get closer to home and further from the U.N. camp.

****

Richard and Tori went on one ATV with Bret and Swabbie on the other. Chris, a 17 year old who was eager to help was on a dirt bike that someone had brought when they came to live at Main Camp. He would run information back and forth if needed and provide an extra set of eyes. The plan was for everyone to head down to Idlewild at first and check the situation out overnight. The next morning, Richard and Tori would head out to find out what was going on at the U.N. camp and hopefully, find Jimmy and his patrol.

They rode out and were soon stashing their machines in the forest and heading in on foot. Several of them had done patrols of Idlewild before but what they saw was not what they were used to. The noise carrying across the cleared area was filled with what sounded like construction and not the usual chaotic "Mad Max" scene. They dropped down into position and scoped the camp.

There were military vehicles on the road and several of the walls had been taken down. It looked like they were dismantling it. People could be seen loading crates, boxes, and bags of stuff into the back of one of the cargo military trucks. Everyone was armed and working together. Richard couldn't believe what he was seeing. It was like something flipped a switch with these people and they were now organized. No one was screaming or being bullied or beaten. In fact, some people were laughing as they helped move stuff out. Richard wasn't sure what to make of it. He could see people watching the tree line while others moved around them. He had never seen them so alert before.

"What the heck happened to them? They are almost acting normal and where did they get those trucks and stuff from? Did they join the U.N. camp?" Tori asked.

Richard shrugged and said, "I know as much as you do right now." She tossed a pebble at him and went back to glassing the area with her scope. About an hour later, an ATV came out of the camp, went off the road and began to patrol the perimeter in a leisurely pace. Richard looked up at the people on the wall and called out, "Eyes down!" Everyone put down their scopes or binoculars.

Chris asked in a shaky voice, "What?! What? Did they see us?"

Swabbie reached over and cuffed him on the shoulder telling him to shut his trap. "You don't question the order, you follow it. You don't need to know if they saw us. The order is given to make sure they don't and you caterwauling like some scared 5 year old will only give them something to hear as well as see, now get it together or head on back." Chris closed his mouth so quickly his teeth clicked and took in a shaky breath, nodding to Swabbie.

Richard said, "They have eyes on the ATV as he moves around. Cover up anything shiny, then don't move and concentrate on breathing evenly until he passes. Keep your nerve, people." He said it mostly for Chris but everyone followed orders and waited until the patrol passed and a few minutes afterward for good measure. Richard got up and glassed the area, noting that everyone was now going inside. The sun was going down and he told everyone to tuck in for the evening. They would take shifts and keep an eye on the changes going on at Idlewild. Richard was going to take the last shift at 2am so he bedded down early. Everyone ate cold rations and Tori shared some oatmeal cookies she pilfered from the kitchens that raised morale considerably.

****

Jimmy found the spot where the trucks that had been taken had stopped yesterday. There were tracks everywhere and were easy enough to follow. When they turned off toward Idlewild, he was certain there would be an attack soon on the camps and told Kory to take them around on the back roads and trails. It would add time to their trip and risk being seen and attacked at night but he was willing to take that risk. A couple hours after dark, he told Kory to pull over but keep the truck running. He jumped out with his radio and transmitted, "Main Camp, a sheep comes in wolf's clothing. Keep the gate open!" He ran back to the truck and heard two clicks come across the speaker as he jumped in and told Kory to haul ass for home.

Kory complied and put his foot into the floor, causing everyone to hold on. They drove across two fields and down a field road before taking a sharp turn across a county highway and down the road to Main Camp. They blew through the gate that had been left open and Jimmy clicked his mic once, then twice as they passed through. There was a two click reply as they pulled to a stop. Captain and several others were already there, armed and waiting. He jumped out of the truck and called for someone to get Doc. As Amie and the others climbed out of the truck, Captain let his guard down and said, "Something tells me you have one helluva story to tell but let me know first: Are we in danger?"

Jimmy helped Hollis down out of the truck and said, "We might be Captain. This is Hollis and in the back of the truck is Bill Allen. I worked with him back in Chicago." Surprise registered on Captain's face and he said, "I will fill in you on those two later. We have bigger fish to fry right now. We can debrief you now but we could use some food. Didn't want to use up the last few MREs if we didn't have to. Oh, we came in pretty hot so--" Jimmy stopped his babbling when Captain put up a hand up.

"Extra security is already on point. Al is sending down some more people and I guess they had a huge score of some military munitions but it will take them a few days to get it all to us. We can't afford to use any resources to get them right now either. This is the first place that will get hit so we need to keep it manned and the supplies we have accessible. Caches are being made again and buried around the forest. We have it in hand Jimmy. Let's get you some grub and we can fill each other in on what we learned. Denise, get on the waves and send the message to Richard to come on back. I know it is a risk but-" it was Captain's turn to be cut off as Jimmy said, "The risk is diminished now Captain. Just send it."

Captain nodded with a raised eyebrow and someone went off to the Comm Hub to deliver the message. They walked to Captain's cabin and began their reports.

****

Richard jerked awake when he heard "Main Camp: A sheep comes in wolf's clothing" come across the earbud attached to the radio. His eyes went wide and he was relieved to hear Jimmy's voice. Then he went back to sleep until it was time for his watch. The evening passed without incident but another ATV came out on patrol at first light which woke everyone up. Before the ATV passed them by, the radio came to life again in Richard's ear. "Round up the cattle and head to the barn." He was surprised that everyone was being called back so early. He wanted to stay longer and gather more intel but orders are orders. He relayed the message and everyone got ready to head out.

****

Jimmy woke up and started to stretch. They had talked late into the night and would finalize their plans once Richard and his team were back from Idlewild, which should be this morning. He went out to the showers and was grateful for the warm water and clean clothes. All of the things that he took for granted before was more work and more appreciated now. It made you slow down and be grateful for something as simple as warm, clean water to bathe with. Once clean, he headed to get some food when Amie called him from across the main clearing. She had a cup of coffee in hand and he was drawn to it, and her, like a moth. Today she wore a pair of camo cargo pants, her usual boots, a t shirt with a flannel over it and had her lengthening hair in a braid. No makeup, no hairspray, or designer clothing. She was the most beautiful thing he had ever seen and told her so as she handed him the coffee.

She laughed and said, "We'll see how you think when there is no more coffee to be had."

235

He grabbed her and pulled her into a kiss and said, "I mean it now, you are beautiful. A beauty to match my beast." She laughed again, this time a little flustered and rolled her eyes at his comment saying, "Oh, please." He knew she liked hearing it though, even if it was corny, by the little grin she had as she walked away.

"Dad wants to see you." Jimmy saluted her with his coffee mug and stopped by the Comm Hub first to ask after how things were at his own camp. There was nothing to worry about, all was well in hand. The first bigger greens were being harvested with some being dried into chips. A group of 15 men were coming down to bolster the forces here without leaving Center Camp defenseless.

He walked into Captain's cabin just as he heard the sound of a dirt bike pulling up into the main square along with the two ATVs. Captain called out, "Perfect timing! Now we can see what Richard has to add and see if our theory is right!,"

Jimmy went inside and sat down before Richard and his patrol could claim all the good seats. Once everyone was settled, Richard reported the changes he saw at Idlewild and was filled in on what Jimmy had seen. Bill and Hollis were doing better and were reported to be fine. Hollis would be good in a few more days though Bill would have to take it easy for several weeks.

After everyone had shared information, Captain said, "Jimmy and I believe that the Idlewild people will be trying to attack us. Since they attacked the military with the religious group and then killed them off, it would make sense they are trying to establish a foothold here more permanent than a place to hole up. Seems they have a leader now who has gotten them all into formation. That poses a problem if they make it to us. I think we should take it to them. They are still getting things loaded up and we can catch 'em with their pants down. If we take 2/3rds of the forces here, we should be able to do enough damage to eliminate the threat. With the others coming in from the northern and Center Camps, they can stay behind and keep the home front safe."

Everyone sat in silence for a few minutes. Swabbie asked about a few details before everyone agreed that tomorrow, they would attack Idlewild.

CHAPTER THIRTY-ONE

Two days after Gordy was made Second in Command, everyone got up and ate the food that was prepared en masse. It was so different than how it had been with everyone hoarding what little they had and being bullied, robbed, killed, or all three for even a handful of rice. Mister had found out that some of the people had found large bags of oats, rice, and barley but had been hoarding it and using it as currency. He calmly shot the two ring leaders and declared in a loud voice that anyone found hoarding food would be killed immediately. That was last night and it looked like the message had been received loud and clear.

As he walked through the group, people called to him in respectful tones, made way and moved aside for him. When he got to the line for food, a person who was serving came around and ushered him to the front, asking him how much he wanted and slipped him a packet of sugar under the bowl with a wink.

"Name's Sparky, Sir. You need anything special to eat, you just let me know." Gordy schooled his face to reveal nothing but he couldn't believe it when the guy actually bowed to him before moving off. Like Gordy was some kind of nobility or something. *Damn, a guy could get used to this!* He went to find Mister who was sitting at a table that had been brought outside. A sheet had been found and was placed over it. There was an empty seat and Gordy sat down. "Amazing how fast things can change. It is almost pleasant this morning. I even got some sugar!"

Mister grinned and said, "Nice to be respected like you should be. You risked your ass out there to bring back the means to make our lives better. Seems to me you should be recognized and treated like it, too. Now, on to business. Today we will meet after breakfast and get everyone out. Then I will explain what is going on and the boys will torch the place. I need you to get snipers in place to take out anyone who tries to run. I can't risk someone telling the military or anyone else about our numbers or plans."

Gordy nodded and sprinkled the sugar into the bowl, stirring it. "What about the valley people? Should we keep some people back to keep an eye out for them?"

Mister snorted and replied, "The farmers? I wouldn't worry about them so much. Besides, we need them and their skills for our food supplies. We need a castle before we can lay claim to the land." Gordy nodded and finished his breakfast.

An hour later, everyone was outside of Idlewild. It disgusted Mister that he had ever thought of it as home. He was better than that now. He was a leader. What better way to start his new role by burning the old way he had done things? He climbed up onto the hood of one of the trucks and the crowd silenced.

"Today we begin a new life. Today we claim a new home. Some of you may die so that others may live on. Any of you who are having second thoughts better speak up now." No one answered and Mister gave the signal. Soon, the crowd of about 70 began to murmur as flames rose higher up the walls and from within the place they had called home. To Mister's surprise though, not a single person ran. He grinned and the light of the flames danced in his eyes as he watched it for a few minutes. Then he told Gordy to move everyone out as he got down from the truck. The black smoke began to rise high in the air and moved on the light breeze of the morning. As Mister climbed into the passenger seat of the truck, he was both impatient and excited to see how the battle that lay ahead would end.

****

The militia at Main Camp was geared up and heading out in 3 teams. One team would be held in reserve and provide cover fire while the other two flanked and sandwiched Idlewild between them. It was mid-morning and they were about 3 miles out when Jimmy smelled smoke. He looked around and saw that others noticed the scent, too. He caught Kory's eye and nodded. Kory replied with a grin and slung his AR15 over his back, walking toward the tallest tree nearby. Everyone halted and dropped to a knee.

Soon enough, Kory was back down and reported a large fire over by Idlewild's location. Jimmy nodded and ordered to have the message passed along. It wasn't long before the scent was stronger and wafts of smoke could be seen the closer they got to Idlewild. Jimmy and his team moved ahead and had to put something over their mouths to breathe through. They came upon the flames consuming Idlewild shooting up over fifteen feet in the air. Nothing moved around the area, there were no vehicles or signs of any life. The only sound was the roar of the flames. The other teams were in place and all stood there a few minutes, trying to puzzle it out. He called Richard and Erik, who were the other team leaders, over to discuss it. They sent out scouts to check the entire perimeter in teams of three. When the team leaders were together, they tried to determine if the military had launched an assault, if Idlewild people had joined the military, or if it was something else entirely.

"Well," said Richard, "They certainly acted more military-like when we last scouted them and were loading stuff up in the trucks. It looked like they had taken down some panels of the walls and whatnot too. Like they were stripping it down. Why would they do that unless they were either taken over by the military or had joined them?"

He nodded in agreement as Erik said, "That would almost make the U.N. presence *more* of a threat since people from Idlewild have scouted us and have intel on our location, numbers, and supplies."

Richard added, "The Idlewild people are not soldiers and have no formal training so if they are reinforcements instead of prisoners, we would still have a fighting chance to take the whole threat out at once."

Jimmy took all of this in and considered his options. They would be able to move about half of their force packed in and on whatever vehicles they had available to get down to the U.N. camp more quickly but it would waste precious fuel. Then again, if they could get their hands on that fuel truck, it would all be worth it plus put them ahead of the game with a supply of thousands of gallons of fuel if it was full.

The scouting teams came back and reported the all clear. Jimmy looked at the people around him and then at the flames that were starting to die down. He sighed and said, "Ok, I need input here. Idlewild is obviously not a threat to us at this time but they could be, later on when the military decide to move through. Then again, if they are prisoners, the military might just move back to their hub. Bill had said they were pulling out after they had cleared the area."

Everyone was lost in their thoughts until Swabbie cleared his throat. Everyone turned to him. He cleared his throat again and said, "Seems to me that no matter how you paint it, these people are a threat to us and how we are living here. One group wants to take everything we have. The other group wants to take everything we have and make us their labor slaves. Worse for the women, too. Way I see it," he paused a moment, looking at Jimmy. "Way I see it is we need to be sure that the threats we know about, and can do something about, need to be handled. They aren't going away on their own." There were some nods of agreement and a few concerned looks. He thought about what Swabbie said for a moment and ended up nodding as well. "Honestly, that makes the most logical sense since this whole ordeal started. Is there anyone who disagrees?"

He looked to the other team leaders who said they were with him. He excused himself to make a radio call to Captain. At this point, he just didn't think the U.N. would have time or resources to track them down from transmitting.

****

Gordy, Mister, and the Idlewild people got out of the trucks several miles from the U.N. camp at the spot they had stopped after the attack a few days ago. Mister watched as people went to their team leaders and waited for orders. *I should have done this months ago,* he thought to himself. The mood was determined and alert. He waited until people had settled and nodded at Gordy who stepped up and laid out the plan they had discussed. Scouts were sent out and Gordy ordered that everyone present check their firearm and ammo supplies. If they were missing something or had issues, they were to take it to their team leads. Additional scouts were sent back down the way they had come from to make sure there wouldn't be any surprises.

Mister didn't really expect any as there wasn't too many people around anymore to cause trouble. He grinned, Just us! The people gathered were quiet and reserved during the wait for the scouts to come back with their reports. A lady came up to Mister at one point and asked, "We gonna have real showers and food after all this, Mister?"

He looked at her a moment and then nodded. "As long as everyone sticks to their jobs, we will be clean and well fed by tonight." She smiled at him and he noted that in her youth, she was probably a good looking woman but the last few months had not been kind. She wandered off just as one of the scouts came running up.

"Sir! The camp looks like it did a few days ago but there are some dead bodies on the road in. The animals have been at em, it was disgusting. Only a few people on the walls. No one going in or out." Mister nodded and thanked the man who looked surprised at the courtesy. He quickly moved off as Gordy came up with a questioning look in his eye. Mister turned and grinned at him. "Time to go home!"

Two hours later, the teams were within visual distance of the clearing that held the U.N. camp. Crows could be heard fighting over the dead but otherwise, it was quiet. Teams started to split up and move into place, going slowly in the bushes and tree line. The quiet was shattered as a noisemaker trap was tripped. The cry of whoever was hit carried across the stillness and there was immediate activity on the walls.

"Shit," muttered Mister and Gordy nodded. They were in a 5th team made up of the best marksman and military veterans they had at their disposal. Mister hadn't said it yet but these people would be making up his personal security and mission team. They watched as guards along the walls picked up their binoculars and looked through their scopes in the direction the noise had come from. They fired a few shots in the general direction but after 10 minutes, decided it wasn't that big of a threat. Mister passed the message on for people to keep moving and be more careful.

The teams were able to get in place without further incident. Mister looked at the sky to check the time. It was just after noon as the sun was a little passed its peak. He turned to Gordy and nodded. A smile spread across Gordy's face and he pulled out a flare gun. He raised it high and pulled the trigger, watching with a grin as it shot up into the air. The battle had begun.

****

"Roger. Say a little prayer for us." Jimmy switched his radio off and turned to look at the people who were gathered, waiting to hear what the orders were. He walked closer and began to speak to everyone.

"Today may well be a pivotal point for us. We come from all over, with different backgrounds but now we are a family. We need each other for help and security. It has been decided that we will continue on to the U.N. Camp and, if possible, take it out. There may be a lot of dead from this. Word has it that the northern camp came across some munitions that will help us rid the valley of the main threats." The few soldiers from north Camp puffed up a little, hearing that their camp was bringing something good.

"We are going to keep the teams we have for now and head out in the following manner." Jimmy laid out the general plan and explained the layout of the area they would be attacking. "Around the perimeter of the camp, right at the tree line, are some places with landmines. It is imperative that you pay attention to where you step. Follow each other's steps to avoid any nasty surprises. There is a fuel truck around back that we must not destroy unless absolutely necessary. We will move out with a team on each side of the road. The third team will provide cover fire and reinforcements as well as watching out behind us. We are hopeful that the northern camp will get to us in time but once we engage, all plans are a mere suggestion." He paused to make sure he had everyone's attention.

"This is the real deal people. You fight for your freedoms from fear, tyranny, and government control. If any of you do not feel they can perform in battle when needed, please speak up now. You may cost some lives from your fear freezing you in place. There is no shame in it and there is still plenty to be done besides pulling a trigger." Jimmy was met with silence. He nodded and said, "Then let's move out. All of this ends tonight."

CHAPTER THIRTY-TWO

The first half of the Idlewild teams began the battle by chucking grenades out from the tree line toward the camp to get the military's attention. Everything started out as planned and Mister was grinning as he watched guards topple over on the wall from his snipers. Some fell into the camp while a few fell outside of the wall. Extra shots made sure they did not get up. When the first grenades exploded, the camp had gone into defense mode with guards lining the walls. Now, only a handful of them were left but there was definitely some return fire.

Mister jumped as a landmine exploded along the edge of the forest and could hear screams from the wounded. His eyes widened as he looked back to the walls. *Very clever*, Mister thought to himself. He hadn't considered landmines. After about an hour of gunfire exchanged, Mister noted there was less return fire coming from inside the walls and he had Gordy give the signal for the teams to move forward. The front doors had not opened once and Mister was getting a little impatient. For this to work, they had to get inside so they could take control of not only the people but also the supplies. He worried they might be sabotaging the food and other goods. It was time to force their way in.

Mister watched as the teams began creeping out of the woods toward the walls. There was an explosion. One team set off the landmines as they moved out of the tree line. Mister couldn't worry about the losses now, he needed to claim this camp! He barked out some orders for people to help plug the hole left by the loss of that team and was pleased when he saw them being followed. The teams leapfrogged to the walls and just as the first team made it all the way there, a soldier on the wall tossed down a grenade right in the middle of them. Mister cursed loudly as more of his people were killed. He turned and looked at Gordy, giving a nod. Gordy smiled and nodded, trotting back down the road about half a mile away from the battle toward one of the aces that they had stuck up their proverbial sleeves.

****

Al from North Camp and his people met up with the reinforcements from Center Camp and was grateful for the offer of using a little homemade trailer to stack the ammunition crates on. They would still have to pull it along themselves, but it was better than trying to carry the crates. While Al understood Captain's situation, he was still a little miffed that no help was sent to get these supplies that could make all the difference in the battle. They ate a little food, refilled their water jugs and headed out again toward Main Camp. It would be about noon when they made it there, maybe a little after. Al sure hoped he made it in time.

****

Jimmy was scrunched in a truck along with about 2/3rds of his force in the vehicles they had available to them and jostled down the road. It kind of reminded him of the scenes he would see on TV sometimes of trains packed with people in rural areas on top, hanging off the sides, and out of windows. Jimmy noticed there were numerous vehicle tracks, and they were pretty fresh. He told the driver to slow down and stop before the next turn in the road. He signaled people to unload and stretch while a team was sent to scout ahead.

Before long, the team was trotting back and reported a clearing that Jimmy remembered from his last time here. There were military trucks seemingly abandoned with boot tracks leaving the area toward the U.N. camp. His eyebrows rose to his hairline. He asked them if they had checked the trucks for any information and they said all they found was a crude map and a few rounds of ammo on a floorboard. He looked at the map and whistled long and low.

"Seems we were all wrong. Those crazy bastards aren't joining up, they are *attacking* the camp. Well, looks like we just got a shot of luck but whether it is good or bad, I'm not sure. LOAD UP!" Jimmy hollered to everyone but motioned Kory over. He wanted to get all the fuel out of those trucks and into their own before going a little further and stashing them. They would head out on foot from there but at least they would have enough fuel to make it back. The other third of his forces were coming in on foot and though they were double timing it, they would likely be there after everything was done. Still, he took comfort knowing there were reinforcements on the way. Before jumping in the truck, he called in a message to Main Camp. "The chicken turned into a fox. Sending in the hounds to clean up the mess." He heard two clicks, a pause, and then two more that let him know his people had heard the message. With adrenaline starting to pump in his bloodstream, he ordered everyone to move forward.

After they drained the truck tanks dry, Jimmy was pleased to see all of his vehicles at over half a tank each. It had been some time since he had seen that on any vehicle gauge. The convoy moved down the road another mile and then pulled off into the brush. People quickly got them covered as best as they could and it wasn't long before everyone gathered to hear their orders. He spoke with the team leads and their assistants, detailing what he saw on the map that was found.

"It looks like they had several teams who were to be

positioned on the corners and then move in. If it was me, I would want to make those inside open the door instead of bashing it in or blowing it up. Idlewild people want to take the camp as their new stronghold. That explains why they burned down the old place. There is really only one way in and out of the camp and that is this road. I want those here to split into three teams. Two will go forward and one stays back. If it isn't us coming back down this road, shoot to kill. The two moving forward will stay off the road and approach from the bushes. Watch out for each other, we have no idea how many people are out there." Everyone nodded and a few whispered some prayers. "Check your firearms and gear. We head out in 3 minutes. I expect it will take us about 2 hours with the slow pace to make it there. Do not rush. Understood?" The reply, though quiet, was firm and determined.

****

Al maneuvered the trailer around the last stump and into Main Camp. With the help of the others, they were able to make it just after noon. The group settled in and got something to eat. Captain came around and asked them how they were and made small talk.

When he saw Al was mostly done he said, "So, I hear you brought us some toys eh? You going to hide them all away or bring em out for show and tell?" Al chuckled and got up, stretching. He led Captain over to the trailer and pulled the burlap cloth off the top, revealing three military crates.

"We have some AK47s, nice pack of 5 in there with some cleaning kits, this one has some grenades and other goodies but this one...well I am not sure."

Captain nodded as Al explained what they had found and asked, "Why didn't you open it?"

Al looked at with a grin and said, "I am no military man and those markings weren't in that book you let me borrow. I didn't feel like blowing myself up."

Captain chuckled and said, "Well, what you have there

could be the key we needed to make sure we are victorious. Those are-" Captain stopped and turned as Denise came running up, calling his name.

"Cap! Cap, we have word from Jimmy. He is heading toward the U.N. camp. He says that Idlewild is attacking the camp, not joining it!" Captain's face registered shock for a split second before he turned to Al and said, "I need you to get those down to them. They will need it if they have to take the camp, too. Take the last truck with half a dozen guys. I will radio ahead." Al nodded and turned to get his gear he had left back at the chow hall. After he had taken 10 steps, he realized that Captain hadn't told him what was in that last crate.

****

Mister waited until he was certain that Gordy was on his way back before issuing orders for the teams to move around the sides to the door. Mister turned in time to see the truck Gordy was sent to get. It had a nice steel cage on the front of it, perfect for ramming a door open. He particularly loved the fact that it was stamped "United Nations" on the side. Gordy jumped out and came around, sizing up their troop movement. He watched as another grenade was thrown over the side of the wall by those inside. It was tossed blindly and didn't explode near anyone.

Mister laughed and said, "Seems like they are grasping at straws there. Perhaps we should let them sweat it out just a little hmm? Let them see how they like being the ones caught in a cage. I may not have agreed with those religious whack jobs, but I sure do hate the military." Gordy nodded and leaned back against the truck waiting for the order.

****

As Jimmy and his group got closer, gunfire could be heard with lower rumbles interspersed here and there. He signaled for his team to spread out and stay low. The going was slow enough to drive him crazy but he knew better than to rush onto a battlefield without seeing how it was playing out and getting your head blown off. After what seemed an eternity, he could just barely make out what looked to be people moving from the tree line toward the U.N. camp quickly. He put up his fist and everyone dropped down where they were. He watched intently as the people assaulting the camp moved forward without turning around to check their backs. He could have given the order to take them out and it would have been an easy counter assault but he needed more information on the U.N. camp itself and wasn't close enough. He didn't want to give away their advantage of surprise.

Once the last of what he assumed was the Idlewild people had moved toward the camp walls, Jimmy gave the signal to move forward to get a better look. As he settled into place, he saw a group of people blown up by a landmine. He watched as the first Idlewild team made it to the walls and saw a grenade launched over the side of the U.N. camp wall. It exploded and blew the people literally everywhere. It also created a hole about the size of a basketball in the wall. He tucked that information away for later. The walls aren't as tough as they look. He scoped around the perimeter and saw some people on the road. He assumed that must be their command but to be so exposed was really stupid. As he watched, he saw someone run off down the road a ways before he lost sight of them. He risked a one-word message to the team leads over the radio, "Observe." He heard clicks in reply and settled in.

The exchange of gunfire was slowing down and there were less guards on the walls, even as more of the offensive group gathered near the walls. Before long, Jimmy heard the unmistakable sound of a truck coming toward them and shoved down a wave of panic. He clicked across the radio again and said, "Hold." Clicks acknowledged the order as he watched the large military truck, complete with ramming cage around the front rumble down the road. It stopped and the guy who he had seen leaving jumped out, going to talk to what he assumed was the leader of the Idlewild group. He watched as the people at the walls of the camp began to maneuver around toward the front and sides. Once in position, a woman fired a single shot in the air.

****

Mister and Gordy watched as their troops got into position and the single shot was fired. Mister turned to Gordy and said, "How about we knock on the door eh? See if they have a cup of sugar we can borrow." Gordy laughed and went to the truck, opened the door and got to work. A few shots were fired here and there while Gordy rigged the wooden log into place so it would fall onto the gas pedal when he yanked the rope. He set the wheel to keep a straight course toward the gate of the U.N. camp and then turned the truck on again. When he came back out, he had a length of rope in his hands that led into the cab of the truck. Mister nodded and then raised his own firearm in the air and gave a single shot. Everyone moved far from the sides of the road to give room for the truck and the people at the walls were ready.

Mister turned to Gordy and said, "Send the welcome wagon!" Gordy grinned and yanked on the rope.

****

Jimmy watched as the scene unfolded before him like something out of a B movie. The truck was unmanned but the sounds of the accelerator being floored rang out across the clearing. Rocks and dirt spit up behind it as it rumbled forward, gaining speed and heading straight down toward the gate of the camp. He was frozen, watching, as it got ever closer. He saw movement on the wall as a soldier popped up over with a bazooka looking device, aiming for the truck. He let fly and the rocket slammed into the back canopy of the truck when it was within 200 feet of the gate. The truck exploded but did not lose its momentum as it careened into and through the doors in a ball of flame.

Those people closest to the gate were killed and several U.N. troops who had been hiding behind the wall came running out, screaming and on fire. The Idlewild people dispatched them quickly and swarmed up onto the road as other U.N. troops fired on them. Before he could decide his next move, the Idlewild people overtook the camp, and focused on getting the fires out. The group of people who were on the road, including the leader, were gone and nowhere in sight. A voice crackled into his ear from the radio, "Activity in rear." He clicked twice to acknowledge and decided that this was the best chance they would have to surprise the attackers in the camp.

Jimmy was not about to let those Idlewild people be an even bigger threat in a stronghold. He got on the radio and gave some orders, not caring who was listening. "Teams one and two, it is time to clean house. Team three, double time it to the turn off."

A crackle came across the radio. "Team three at turn off already, awaiting orders." Jimmy was surprised until he looked at his watch, it was after 2 already. He did not want to be fighting after dark. He wanted this done *now*. He was sick of being shot at, shooting at others, and looking over his shoulder all the time. He wanted peace in this valley and he was going to have it or die trying. "Team three, line the road and shoot anything that comes along that isn't us." Two clicks came back at him and he turned to those in his team.

"Alright, let's go clean up."

****

As the truck moved forward toward the gate, Mister and Gordy dropped back to one side of the road and watched as the truck exploded but still barreled through the doors, setting people and the area on fire. Screams could be heard from both his people and the U.N. troops who had been hiding inside. While he didn't really care about those on his side who died, he would use their 'heroics' to bolster the survivors of this battle to build up both them and his image. He did have a bit of pride as he saw his 'soldiers' swarm over and into the camp. Shots could be heard inside and then a flare went up. This was the signal that they had secured the fort. Mister whooped out a victory cry and called everyone to move forward.

As the teams got up on the road and began to run into the camp, gunfire began raining down on them from seemingly everywhere. Mister was hit in the shoulder and knocked over. Gordy quickly picked him up and half dragged, half ran with him into the safety of the walls. Their people were getting the truck fire under control by throwing dirt and sand from the sandbags inside the walls on it. The last few people were trying to run in but were gunned down just before they crossed the threshold.

"Close the damn gate!" Mister yelled. A few people ran and worked hard to push the dented, soot covered metal closed. More than one person was picked off and fell where they were by a single bullet in the head. Mister screamed again through the pain in his shoulder.

"Hurry the hell up!" He pushed Gordy toward them and told him to get these idiots in line. Gordy looked uncertain but did as he was told. Just as the gate was coming together, Gordy felt a blinding flash of pain and then...nothing.

****

Jimmy watched as people began to stream toward the camp and he opened fire. He saw several people fall or reel from being hit but even still, the majority of the people made it inside. He focused his fire on those trying to get the gate closed and aimed for the head. *One shot, one kill, one less threat,* he thought to himself.

The gates closed and everyone ceased fire at his command. He didn't want to waste ammo on walls. The silence was broken only by the moans of the wounded and dying. He decided to wait and see what the Idlewild people would do for a few minutes as the radio crackled in his ear. Jimmy was surprised to hear Captain's voice.

"Team Alpha, this is the barn."

Jimmy quickly replied, "Go ahead for Team Alpha."

There was a pause before he heard, "Friendlies incoming with brooms for a final clean up." Jimmy couldn't help but grin. "Roger. Alpha Team out." He called out across the field loudly.

"We got more coming in to clear these bastards out!" Jimmy hoped like hell they heard it inside the walls, too. He wasn't about to wait for them though, he wanted to keep these people off guard and not give them a chance to think of any strategies. He gave the order to move forward slowly and keep suppression fire on the walls. "If anyone pokes their head up, shoot to kill."

CHAPTER THIRTY-THREE

Mister watched in shock as Gordy dropped to the ground in a heap. The gates were closed as best as they could be and people were dragging bodies away while others brought stuff to brace the doors with. Mister screamed for people to start looking for weapons, especially any grenade launchers and more ammo for the bazooka-looking weapon that was shot at the truck earlier. People were running everywhere.

"Someone find out if that is the U.N. or someone else out there!" A few ran up the stairs to the upper catwalk on the wall and peered over. The first two had barely poked their head up before they were shot clean off the catwalk and fell a few yards from Mister. *This was not how it was supposed to be!* Everything was unraveling before his eyes.

He heard someone call from outside the walls, "We got more coming in to clear out these bastards!" He began screaming for people to find the biggest weapons they could and get ready to defend their new home. He noted that when he called it home, people's faces that showed fear now had some determination creep in, too. He hoped it would last but one thing was certain of: He was not going down without a fight.

****

Al and 6 others were speeding down the road as fast as they could without wrecking the truck. One of the crates had been opened and all but one man had an AK47 with 3 magazines each and they were thrilled to see two ammo cans in the bottom. The other two were in the bed of the truck and Al hoped that all the bumping around wouldn't set any of the older ammunition off. He still didn't know what was in the one crate but once they got to the turn off that they had been told about, he was going to crack it open and find out. As long as they didn't run into any trouble, they should make it to the turn off around 3 or so and Al sure hoped he made it in time to help.

****

Jimmy's team worked with the others as they moved forward little by little. Some stayed back in the trees to provide cover fire. When the teams were clear from the trees and brush, grenades started being lobbed over the walls towards them. His eyes went wide as one exploded near two people from his camp and he hoped they felt no pain as he hollered, "Spread out! Don't bunch up! You see a target, you shoot it!"

The amount of grenades being tossed out made Jimmy believe they had found some kind of stash inside and until they ran out of them, there was no way that he could get the majority of his people to the walls. He needed something he could toss back at them too. Otherwise, this would be a long wait and likely turn into a siege battle. Jimmy knew they did not have the supplies, nor were they able to draw this out for any length of time. Jimmy just hoped those 'brooms' Captain talked about were big and plentiful enough to do the job.

He was just about to order a retreat until backup arrived when he saw someone pop up over the wall with a missile launcher on their shoulder and fired toward the other team. He screamed out a warning but it was too late: the missile exploded in the middle of the field and sent bodies flying.

He heard a scream from behind him and turned to see Amie with a look of shock on her face.

He screamed at everyone to fall back and had to grab her arm to get her moving. Her eyes were dim, like she wasn't really here but moved easily enough as he pulled her along back to the tree line. He pushed her to the ground and got on the radio. "Alpha Team taking heavy fire, where are those brooms?!" He watched in horror as another person from inside popped up with a loaded missile launcher pointed in their direction. He said a silent prayer of thanks as a bullet snapped their head back before they could pull the trigger.

"Get back! EVERYONE GET BACK!"

****

Mister was inside the medical area of the camp getting his shoulder wound bandaged. It had gone clean through and hadn't hit anything vital. His adrenaline was pumping so heavily that he refused any anesthetic to dull the pain. He heard explosions and screams of the wounded outside the walls making made him grin and the adrenaline pump harder. Someone came in as he was getting his shirt back on and told him about the missile launchers and grenades they had found and what they were doing. The attackers were moving back to the woods and Mister heard someone scream for everyone to get back as he stepped into the main area of the camp.

He turned to the younger guy and said, "Push them back as far as you can and then start lighting the trees up with those missiles. We will burn 'em all out so they can never come back. This is OUR CAMP!" The man stepped back from Mister's intensity nodding. He saluted and took off to give the message. Mister saw Gordy's body lined up with the others and noted that his pockets had been picked clean and his shoes were gone. He didn't begrudge anyone from trying to get shoes since there wouldn't be any new ones made for a long time. People trotted by carrying various firearms and he watched as pins were being pulled on grenades and tossed over the sides.

"Hey there! Make sure you toss em out far enough, we don't need any more holes in our walls," he said as he went to assess the situation for himself.

****

Al heard the frantic call over the waves and he told the driver to punch it. "To hell with anything else!" He got on the radio and said, "The brooms are coming in! Clear a path and we will bring em right to you!" They turned a bend after a few more minutes and saw all of the other trucks, including a line of people – his people – across the road with guns aimed at them. The driver slammed on the brakes and Al stuck his head out of the window showing his face clearly. The person in charge barked an order and everyone moved to the truck. Al got out and the guys in the back pulled the crates out.

He turned to those who were assigned to this location and said, "How far down to the camp?" He was told it was roughly 2-3 miles down the road. Al nodded and grabbed a crowbar from the behind the seat of the truck and told everyone to move back so he could open the mystery crate. Just as he was about to crack it open, a female's voice said, "Sir, I can tell you what those are. That crate has 3 M72 LAWs (Light Anti-Armor Weapon) in it with munitions. Looks like 2 shots for each one."

His jaw dropped and he glanced at the crate. "No wonder it was so damn heavy. This should help level the playing field nicely! Anything ahead I should be worried about?" The man who spoke earlier shook his head and informed Al that reinforcements were sent ahead and on either side of the road but that they should be fine, as everyone knew they were coming. Al nodded and thanked him. He turned and told his people to load up the crate and get back in the truck. Several others loaded in as well so they could help provide cover fire. They were going to deliver these right into Jimmy's hands.

****

"Brooms incoming. Repeat, brooms incoming. Big ones." Jimmy felt some relief hearing that there were reinforcements and some bigger guns coming in to help. As it was, they were at a standoff with the people inside having large munitions to fire and him being unable to move forward without taking heavy casualties. Brad made his way through the brush over to Jimmy and gave him a questioning look. He explained what was going on and sent one of the other people to spread the word.

"Tell them to sit tight, save ammo. The big guns are coming." He turned back to Brad and told him about the reinforcements. Brad grinned and said it was a better party with more friends. Jimmy shook his head with an amused look on his face until he focused in on Amie again. She was still a little dazed and though he loved her, she really needed to get it together.

He snapped his fingers in front of her face and said, "Hey. Come on back to me here. Captain didn't raise some wallflower, some fragile woman. I need you right now, Amie, so come on back to me." She didn't respond until he said Captain and then she looked right at him. He watched her face go from offended about being called fragile and then haughty when he said he needed her.

She cleared her throat and said, "Well of course you do. Every man needs a woman to keep him out of trouble." He sighed in relief knowing that for now, she was OK.

Another missile was shot, this time into the forest itself. The explosion caused a fire to start and smoke billowed through the brush and trees. Jimmy cursed and had Amie give word that everyone was to sit tight for a little longer. Unless they were in direct danger, stay put. While he watched her move back into the woods, Brad said he wanted to see if the fuel truck was still around the back and now was a perfect time to scout it while all the focus was on the road and in front of the camp. Jimmy nodded and Brad slipped back into the brush.

****

Mister climbed up the scaffolding to the catwalk and risked looking over the side before ducking back down and moving to a different location in case anyone wanted to shoot the spot he had just been. The area around the camp was cleared and there was a fire from the last missile that went into the forest. He called for a cease-fire when he thought he heard the sound of an engine coming down the road. After about 10 seconds, he was sure it was a truck and ordered people to aim for it because whatever it was or carried was not theirs or their people. Those on the catwalk nodded and got set up. A few people lobbed some grenades out there to make it look like they hadn't heard the truck coming and were focusing on what was in front of them. Mister hoped it wasn't a tank. They couldn't stand up to that.

****

Al saw smoke rising from the forest as he came around a turn in the road and could see down the final straight stretch about half a mile to the camp itself. He ordered them to stop and pull off the road into the brush and didn't care if it got stuck right now. Everyone jumped out and Al clicked the radio on.

"Alpha Team, the brooms are here. Need a loc for delivery." Al had his 6 people from Main Camp take the M72 LAWs and two missiles each. The radio crackled with a rough estimation of his location and they began to make way through the brush. As they crossed the road, shots rang out from the direction of the U.N. camp toward them. They ran down the other side and into the denser brush just as another explosion sent debris and dirt showering down on them. Al looked down the road and saw the hole it had created. He was grateful that the missile was over shot, otherwise all might have been lost.

Amie came out of nowhere and startled the group. She

grinned her saucy smile at having caught them unawares and turned to lead them to Jimmy. When they came up, Jimmy's eyes were big as dinner plates and said, "That's one helluva broom there, Al." He smiled and clapped Al on the back. "I sure am thankful for you. You may have just saved the day."

Al nodded and looked down at the praise and replied, "I wouldn't be here if you hadn't taken us in all those months ago. We're family now, it's how we do things." Jimmy nodded and quickly laid out a plan for the attack. He wanted one M72 positioned in front and the others on either side of the camp. The two on the sides would fire first with the one on the road held in reserve. All those fighting for the valley would create a circle around the camp in the trees and brush to take out anyone who tried to escape from the camp. Al nodded in agreement.

Amie said, "Wait, shouldn't we try to salvage some of the supplies in there? That is valuable stuff! Seems a serious waste, Jimmy."

He shook his head as she spoke. "No, I don't want anything in there. There is no way to know if today will end things or not. I don't want to risk having anything of the United Nation's military in our camps if we can help it. It will only draw trouble and right now, we are trying to rid ourselves and this valley of a lot of trouble."

He could tell Amie didn't like the answer much but she didn't argue. Jimmy gave the order to move out

****

Mister watched from a more secured location than the top of the wall. He saw the truck pull off the road down to the side and then watched as people with something over their shoulders ran across the road. He had a sinking feeling in his stomach and barked out orders. He left a dozen guys on the catwalk with another dozen ready to chuck grenades. All of the rest he had gather in the middle of the camp.

"I have no idea who these people are but this is OUR home now. They are planning something and we need to be ready. How many more of those missiles we got?" He nodded when he was told there were 8 left and replied, "Good. I want two put at each corner platform with a shooter. I want snipers with them, too. Pick off anyone you see out there, especially if they are aiming anything at us." He paused for a moment and realized there was no more gunfire except what his people shot.

"Stop shooting you idiots! You're only wasting ammo!" He turned back to the group gathered and said, "Anyone not fighting to protect our home will be shot. Anyone who runs will be shot. There is no freedom right now. You are either fighting until you die or will die for not fighting." A few people glanced around to see the reactions of others. Most of them were exhausted and just stood there. Mister noted those who glanced around as potential dissidents. He ordered them to get into position and not let anything get near the camp. He wanted the area that had already been cleared of trees to stay clear of anything else, too.

****

Brad was watching the fuel truck closely. There were only three guys on guard now. One was always in the cab of the truck in case they needed to drive away while the other two nervously watched the tree line. They had looked right at his location more than once but never saw him hidden in the brush. *Talk about greenhorns*, he thought to himself. He waited until they had turned away and then fired a single shot that took one guard out. He simply fell like a sack of laundry in a pile. The other two jumped into action and were looking around frantically. The guy in the cab jumped out, gun ready but visibly shaking. Brad aimed again and took out another one. Realizing that he was the last guy alive, the man dropped his gun and took off running, screaming his head off around the side wall. Brad tried to get him but the guy had the fear of God or the devil in him and his feet barely touched the ground as he fled. Brad waited to see if there would be any action on this side of the walls but he could hear someone inside giving orders. Though he couldn't make out the words, he did notice that the gunfire had calmed down considerably and then stopped. He wondered what was going on out there. He wanted to get that fuel truck safely out of here; they could really use whatever was in there.

Brad risked moving forward and was able to get to the truck. He grabbed the guns and magazines off the dead and tossed them in the cab, climbing in after. He wanted to wait until things started up again and then move the truck back or, worst case, when that guy brought more people. He already had an exit strategy in mind but decided to make another one just in case. He would simply go right into the woods and hope he made it far enough.

****

The area was eerily quiet. All gunfire had stopped. Jimmy's people were getting into position and it seemed an eternity already. His nerves were getting frayed as the silence stretched on and there was no activity from within. He worried about what they might be doing in there but knew there wasn't much he could do about it right now. His heart began to race again as he heard one and then two clicks across the radio. He clicked back once to acknowledge. The east side team was in place. Not long after, he heard two clicks and then one. West team was in place. He clicked back once and then turned and nodded to the team he had near the road. He was silently saying a prayer when the sound of a truck suddenly kicked to life, echoing through the clearing around the camp. At the same time, people popped up over the walls and on the platforms in the corners of the camp.

"Shit," he muttered as he noted that there were other shoulder-fired missiles in each corner. At the same time the fuel truck behind the camp came into view, the people on the walls opened fire and the grenades were being tossed closer to the tree line toward their direction.

Bullets zinged by him and he watched in horror as one of

the rockets was shot into the forest on the west side. He got on his radio and screamed "FIRE!" Seconds later, he saw the trail of smoke left behind as the M72 released its payload and slammed right into the walls on either side as planned. Screams could be heard inside along with someone cursing at them, adding to the gunfire and grenade explosions that made for a scene of chaos. The Idlewild people managed to get more rockets of their own fired into the woods and within minutes, there was fire everywhere. Just as Jimmy and his team were forced to relocate, he saw the fuel truck driving into the forest around the back side of the burning camp and hoped that was Brad driving it.

****

Brad watched closely for any signs of movement. He saw people climbing on the platform at one corner and noted they had a shoulder-fired rocket they were loading. There were also several people with guns getting in place.

Time to go! Brad thought to himself and decided that going off into the trees would be the best bet, even if he got stuck. As he started to pull out, he glanced at the platform and saw guns being aimed at him and then heard and felt an explosion on the other side of the camp. He floored it and drove the truck into the woods, hoping he didn't get stuck too soon. He turned to position the truck into a semi-cleared area and then everything went black. The truck slammed into a stump that was hidden by bushes and stopped, steam spewing from the radiator.

****

Jimmy moved quickly with his team and saw people starting to pour out of the burning camp. He got on the radio. "If you have a clear shot, fire again at the camp. Perimeter, you have runners incoming. Try to be sure before you shoot to avoid friendly fire!" He repositioned in a relatively smoke free spot and took aim at the gate. The ground shook and the scene in his scope said that another rocket was fired at the camp as he took out three people fleeing from inside.

****

Mister was knocked to the ground and landed on his back, his breath *whooshing* out of him, leaving him gasping for air. All sound was muted and he struggled for breath. He saw the fire and a huge hole left where a rocket had hit the wall. People were running everywhere, trying to escape. He wanted to scream at them to stand and fight but the lack of oxygen and landing so hard made him begin to pass out. The last thing he remembered was being picked up and dragged toward the hole in the wall.

****

People were dropping almost as quickly as they came out from the U.N. camp. Some made it to the tree line but Jimmy would let the perimeter deal with that as best as they could. When no more were coming out, he called a 'cease fire unless otherwise currently engaged' over the radio. A few shots could be heard in the forest around the camp before that eerie silence washed over the area again. Jimmy ordered everyone to hold position unless in danger.

After a full ten minutes of hearing nothing other than the explosions of ammo and fuel inside the camp and seeing nothing but the 20 foot flames licking at the sky, Jimmy let out a deep breath of relief. He got on the radio again and ordered the wounded to be helped out to the road and for the people at the turn off to bring some trucks forward with medical supplies.

He turned to Amie who had stuck with him the whole time. She smiled up at him while searching his eyes to see if he was OK. He looked back at her and then reached out, bringing her in for a hard kiss that hurt her lips but she returned it with the same intensity. When he broke the kiss, he took a couple more deep breaths and said, "Okay. Let's clean up."

****

Richard was making one last pass around the area when he got to the fuel truck that had made it about 50 yards into the woods before hitting a stump. He approached with caution and came around the side, weapon up and ready. When he saw the driver slumped over the wheel he opened the door. Brad's limp body slid to the side and began to fall out. Richard caught him and guided him to the ground. He checked for a pulse and when he found none, he radioed it in to Jimmy. "We need a wagon on the back side and help to get the fuel truck."

Jimmy's voice crackled on the radio. "The truck is still intact? Way to go Brad! We will send someone over right now."

Richard had a lump in his throat the size of an apple and said, "Brad is gone, sir."

****

"All told Captain, we lost a total of 48 people but that may be higher depending on the extent of some injuries."

Jimmy sat at the table in Captain's cabin at Main Camp with Amie, Richard, and Al. The battle had happened 2 days ago and it had taken that long to get everyone back to their camps and things sorted out. There was nothing left of the United Nations deployment camp. Oddly enough, nothing had come over the waves yet about the attack which both relieved and worried him.

The news of losing Brad was a blow to him personally. Brad was Jimmy's right hand when it came to the camp buildings and infrastructure. More than that, he had become like a brother and the loss hurt more than the other 15 or so people from his camp that had been killed. Of course, that only added to his guilt. Amie sat next to him and reached over to squeeze his hand and held it.

Captain nodded at the report and didn't say anything for a few minutes. He asked about their plans for the dead and

Captain told him about an area they had already scouted as a graveyard. It was being cleared and prepared. They didn't have wood for coffins and made sure the location was far away from any water sources or close to the camp. The holes would be dug extra deep to help keep predators or scavengers from digging them up. Hopefully there would be no smell, either. They discussed plans for the next few days and would call down everyone who wanted to come for the mass funeral.

There would be special mention for Brad whose forward thinking had netted them about 400 gallons of fuel. It would put them ahead of the game on better housing and protected areas to grow food. That made many tasks go much easier and faster like building, digging trenches, or sadly, graves. They agreed that they would need to get it done sooner rather than later and would send trucks to pick people up. It was a lot of fuel to be used but in this case, honoring the dead was more important for everyone involved.

EPILOGUE

The tenth of September dawned warm and clear. The wind gave a hint of cooler temps coming soon but for today, Jimmy Walker was content. He sat on his front porch with a cup of coffee, precious coffee, in his hands. Buildings had sprung up around the main square and "Town Hall" now had large flat slabs of granite leading up to it and more were being added in front of other buildings to help combat the mud that would build up when the snow melted next spring.

There had been no talk across the waves or mention of anything about the U.N. camp they took out and no suspicious people or activity had happened in at least two months. He savored the feeling of being secure and in charge of his own destiny. He wouldn't have chosen to live this life before IT had all happened but he felt more in control over his own life and more alive than he ever had before.

The crops had done pretty well considering no one was really a true farmer before things had changed. They lost some tomatoes to pests but Main Camp had a bumper crop going. This weekend was going to be another gathering for market between the camps though at the last one, some traveling traders had come in and asked to set up as well.

After being checked out and then followed after the market, Jimmy and Captain had felt that these people were the real deal and this was going to be the new norm. Just like olden times, traveling traders were going to be more and more common. Not only did they have some stuff from the old world, they also usually had news. Jimmy took a drink of his coffee and sighed again in gratitude for everything he had been blessed with. He smiled as he heard the door open behind him and turned to look at Amie, smiling. She was absolutely glowing and the barest bump peeked through one of Jimmy's old t-shirts.

"Good morning, handsome," she said, taking her chair next to his. He reached out to hold her hand and she said, "I felt a kick this morning. It was weird, like a flutter of wings or bubbles inside."

Jimmy looked at her, eyes filled with emotion as he set his coffee cup down. Kneeling in front of her, he laid his head on her legs, putting a hand on her baby bump and said, "Welcome to the valley, my little one."

ABOUT THE AUTHOR

LeAnn lives with her husband and fur babies in beautiful
Southeast Alaska. She writes on homesteading and
preparedness on her site, www.homesteaddreamer.com.
LeAnn also writes for PREPARE Magazine and is a member
of the Professional Prepared Bloggers Network.
Her biggest dream is to have a cabin in the woods... and high
speed Internet.

Made in the USA
San Bernardino, CA
08 December 2014